AURORA'S WINTER

K.J. GILLENWATER

AURORA'S WINTER

By K. J. Gillenwater

First Kindle Edition, March 2024
Copyright 2024 by K. J. Gillenwater

Cover art design by Miblart
http://www.miblart.com

CHAPTER 1

I cranked up the music in my earbuds—something hard, driving, and loud—to block out the chop of our Polaris snowmobile and give me focus. As my boyfriend, Ben, and I rode along the edge of the Bering Sea, we bumped and jostled over hard knots of frozen water. Sea ice was nothing like the smooth ice of a rink. There were no Zambonis out here.

The snow machine jolted forward as I gunned it, guiding it around ice heaves and other gold dredgers. Its skis skated across the hardened surface, which had thickened even more after last night's below zero temperatures. Each year in March the conditions were different. Every dredge team wanted to have maximum time to search for gold, but Mother Nature didn't always play along.

Ice season was the cherry on top to insulate a miner from a bad summer season or fuel him into next summer when the real action happened. But limits existed with ice diving—not only the U.S. Army Corp of Engineers in concert with the Alaska Department of Natural Resources regulating the dates dredgers were allowed out on the ice in the first place, but there was a higher amount of risk.

Diving for gold was the only life I knew. The only life I ever wanted. Ben supported me in that goal and had become an extraordinary underwater dredger in a matter of weeks last summer. We'd scraped by through the fall counting on ice season to save us from going broke and to help fund the purchase of our own summer floating dredge. Everything was dependent on our success. I turned my mind off to the possibility we wouldn't earn enough money to achieve the dream. That kind of thinking was for losers. And Buck Darling's daughter didn't lose.

The Bering Sea ice could be unforgiving, but at least we were within a thousand feet of the Nome shoreline if something went wrong. If we followed the safety rules I'd learned over the years from my dad we should be fine.

Last summer we'd found a good pay streak we'd marked on my father's GPS device, but we'd lost that data when we'd sold our family's floating dredge, the *Alaska Darling*, piecemeal to pay my dad's staggering medical bills. I'm not sure who ended up with the gadget, but I'd made sure to clear out our labeled points so we didn't give any information to our competition. The best we had to work with now was a notebook of coordinates I'd hastily drafted before the sale and entered into my phone's mapping app.

I took a quick glance at my phone to compare our position to the coordinates I'd entered earlier. Our summer gold streak seemed cursed—located too far from shore. Not enough solid ice had formed to travel that far out, and the authorities had made sure all the dredgers knew it using their orange cones to delineate a restricted zone. But I had a back-up plan after studying the public mining areas and knew exactly where I wanted to set up our winter dredging operation. Hopefully, this new location was one with plenty of gold. I didn't know what we'd do if we couldn't come up with the eighty grand or so it would take to build our own summer dredge.

The challenged fueled me—the promise of thousands of dollars in gold hidden beneath the ice if we only took a chance, made a hole, and worked harder than anyone else out here. It had to work.

My heart thumped. I loved driving the Polaris, but I loved diving for gold even more. Nothing else compared to that rush of excitement when you were on the gold—the flecks visible beneath your hands as you swept the suction hose back and forth through the cobble. I don't know if there's another job on earth as satisfying when you end the day with a sluice box full of gold and pickers in your glove.

The town of Nome grew smaller and smaller in my rearview mirror as the edge of the ice grew more visible. Beyond the icy frontier, the wild and unpredictable winter seas seethed.

I swerved to the left, past summer rivals who'd already set up shelters. I gave a wave and a nod trying not to show my annoyance that they'd beaten us out on the ice for Opening Day. When I reached our spot, I let the snow machine glide to a stop. Ben patted my hip and slid off.

As a strong, icy breeze cooled my face, I smoothed loose strands of hair that had escaped my ponytail during the ride. "Before we unpack the sled of equipment you bought for us, let's grab the auger, make a hole, and use that camera you nabbed." The sight of those other miners with holes cut and equipment assembled made a cold sweat break out on my brow. We had to move more quickly.

"Roger that, Captain Aurora." Ben gave me a mock salute, a tribute to his days in the military. It was our inside joke as I'd been the captain of my family's dredge last summer when we'd met.

I grinned. "At least you know your place." I shoved him playfully out of my way to search for the underwater camera Ben had stashed in the storage compartment of the Polaris. With his earnings from gold diving last summer, Ben had wanted to fund our ice season. At first, I'd been hesitant to let him go to the used equipment sale without me. But I didn't want to him to think I didn't trust him, and guys were supposed to be good with mechanical know-how, right? Ben had staged everything in town before our arrival with the snow machine this morning. Today would be the first day I'd get a look at what he'd purchased for us.

Matt's GMC Jimmy pulled up, towing the shelter and some of our heavier equipment, like the used generator and the pumps, on plywood skids. Stella, my best friend, waved at me from the passenger seat. She wore a bright pink and purple striped knit hat on top of her dark curly hair and a matching scarf around her neck. She'd dressed more for a short stroll through town rather than a day on the ice. But I was grateful for their help and knew it would speed us along to a completed set up in a few hours.

When her boyfriend stopped the truck, my friend hopped out. "What can I do to help, Rory?" she asked brightly. "I know you said I didn't need any experience to help you guys, but looking at all of this stuff—" she captured her thumbnail between her teeth for a moment. "—I might be in the way."

I waved off her concerns. "First things first, Matt, can you unhook the shelter and then move the snow off this piece of ice?" I pointed at an empty patch located quite distant from the other miners who preferred to stick closer to shore. The competition might be mining sooner than I would, but I knew the big gold came from unworked ground farther out.

"Got it." Matt went around to the back of his truck to detach the chain used to drag the shelter on skids.

"Ben," I barked out with a no-nonsense demeanor, though a twinge of worry about sounding too commanding crossed my mind. "Can you work with Matt? Make sure he clears enough?"

"Absolutely." Taking my direction like a champ, Ben scuffed along the surface so he wouldn't slip and climbed into the passenger side of the truck.

Matt got back into his truck, started it up, and lowered the plow attached to the front to make a snow-free space for our shelter.

"What should I be doing?" Stella lingered on the periphery, uncertainty written on her face. "I don't want to mess anything up."

"Aw, sweetie." I left my work digging for the camera to reassure my best friend. Her round, earnest face lifted my spirits. She'd always been my cheerleader, even if she didn't always trust my judgment. "We're only unpacking things. Nothing to mess up. And can I tell you again how grateful I am you and Matt could help us?" I put an arm around her shoulder.

We watched as the two men cleared a strip of ice and pushed the snow off to one side.

"What are boyfriends for?" Stella smiled.

"True," I said with a laugh.

Ben rolled down the window. "Hey, should we clear all the way to that heave so we have space to move the shelter?"

I was impressed. He was thinking ahead. He'd learned a little something over the summer about how hard it can be to find the perfect dredging spot. "Go for it!"

"You want me to unload things off the sled?" Stella asked.

"Not yet." I gave her shoulder a squeeze. "Stuff might've shifted on the ride over. Plus, if this hole looks to be in a bad location, we might be moving elsewhere on the ice."

Stella had already unzipped a large duffel bag strapped to the sled that Ben and I had hooked up to the Polaris after riding into town from his cabin, which was a dozen or more miles outside Nome.

"Wow, these are heavy," Stella said as she lifted two cold diving suits out of the bag and set them on the ice. "You dive in these?"

"Yep." I barely gave her a glance as I spied the underwater camera under a folded up stack of miner's moss, used to trap and retain fine gold particles in our sluice box, and plucked it out. "Got it. Can you repack the suits?"

She nodded and stuffed the cold suits back into the duffel. "What's the camera for?" she asked with the inquisitive innocence of a dredging newbie.

"Need to find the right ground," I explained, turning on the camera to ensure it was working. "Don't want to take the time to make the hole we need and then find out we're in the wrong place."

"Oh?" Stella asked, her brow furrowing with genuine curiosity. "Would that be a big deal?"

"We only have a month to dredge before the ice starts breaking up." I cast a glance toward the distant roiling sea. "If we have to relocate our operation, that could impact the limited time we have to dive."

As the guys finished plowing, a pickup drove across the ice toward us. My gut clenched as the truck came into view.

It was my father.

He'd been back in town for about a month or so, I'd heard. Living out at Ben's cabin had kept me away from the goings-on in town, and from the drama Buck Darling's return would cause. The legend.

The thief, I reminded myself.

CHAPTER 2

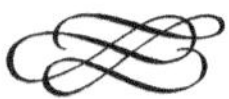

"Isn't that your dad?" Stella asked, tucking her hands inside the pockets of her parka.

The wind whisked across the open surface of the ice, which clung to the shoreline like a child to its mother.

I shivered. "Yep."

My gaze followed the track of his truck, still distant enough that all I could focus on was the blinding glint of the sun on the windshield.

My friend turned her attention to the boys while they finished plowing.

As Buck's truck drew closer, I wished he would turn and choose another location for his winter set-up. But I was his daughter and had mined with him for years. I knew his strategy. I should've guessed he'd show up eventually.

Seemed hard to believe only a few months ago he was recovering from heart surgery. Surgery I'd worked hard to pay for with my own two hands…and the help of Ben. I didn't want to dwell on it. I'd taken on the responsibility wholeheartedly as his only child, the only successor to take over the family business. I'd had to step up, and I had no problem doing it.

My father peeled off to the right, farther east of our location. I breathed out through my nose in relief.

"How's this?"

I recognized Ben's voice and refocused on him and Matt. Ben stood next to the truck and swept his hand in a grand gesture at the swath of ice they'd cleared.

It was more than enough for us to begin the first stages of setting up our temporary gold claim.

I gave him a thumbs up, handed Stella the underwater camera, and grabbed the auger so we could create our first test hole.

The ice was four feet thick—a nice, safe amount. The last thing we wanted was thin ice, but this close to shore with the weather we'd had lately, I knew that wouldn't be a problem. Plus, the representatives from the Alaska Department of Natural Resources were meticulous with their measurements—at least at the start of the season.

"Here it goes." I slipped the camera, set to video, into the hole. I made sure it sank deep enough to give us a good look at the sea floor.

Stella leaned over and stared into the narrow hole, supporting herself with her hands on her knees. Matt and Ben coolly leaned against the truck hood with their arms crossed over their chests.

I waited thirty seconds and then pulled it up.

Stella crowded me. "Well, is it a good spot?"

"Give me a second." I took off my insulated gloves, so I could more easily fiddle with the buttons. Ice cold water dripped from the camera. "Come here, guys, look."

Matt and Ben joined us near the hole. Ben was tall enough that he could stand behind me and still see the small screen on the back.

I replayed what I'd captured.

At first, disappointment soured my stomach. The video displayed a murky view of a sandy bottom. We didn't want sandy. We wanted rocky and filled with cobble—rocks and pebbles that would capture the gold deposited by glacier flow into the Bering Sea.

Then the camera spun to the left. The bottom grew less sandy. Larger and larger rocks appeared, revealing undisturbed ground that hadn't yet been mined.

"Yes." I punched a fist in the air. "I hoped coming out this far would pay off."

Ben wrapped his arms around my middle. "Way to go, Rory."

I leaned into his solid body. "Maybe you were right. Maybe we can figure this out on our own."

The sound of multiple chainsaws carving through ice drowned out our conversation.

We all turned our heads.

My father and a very recognizable figure, his old business partner, were cutting their dive hole near his truck.

"I can't believe him." Disgust filled my words.

"Who?" Ben asked. He squinted at the pair of men.

"My father and Nate. Together." The saw blades sheared through the thick ice inch by inch, and the buzzing annoyed me like a hungry mosquito in July. "After Nate was fired last summer, I thought the two of them would never work together again."

"Didn't you punch Nate in the nose?" Ben gave me a pointed look.

My face heated. It hadn't been my best moment on the *Alaska Darling*. "He was being a jerk, and I'd never seen him so angry. It was the drugs screwing with his head. We settled our differences, but he's just out of rehab." In October, Nate had called me from group therapy and had asked for my forgiveness over several confrontations we'd had. "Should they really be partnering back up?" Didn't addicts in recovery usually try to avoid their triggers?

What I didn't voice were my concerns about my father's health, because it irritated me that I cared so much after learning the truth about him. Should Buck be anywhere near a dredge operation after barely surviving major heart surgery? Did his doctor clear him for that?

"I'm sure they'll be fine." Stella liked to play peacemaker. "I think they're a good fit for each other. Who else was going to work for your dad? And who else was going to hire Nate?"

"I heard Nate moved in with him," Matt said.

"When?" I asked, my muscles tightening. "And why didn't anyone tell me?"

I scanned Matt and Stella's faces to find the guilty party.

Ben rubbed my arms. "I knew it would upset you."

"Wait." I turned out of Ben's arms. "I can forgive Stella and Matt for not telling me about this because I've hardly seen either them all winter, but you?"

How could Ben keep that kind of information from me knowing how I felt about my father and his deceit? I thought he had my back.

"Are you really going to hold that whole map thing over your dad's head forever?" Ben headed straight for our makeshift sled and the equipment we needed to unload now that we'd found our dive spot. Matt followed him wordlessly. Stella's boyfriend was the type that put his head down and did the work. He wanted no part in any arguments.

I gave Ben a look. "He stole that gold map from a dying man, used it to build up his reputation as the best dredger in town, and then lied about everything."

"Everything?" Ben untied the two corners of the tarp that covered everything. "I think you're exaggerating a little bit, don't you think?" He held his fingers a few centimeters apart.

Stella's eyebrows shot up, and she hurried over to the truck to busy herself with a cooler full of snacks and drinks they'd brought.

As my friend fled the scene, the burn of embarrassment hit my stomach. "I can't believe you're on Buck's side. You haven't even met him." I joined Ben and Matt at the sled to help them set up.

Ben whipped off the tarp, and I got my first look at what he purchased for our winter operation. A knot formed in my stomach. "This is what you bought? It looks like equipment found at the dump." I picked up the stiff, cracked rubber hoses used to deliver air and hot water to the diver, which had been patched badly.

Ben frowned. "This is what Stu's friend was selling. Beggars can't be choosers out here. You know that, Rory."

As he hauled out the second-hand sluice box and set it on the ice, I could see it was corroded and discolored from years of hard use.

"What I know is that I never would've spent my hard earned money on this junk." Although I knew the words coming out of my mouth were harsh, I couldn't hide my disappointment. Ben had spent most of his summer gold earnings on worthless equipment. We didn't have any more stake money to risk on our winter opera-tion. I couldn't just pretend everything was fine. How were we going to find the gold we needed using this stuff?

"I didn't have much choice." His face flushed a deep red.

My mind was blank. I didn't know how to fix this. Our first day on the ice might be our last. "I thought the listing online said the equipment was only a few years old." I felt nervous sweat coming on. I needed to solve this debacle...but how?

"Not as if I was the only buyer."

"Someone *else* wanted it?" As I got a closer look at the most vital piece of equipment for any dredging operation, the Aquacom unit, it was clear it had worn-out cables with their protective coatings peeled away, exposing the inner wiring.

"The seller had a storage unit filled with a bunch of things. I had to fight to make sure we had everything we needed." He wrapped his arms around himself as if creating a protective shield. "Nate convinced me this would get us by for the season."

"Wait, Nate was there?"

Matt quietly unloaded the rusted generator. He smartly avoided even getting involved in the argument. With that much rust would it even be able to start?

I looked across the ice at my father and Nate setting up their own diving venture with much newer equipment. Where did they purchase theirs from? I'd sold every bit of the *Alaska Darling* last summer. They would've had to start over from scratch, too. "You got played." I shook my head. "Nate lied to you so he could buy the good stuff without it turning into an auction."

Ben blew air out his nose. "Fuck." He kicked the rickety sled made of old plywood and broken bits of lumber. "He made it seem as if I'd made a good deal. Was real nice to me, too. I'm sorry, Rory, I screwed up. I never should've trusted him."

It ticked me off that Nate would do that to Ben. I thought we'd buried the hatchet after last summer's falling out. But clearly he was more loyal to my dad, rather than caring much about me. Maybe Nate would always be striving to earn my father's admiration. I sighed and rifled through each piece Ben had bought to find a silver lining. What else could I do? These were the cards we'd been dealt. "Okay," I said, touching the frame of the sluice box, "we can probably weld these corroded points back together. It might look ugly, but it should hold. The hoses we could try repatching in the worst spots, test them out to make sure they don't leak, and then keep an eye on them after every dive."

Ben inspected the rusted generator. "I'm sure I can get this going again."

Matt raised his brows.

I wanted to believe Ben, so I brushed past my best friend's boyfriend to dig out our tools and extra parts we kept on hand for repairs. I could be ticked off and work at the same time.

The buzzing stopped. I looked over my shoulder at my father's dive spot. Someone stood staring in our direction. I frowned. *Who was that?*

A few seconds passed, and the figure ducked behind the canvas and wood structure that served as a dive shack.

My body flashed hot and cold—as if I'd seen a ghost.

It couldn't be...he was in jail. I must be seeing things.

"Are you sure this is where you want to set up?" Ben asked. "I'd like to get to work on the genny."

I kept my gaze on the distant structure, hoping for another glimpse of the familiar figure to reassure myself I'd been mistaken. "This is our spot, and I'll be damned if Buck Darling is going to scare me away."

CHAPTER 3

As Ben and Matt worked together to restore the generator, I patched hoses and taped exposed wires. With such a bad start to the day, my thoughts drifted to the unknowns about this ice season. My very first one with me at the helm. Deep down I was nervous, but I didn't want any of them to know—especially Ben. The equipment debacle only added to my worries. After I snapped at him, guilt ran through me like a cold ocean current. Nate had done him dirty. Had that been my dad's idea? To sabotage our gold mining efforts to benefit himself?

Nome was a hard place to eke out a living, but its remote emptiness held a certain charm for people. It beckoned both the adventurous and those seeking solace. Despite the hardships, Nome acted as a magnet, pulling in those captivated by the idea of striking it rich or wanting to hide from the rest of the world.

I had to admit, even at twelve I had the same thoughts. My mother had disappeared. My stepfather had been rigid and cool to my hurts. Running away to a just-discovered biological father in an exotic locale seemed like the perfect solution to my pre-teen mind.

Running away had worked for a time. I'd lost myself in learning all about Buck Darling and what kind of father he would be: loving, yet tough. He expected me to grow up quickly and work as hard as any of his crew on the dredge. But I'd relished the opportunity to feel wanted, to have a purpose, to be noticed.

I taped up the last of the exposed wiring on the comms equipment and prayed that it worked. Without communications from the surface to the diver below, the danger would be too great. I tallied up the rest of the repairs we'd have to make before we could start dredging and sighed.

Stella honked the GMC's horn. "Come sit with me!" After the wind had picked up and dropped the temperature a few degrees, she'd retreated to the refuge of the truck's cab.

Turning from the boys, I went and joined Stella in Matt's truck. I felt a little guilty for leaving. This was *my* operation. I was the expert, but Ben had gotten us into this mess and seemed determined to fix things with or without my support. Later, I'd have to apologize for my sharp tongue. It had been hard to give up the need to control everything about our winter dredging plans. But if I wanted to keep Ben in my life, I needed to learn how to loosen up a little.

Climbing in, I said, "My hands are starting to cramp up. Ben probably won't mind if I take a break. He thinks I work too hard as it is." As I rested for a moment, I hesitated to disclose the extent of the repairs needed. The truth was, a ton of work needed to be done on our equipment, and I didn't want to burden Stella with the full reality of the precarious state we were in.

"Don't worry about what he thinks," Stella said with a dismissive gesture of the hand. She scooted over to the driver's side.

Instantly, she rolled up the window with the driver's side controls. "See? So much better in here."

I let out a breath. A puff of white smoke evaporated in the truck cab. I grinned.

Stella laughed. "Well, at least you're out of the wind."

"True."

My friend took out her earbuds and set her phone on the dashboard. "I've missed you. I feel like I've hardly seen you this winter."

"I missed you, too, Stel."

She pushed my shoulder playfully. "You did not. You got all snuggly with manly man there." Stella shifted her gaze to Ben who crouched with Matt next to the generator.

My cheeks grew warm. "I had to move out of my father's apartment. You know that." I bit the inside of my cheek. "Ben offered, and I…well—"

"Jumped at the chance to move in with your boyfriend? Yeah, I get that." Her eyes misted over. "I remember moving in with Matt and how much fun we had."

"You act as if that was eons ago, and it's been, what, a couple of years?" I couldn't avoid the pierce of jealousy. Stella and Matt went together like two peas in a pod. They just made sense. I never felt as if any of the men I'd dated made sense. Even Ben, and God knows I loved the guy, had his secrets. Depths he hadn't yet shown me. I knew there was more to his past than a dead fiancée. I just hadn't had the guts to ask. I didn't want to screw things up like I usually did.

"Yeah, but Matt's little sister showed up on our doorstep six months later," Stella muttered with a roll of her eyes.

"Hm, Alisha. I forgot about her."

"Anyway, I miss our binge nights—the pizza, the beer, the gossip." The idea of gossip lit up her face with a happy glow. "I almost forgot."

Stella always kept track of the latest news in Nome. Who was dating whom. Who got fired. Who got arrested. And if she didn't know the people involved very well, she was an expert at internet sleuthing—Facebook stalking, Google searches, Instagram posts.

"Oh?" Last time she'd brought something to my attention had been when she'd thought Ben had murdered his fiancé. Since then I'd made a point of double checking her 'news.' "What's going around town?"

"A mysterious arrival the other day." Stella grabbed her phone and brought up her Facebook app. "The *Nome Tidbits n' Tales* page had a post about it." She scrolled through the latest news.

"What makes it so mysterious?" I leaned in to look at her screen.

Stella's eyes lit up. "Well, this guy's been seen all over town asking questions. Some say it was stuff about your dad." She clicked on a group link. "Here it is. Someone took a pic of him leaving Ernie's Pub around lunchtime on Monday or maybe it was Tuesday."

Stella handed me her phone. On the screen was a blurry picture of a figure exiting the pub wearing an orange and black parka and a shearling sheepskin trapper hat. Lean. Narrow. Medium height.

"I don't recognize him."

"Well," Stella took back her phone and read the details of the post, "Sandy at Trini's Nail Spa says he was in Ernie's asking about *you*."

"And?" I shrugged even though it made me nervous to think some stranger was asking for me specifically. And why at Ernie's? The pub was a nighttime place where rougher types hung out. A few minor drug busts had happened within its walls as of late. "Are you sure it wasn't someone visiting for the races?"

Stella let out a sigh. "The Iditarod ended two weeks ago. Alisha said all the teams left right after the race."

Matt's younger sister had an obsession with dog mushers. She'd been tending to a half dozen dogs at some property her parents' owned for the last few years, and I often wondered about her plans for them. "Well, if Alisha said—" I said with a grin.

"You might not believe me," Stella huffed. "But something's going on. He's been seen all over town."

"Why don't one of these people in your little group go ask the guy what he's doing here? That might end all the speculation. You know how I feel about that sort of thing. I learned my lesson."

Stella's face reddened. "This is totally different, Rory."

"You had me convinced Ben was a murderer." I cringed at the memory. Since last summer things had changed considerably. Now I couldn't imagine not having Ben in my life.

"I apologized for that, Rory."

"You're right, Stel. You did," I began, my tone gentle and conciliatory. "And I have to admit some of the evidence was pretty damning." I gave her a wry grin, hoping she understood I didn't blame her for what she'd done. Stella had only wanted to protect me.

I gazed through the windshield at Ben filling the generator with diesel from one of the full cans we'd brought with us. Could he and Matt have fixed it already? Even though he'd come to Nome not knowing a thing about diving for gold, he'd proven himself a quick study. It helped he was good with mechanical things. I liked to think of myself as knowledgeable about all the equipment since I'd been using it for a decade, but Ben definitely had a leg up on figuring things out when we hit some kind of snag that went beyond the obvious. The equipment out here on the ice couldn't fail, couldn't break, couldn't be down for a moment, or someone's life could be at risk.

"Well," said Stella, interrupting my thoughts as I watched the men work. "Do you think they did a good job?" She cocked her head to one side as if that would make it easier for her to understand how the mess of equipment fit together.

"Let's go find out." I hopped out of the truck praying the repairs had done the trick.

Ben looked up from his work as we came over, his face ruddy with the cold.

"Did you fix it?" I asked with a smile. Ben needed a win.

"Aye, aye, captain." He finished adding the fuel. "Here we go." Ben turned the switch and, miraculously, the battery had enough charge to turn the engine over. After a few cranks, however, it wouldn't start. He slid his gaze to me and swallowed.

If I could've crossed my fingers in my big winter gloves, I would have. Everything depended on our second-hand generator working.

Ben slid the lever switch to choke it and then cranked it a few more times. The engine caught, roared to life, and blew out a cloud of blue smoke.

Despite the decrepit condition of our equipment, our operation was somehow coming together, and my pre-dive nerves kicked in —but no one needed to know that.

Ben touched my shoulder as he passed behind me. "We need to test everything today to see if we can even dive tomorrow."

I scanned the bits and pieces of equipment strewn across the ice. Sure, I'd repaired a few hoses and the wiring, but the sluice needed welding and the pump looked as if the casing could be cracked. "We've got a lot of work to do here before we're ready to test."

Ben let out a sigh. He knew it was the truth, but it didn't mean it was any easier to hear.

I turned to Stella. "Look, we need to spend probably spend the rest of the remaining daylight hours working on repairs. You don't need to hang around for this. Why don't you meet us over at

Miner's around five, and we'll buy you dinner to thank you for all your help."

Ben gave me a surprised look. I hadn't exactly clued him in on the fact we'd be spending some of our dwindling cash supply on a meal for four.

Stella gave me a hug. "That sounds great."

CHAPTER 4

Miner's Bar & Grill stood on the main strip, which ran along the famous Nome beach, where in the early days folks had panned for gold right in the sand. Miner's was one of the few restaurants in town that sold beef steaks as a regular menu item. Although moose and caribou were easy to come by, nothing hit home like a big, juicy T-bone from an actual cow. They had them flown in from Anchorage in between storms in the winter time, but since the Iditarod had only finished up a couple of weeks ago, they were sure to have some leftover.

We entered as a foursome: Ben with one massive arm around me and Stella and Matt walking in side by side. Matt wasn't the type to outwardly show a lot of affection. He hid his face behind a bushy dark blond beard—probably to compensate for his receding hairline. The beard hid his expression, which tended to move from glum to serious to emotionless.

Okay, that was harsh. But Matt could be a hard one to read.

Against his nature, Matt broke out into a smile when he saw who was tending bar. He left our little group to talk with Marla Stearns. She managed the restaurant as well as tended bar and played server when need be. Back in high school, Matt had worked at Miner's as a bus boy and dishwasher in the summers. He'd mentioned a few times what a great boss she'd been.

The practically empty room told me Marla was playing all three roles that afternoon. After the crush of the Iditarod crowd, it was nice to have our little town back with all of its hushed winter quiet.

"Let's sit by the window," said Stella. She grabbed three menus off the bar and headed toward an empty table with a good view of the street.

"So, we're buying, huh?" Ben whispered to me as we followed Stella.

"They deserve it." I should've consulted with Ben first, but sometimes my mouth was a few steps ahead of my brain, and I was still a little ticked at Ben for buying such crummy equipment. A buffer of friends would help me work through my annoyance before Ben and I were alone in our temporary quarters—a rented yurt on the beach. "They were out on the ice with us for hours."

"True."

Stella handed me two menus, and I passed one to Ben. It was his first time at Miner's. "Here. Most everything on the menu is edible. But if Marla's cooking, too, I wouldn't pick anything more complicated than a burger and fries—"

"Or a steak," Matt said, taking a seat next to his girlfriend.

"How's Marla doing?" I asked, deciding on a large bowl of chili and a side of cornbread.

"Once again, she's running the whole show. Her cook's in Arizona for the next two weeks." Matt didn't even glance at a menu. "She wanted to know what Alisha was up to. Guess she was tearing through town the other day on that used sled she bought."

Stella gasped. "She actually hooked up those dogs to a sled?"

"I didn't know she'd gotten so serious about it," I said.

Matt shrugged.

Marla approached with a pencil behind her ear, a notepad in her hand, and her red framed readers perched on the end of her nose. "What can I get you, hon?" She turned her gaze expectantly on Stella.

"I'll have the steak. Medium. Baked potato. And a beer."

Marla scribbled furiously. I wondered why since Matt had intimated Marla would likely be filling in for her vacationing cook.

"Same," said Ben and Matt simultaneously.

I felt like the oddball when I gave Marla my order. Although I'd lured everyone here with steak, I wasn't much of a steak-eater myself.

Marla headed to the kitchen.

"I really wanted to thank the both of you for helping us set up today," Ben said.

That surprised me. Ben was beginning to shed his reserve. Last year, his words had been sparse and clipped when with my friends.

"Yes," I said. "We couldn't have done it without the two of you."

"Well, I don't know about me," said Stella. "I probably got in the way more than helped." Her cheeks flushed red.

I reached across the table and grabbed her hand. "You did just fine, Stel."

She smiled a little smile at me. "Thanks."

"It was really hard to see my dad out there today, so having some friends around me was helpful."

"We just need to focus on what we're doing," said Ben. "Don't worry about your father or Nate. We managed last summer without them…we can do it again."

My brow furrowed. I really needed to tell him about the risks, especially now that our equipment was not in the condition I had been expecting. I tried not to dwell on what might happen if any of our repairs failed.

Ben didn't miss a beat. "Hey, everything okay?" He brushed the hair from my eyes.

I couldn't lie when he looked at me like that. "I'll figure it out."

Before he could call me out, the door to Miner's swung open and my gut clenched for the second time that day.

My father, Buck Darling, and his long-time partner, Nate Frazier walked in.

Marla, who had exited the kitchen with a basket of breadsticks for our table, greeted my father and his partner, "Hey! Good to see you both. It's been awhile, Nate. Looking good."

"Thanks," Nate replied.

He did look good. No longer so thin, his face shaven clean, and his once red-rimmed eyes clear as day. Rehab had worked wonders.

"We can scooch another table over, so you all can sit together," Marla said. She plopped our basket in front of us and reached for another table a few feet away.

I grabbed Ben's hand under the table and squeezed—hard. I wasn't ready to talk to my dad. The last time we spoke, we ended up in an argument.

Ben looked down, surprise on his face, then assessed my expression.

Before he could react, my best friend, who was too sweet for her own good sometimes, rose from her seat and helped Marla move the table to abut ours. "Absolutely. So good to see you back, Mr. Darling." Stella's round face lit up with a smile, and she even moved the bread basket closer to the center of the joined tables. My friend had no idea how the relationship between my dad and I had changed for the worse over the last few months.

My father's face turned red. He open and closed his fists, avoiding eye contact with me. "No, that's all right," he said. "We can sit over here so that you kids can have some time without us old guys bothering you."

Stella pulled out a chair nearly tripping my dad as he attempted to get away. "No, I insist. Please."

Nate took a seat without comment and tucked into the breadsticks.

Marla touched Nate's shoulder. "I'll bring you a coke, honey?" she asked the recent rehab graduate.

"Sure. That'd be great." Nate slipped a glance my way and then focused back on his half-eaten breadstick.

He knew I knew about the dirty trick he'd played on Ben to convince him to buy substandard used gear. I hope it ruined his appetite.

My father hung back for a few seconds, then gave in and sat next to Stella, whose face glowed in delight at the possibility she may have healed a family wound. She just had no idea how deep that wound had grown after my dad found out I sold the *Alaska Darling* out from under him.

"I was just telling Rory you'd come back to town, wasn't I?" Stella said in a rush.

"I—uh—" I had no idea what to say.

Ben stuck out his hand. "I'm Ben Abel, Mr. Darling. Nice to meet you. Your daughter and I worked together last summer on the dredge. She taught me a whole lot. You should be really proud of her. One tough cookie."

Buck shook my boyfriend's hand firmly. Ben's huge one overpowered my father's finer, more delicate one. "I see."

Marla returned to the table with a plastic glass full of ice and coke for Nate and a bottle of beer for my father. Buck snatched it out of her hand and took a long swig.

Stella tried once more to smooth things over. "Looks as if you and Rory are going to be neighbors during ice season. I had no idea how much work it takes to set up your shelter, dig the hole, all that equipment."

"Expensive equipment," my dad said bitterly.

I felt my ire rise. How dare he bring that up after sending his partner to trip up Ben at the equipment sale?

Ben touched my leg.

But that wasn't enough to stop me. "I did what I thought was best. Did you want me to let you die?"

My father gripped his beer bottle. "What I wanted you to do was keep the business going, not sell it to the highest bidder," Buck said raising his voice. "What I wanted you to do was work your ass off and not give in when things got a little tough. I never thought a daughter of mine would take the easy way out."

"Easy way out?" I gasped. "Are you kidding me?" I opened my mouth, wanting to spew out exactly what I thought of Nate convincing Ben to buy junk.

At that very moment, Marla showed up at the table with three steaks and a bowl of chili. "Who had the chili?" she squeaked.

An awkward silence took over the table.

I pressed my lips together.

Matt, who had been quiet the entire time, said, "I ordered steak. Put one of them bad boys right here." He pointed at the spot in front of him, seemingly unbothered by the argument that had erupted.

Marla handed out the rest of the food, turned to Nate and Buck, and asked, "Do you know what you want?"

My dad kicked back his chair, took his half-drunk bottle of beer, said, "I don't need this shit," and walked out.

Nate looked longingly at the steak dinners in front of Stella, Matt, and Ben, sighed, and said to Marla, "Guess we'll come back another time." He tossed ten bucks on the table and followed Buck out the door.

CHAPTER 5

The sun was setting in the sky: a low orange orb distant beyond the ice shelf. I squinted to locate our dive shelter. Several tarp-covered frames dotted the ice, but I couldn't figure out which was ours.

After the argument with my father, my mind was muddled. We'd never been the type to argue. He'd been the one in charge, and I had been the daughter, helper, believer, supporter who'd followed his lead in everything. Since his accident and finding out he had stolen an old man's gold map, however, our relationship had developed a deep crack.

I hugged Ben closer as he pulled up next to our yurt. He'd become the new rock in my life. A falling out with my dad needed to be set aside so I could focus on the prize: big gold. My intent had been to find it as quickly as possible before the ice melted. But now I wondered if we'd make it through a full winter season with the dilapidated equipment we had to use. Without a good boost in our finances before the summer gold season, we wouldn't be able to buy the floating dredge we required. This whole thing was turning into a nightmare before my eyes.

Stu, who owned Alaska North Assayers, rented out yurts in both summer and winter to gold dredgers. He also exchanged raw gold for cash and sold new and used mining equipment. I'd had my eye on a used floating dredge he had acquired for resale that I hoped we'd be able to afford come spring. But after the horrible experience Ben had with buying used equipment through a friend of Stu's, I was wary of trusting him for something as important as the watercraft that would be the foundation of our summer operation.

Ben switched off the machine and shook out his shaggy hair. "Home sweet home. This is the right one, yes?"

"Yep. Number twelve." I slid off the back and approached our makeshift sled that we'd left behind before dinner. "That's our stuff right there."

I uncovered the rest of our gear and grabbed a duffel bag, which I'd crammed full of layering pieces, wool sweaters, snow pants, and enough underwear to carry me through until we could find time for the laundromat.

Ben popped his head inside. "Pretty basic, but it'll do." He reached for a battery-powered lantern I'd uncovered and disappeared inside.

Meanwhile, I unloaded two arctic-rated sleeping bags and some plastic grocery bags filled with easy-to-make meals we could reheat over the propane stove. Reviewing the limited selection, I was glad we'd splurged on a good meal at Miner's. Loaded down with the duffel and a sleeping bag, I entered the yurt.

It felt about as warm inside as outside, but Ben was already working on getting a fire started in the small wood stove. Stu had supplied some kindling and a few larger logs, which would keep us going until tomorrow.

"Thanks for getting started on that."

"My pleasure." Ben smiled. "I have to make sure my baby doesn't freeze." He winked.

I knew he wanted to coax a smile from me, but I didn't feel much like smiling. My mind was loaded with worry about the sorry state of our equipment. How could he be so cavalier about it? "I'll be warm enough after hauling in all our gear." I headed back out for more supplies.

Ben appeared at my side. "Here, allow me." He scooped up as much as he could in his massive arms. "Fire's looking good. Should be warm in there in no time."

We arranged our cots on one side of the yurt near the stove. All

I wanted was to climb into my sleeping bag, shut my eyes, and sleep, but I knew Ben sensed my change in demeanor since we'd unloaded the equipment.

While I rustled up my courage to clear the air between us, he unfolded two collapsible camp chairs and flipped over a cardboard box we'd used to transport some of our dredging gear to use as a table. "We can figure out the rest tomorrow, no?" He sat in a chair and stretched out his hands to warm in the now crackling fire.

"Sure." Kicking off my boots, I slid inside my sleeping bag and sat upright on the cot. "About that. Tomorrow, I mean." I let out a breath, which turned white in the cold air. "I'm worried about the safety of our equipment."

Ben frowned. "I don't know what you want me to say, Rory. I'm sorry I'm stupid and bought crappy stuff."

"Look, it's too late to do anything about it now. We're stuck with that junk."

His face turned red.

"We have to make the best of it. We don't have any choice."

"We could choose not to dive this winter," he said quietly.

"What?" His statement shocked me. How long had that idea been zinging around in his brain. "Are you serious? You want us to give up?" He'd shocked me into silence. All I knew was dredging. I had no greater aspiration than to be the best goddamn female dredger in Nome.

His blue gaze burned into me. "You said it yourself—you're worried about the safety of our equipment. Do you really think it's worth it to dive when we don't trust our gear? I'm sorry I ever trusted Nate and spent all that money on junk. It took everything in me not to punch him in the face when they showed up at Miner's."

I leaned back at that confession. I had no idea he'd been hiding such a deep resentment earlier. "We're going to dive." I'd been on the hunt for gold for so many years, I couldn't imagine stopping now. Yes, the equipment sucked, but we'd figure it out. "We'll just make sure to have plenty of parts on hand and do an equipment check every day. If you see anything hinky, we pull the plug until we can make a fix." Aurora Darling did not quit—no matter what.

Right then I should've confessed that I've never ice dived myself, but I couldn't make the words come out. That would've added to his reasoning for us to quit. But I'd seen my dad and Nate do it a million times. There was no point in worrying him. But if that was true, why did my palms grow clammy?

"*Anything* hinky?" Ben left the newly lit fire and joined me on the cot.

"That's right," I said. "If you see anything weird when you're tending, you're allowed to end the dive, and we make sure to fix the problem before we continue."

In a flash, he had lifted me onto his lap—sleeping bag and all. I squirmed in his arms. "Hey, this is serious."

His eyes flashed with a blue fire. "This is serious." He leaned in and kissed me.

The chill I'd felt after I'd entered the yurt fled, and desire rushed in. All my worries about my father, the equipment, finding enough gold disappeared when he kissed me, and I wound my arms around his neck.

As we kissed, thoughts of all our lazy mornings came back to me. We'd spent the entire fall at Ben's cabin enjoying ourselves. We'd eat in bed, snuggle under the covers, and make love.

I broke off our kiss and leaned my cheek against his rough one, breathing in the wood smoke smell that permeated his clothes. "I wish we could stay just like this," I whispered. "Always."

He stroked my hair. "Me, too." He let out a long breath.

After a few minutes, he gently pushed my legs off his lap, and I sat back on the cot. He pawed through our pile of things on the other side of the yurt and grabbed his sleeping bag.

I didn't mind the abruptness. The flash from passionate to serious. That was Ben. Although he appeared unbreakable, tough, a mountain of a man that couldn't be touched by anything, his emotions ran wildly underneath it all. Every now and then, something would remind him of bad times. I accepted that part of him. We were both broken in our own way and understood each other because of it.

Ben lay down, zipped up his sleeping bag all the way to the top, and stuffed a jacket under his head as a pillow.

I rolled on my side, crooked my arm, and rested my head in my hand. "I'm sorry I freaked out about the equipment earlier. I could've handled that better."

His expression shifted from tiredness to a subtle sadness. His eyes, once bright, now held a shadow of hurt, and his lips tightened as if wrestling with the sting of my earlier criticism. The heaviness in the air was tangible, as if the weight of my doubts lingered between us.

"It's all right."

But I didn't believe him.

A sharp rap on our yurt's plywood door broke up our conversation.

We both sat up.

"Who is it?" I asked.

A long pause of quiet.

"Hello?" I called out.

"It's Nate. I have some of your stuff."

I swallowed, thinking about Ben's confession only minutes ago. He had wanted to punch Nate. Maybe I should've told our surprise guest to go away or come back in the morning. Whatever it was Nate had to give me, it could wait. I glanced at Ben. He nodded.

Was I inviting trouble into our yurt?

"Come in," I answered.

Ben climbed out of his sleeping bag to unfold a chair and chuck another log in the wood stove. He was being more welcoming than I would've been.

The door opened. Nate stood just outside carrying a cardboard box. Darkness had settled quickly even though it was only early evening.

His gaze warily swept from me to Ben.

I gestured at him to enter. "It's cold out there. Let's not lose the little bit of heat we've managed to build."

"Sorry." Nate came inside and shut the door firmly behind him. "I hope I'm not interrupting anything."

I felt my face heat. I knew what he was implying. I'd known Nate since I was twelve; he was like an uncle to me. "Not at all. We just finished unloading our gear."

"Buck wanted me to bring this by." He set the box on the floor.

"Some of your stuff was still at his place. Oh, and he wanted me to thank you for keeping up with the rent while he was in Anchorage."

I gave a nod of acknowledgment.

I'd been planning to pick up the few odds and ends stored at my dad's apartment while we were in town for ice season, and it looked as if Nate had included some of our mail. At least I could check that off the list of things to do.

"Here," offered Ben gruffly. "Got a chair for you."

The tension between the two men was palpable. I prepared myself for an intervention in case things escalated.

Nate whipped off his ever-present baseball cap and ran a hand through his thinning hair. He'd trimmed it since last summer. "Thanks."

"You look good." I feigned friendliness as he took a seat. "Sobriety really suits you." It had been only a few months since he'd successfully completed a rehab program down state.

Why the heck was Nate sticking around after his errand? He had to know we'd figured out the equipment was trash. Did he have a death wish?

"Thanks," Nate started awkwardly, "I know we had our run-ins last year and all that. I wanted to tell you in person that I never meant to take it out on you—the problems I had with Buck." With lowered eyes and a slight slouch, Nate's posture suggested an unspoken admission of guilt.

Ben crouched by the small wood stove and poked around in the coals.

"Hope you're happy with the set up you and Buck have going." Ben's voice sounded low and dangerous. "That's some nice equipment you got."

Nate's demeanor shifted subtly, his shoulders tensing. "Buck sent me to the sale to buy the best equipment I could lay my hands on." His gaze sharpened, and a guarded expression emerged. "Is it my fault if you don't know crap when you see it?"

The Beast was unleashed.

Ben rose from the fire and hit his full height—a good four inches taller than Nate. "Rory trusts you. I never thought you'd screw her over like that."

Nate hopped up in a flash.

"Whoa." I quickly climbed out of my sleeping bag and got between the two men. "Ben, he's not worth it."

I could easily envision my boyfriend pounding Nate into the sand without mercy, which could turn into the police getting involved. Not what we needed right now. Nome had only recently gotten over the idea Ben was a murderer. I didn't need people giving him the side eye for a different reason.

Nate had his fists balled up and fire in his eyes. The same Nate from last summer who'd been high on something when he demanded I owed him money because of his twenty-year dredging history with my dad. He'd tossed me around and possibly would've done worse if Ben hadn't shown up and punched him.

I placed the flat of my hand on Ben's massive chest. "You don't want to do this."

Under my palm I could feel his heart beating steadily. The control Ben had surprised me. Mine beat in my chest like a wild bird trapped in a cage.

"You'd better pray nothing breaks when we're diving. Because if Rory gets hurt—" Ben warned.

"I'm not going to get hurt," I soothed. I didn't believe my own words, but I had to calm him down before something bad happened.

"I don't need this shit from you," Nate spat out. "I came to apologize to Rory. That's it."

I looked up at Ben to gauge his expression. The furrowed lines on his forehead and the slight clenching of his jaw hinted at his growing anger. "I think it's time to leave, Nate," I said.

"Get the hell out," Ben said between clenched teeth.

Nate, his face tight with tension, abruptly stood up and headed for the door of the yurt. "You got it." Without another word, he pushed through it and disappearing into the winter blackness.

I perched on the edge of the ice hole in my dive suit, looking into the deep dark blue of the Bering Sea below. A chill ran through me. At first, I dismissed it as a reaction to the freezing temperatures out on the ice, but if I thought about it for more than a minute or two, I knew what it was: fear.

"Everything good to go, Rory?" Ben asked as he stood behind me at the comms station.

Dread coursed through me. Instead of the familiar surge of excitement I usually felt before a dive, the tips of my fingers and toes tingled, and a deep, unsettling sense of foreboding took over. The morning light accentuated the dismal state of our equipment. Would the repaired hoses hold? Would the pump fail in the middle of my dive? I did my best to shove the worries to the back of my mind. Ben didn't need to be reminded, once again, of the unfortunate decision he had made in purchasing this old, broken junk.

I forced my face to remain neutral and nodded.

As I lowered my mask over my face and adjusted the umbilical of air and hot water hoses so they wouldn't get in my way, I clenched my jaw. I could handle the fear. Aurora Darling, daughter of legendary underwater dredge miner, Buck Darling, didn't get scared. Being scared was for chumps.

I gave Ben a thumbs up, slipped into the hole we'd made, and chased my worries to the back of my mind. We didn't have time to waste, and there was no time to find better equipment. Ice season didn't last long, we needed the money badly, and with only a two-person team to work the gold-bearing ocean bottom, I couldn't back out. Not an option.

Once I was fully submerged, the closed-in nature of being under a thick sheet of ice gave me pause. Even though it was light outside, the daylight didn't penetrate the thickness of the frozen surface and all that met me was an enigmatic stillness and murky depths. The water, almost ink-like in its obscurity, held a shroud of mystery I found unsettling. Not only that, but the ceiling of ice above me looked like the inside of a crystal cave with stalactites hanging—not great for keeping my hastily repaired air and water lines unsnagged and free floating. I continued down about twelve feet. When I reached the bottom and a field of untouched cobble, gold sparkled under the light attached to my visor. I panned my head back and forth, and the bright pops of metallic yellow lit up under the glow. I focused on the slivers of gold, hoping the rush of the discovery would help me ignore the sick feeling in my stomach about whether or not the hoses would hold and the pump would continue pushing fresh air into my mask.

I propelled myself forward to reach the suction hose waiting for me at the bottom. Even though my heart raced at the thought of being trapped down here if the generator failed, I forced myself to take deep, slow breaths.

"How's it looking," Ben asked as he tended the machinery above that kept me alive and warm.

His voice calmed me. The communication system worked fine despite appearances. I scanned the ocean floor below and saw cobble in all directions. No sand. "Looks good down here. I think we found an excellent spot."

"Fantastic," he replied. "I've got nothing to report up top. All the repairs are holding. We can check them again between dives. Looks as if we have a bit of competition to the east of us and—" He hesitated.

Although I was working hard to remain calm, I knew why he did that.

"My dad? Is he out there now?" Buck would have a fit if he knew

I was ice diving, not only because of the shoddy state of our equipment, but due to my inexperience with winter diving.

He was right.

When we'd driven the snow machine across the ice that morning, my dad's shack had been empty. Its canvas cover rippled in the steady breeze that blew in from the Bering. Even though it was windy, the conditions weren't bad. No way would he stay away from mining on a day like today.

"Not yet," Ben replied.

Last summer I'd been able to get my sea legs and figure out how to manage a dredge mining business on my own. I'd been forced to hire Ben, a diver who had no history of gold dredging in Nome. He'd given me the freedom I needed to make mistakes, forge my own path, and learn things. Although I'd dived for years under my dad's meticulous guidance in the warmer ice-free waters of summer, winter diving was new to me. But how different could it be? I possessed the necessary diving skills; now, I just required practical experience.

My breathing grew shallow again. I wasn't sure if it was my regulator icing up or my nerves throwing me into a mini panic attack. Why did I think this would be so easy? I clung to the umbilical and focused on the gold-bearing ocean bottom below me. My light swept the bumpy terrain.

Slow down, Rory. Breathe deep and slow.

"Forget about him, Rory," Ben's voice drifted over me. "You got this."

His encouraging words calmed me again. He had no idea how much I needed his voice in my ear. After we'd spent months alone in his cabin, the two of us had figured out the right way to communicate.

"I got this," I said to myself in a whisper. My years of training came back in a rush: keep your cool, breathe steady, find the right ground, sweep for gold, repeat, repeat, repeat.

Above me the ice had grown unevenly. Some pockets were shallower than others. I needed to be careful with my lines here.

My vision narrowed to a small window of cobble, and my light glinted off gold flakes. To the untrained eye, it would be hard to see, but I knew gold when I saw it. I reached the bottom and followed the end of the suction hose until I had a good grasp of the handles on either side. I forced my body perpendicular to the ocean floor and straddled the hose.

"Start her up!" I shouted into my headset. The sick feeling in my stomach dissipated at the sight of gold.

"On it," Ben responded.

Within moments I felt the kick of the powerful suction hose. Sand, rock, and gold flakes swirled up into the six-inch opening.

Nothing like that feeling. Gold. Brilliant beautiful gold. Each flake one step closer to our dreams: our own floating dredge operation by summer.

As I cleared away the sand and rock, the gold flakes kept appearing. Not a bad start to the very short season.

I had a hard time keeping the excitement out of my voice. "I found a good streak. Hope it lasts."

"Sweet! I knew we could do it, babe."

I ate up his compliments as if they were a good meal. "*We* did it," I emphasized.

"Everything good with the heat in your suit?"

I did a body check. "I think so." I wiggled my toes in my wetsuit and boots. They moved.

"If anything starts to go numb, let me know. Don't want you staying down there too long."

I wanted to snort. No gold diver wanted to be told to come up before she was ready, but I knew he was right. I should know better than to push boundaries on my very first day, especially not knowing how reliable any of our equipment would be. "Got it."

"I'm going to check the fuel and grab a snack. I'll be right back."

"No prob, babe." I continued sucking up the flecks of gold that twinkled in my light.

Out of the corner of my eye, I saw quick movement, and startled, the suction hose leaping up in my hands.

A seal glided past.

A stupid seal.

I tried to slow my racing heart as I grabbed the hose again. The seal seemed curious and took a pass around me, keeping at a respectful distance. As he glided by, he rolled over on his back, then to his side as he swam off into the turbid water.

I smiled at my jumpiness. Mentally, I wished a friendly goodbye to the ringed seal and went back to sucking up gold. I moved forward, following the trail.

"Everything looks good up here." Ben's voice lit up my comms. "Generator seems to be working fine, but maybe a little rough. It could probably use some tweaking between dives. The wind has died down some. And I'm eating a PB and J. Made by yours truly. How about down there?"

"Everything's good."

"Those hoses holding up okay?"

Did he think I didn't do a good repair job? "I made sure to tape up every single weak spot. You think I want to risk a leak?" I snapped. I was the one diving with ancient, cracked hoses while he ate a sandwich and kicked back up top.

"It was only a question. Jeez, babe, why so touchy?"

I wanted nothing more than to go back to sucking up gold and forgetting about the worries I had about everything, but his questions set me off. "Look, I did the best I could with the time we had yesterday." My breathing sped up. "Why do you think I chose to dive first? If I screw up, guess who's going to suffer the consequences?"

"Sorry I care about your safety." His words came out clipped. "Next time I'll just keep my concerns to myself."

"Next time, maybe I should do the buying," I mumbled.

"Wow, I can't believe you said that."

The hurt in his voice pained me. I didn't want to be in this argument with Ben. Why did I have to say something so mean to him? He didn't deserve it. My heartbeat throbbed in my ears as my blood pressure rose. I wanted things to be smooth and calm between us. My life beyond our dive shelter was screwed up enough. Was I destroying another relationship because I couldn't leave things well enough alone?

I answered him with a grunt. I was too worked up to offer any kind of apology. I'd probably say more mean things until my emotions burned off.

As I picked up the suction hose to continue, I thought about my prickly reaction to Ben. Why couldn't I listen more and argue less? I'd taken Ben's simple question and turned it into a personal attack.

My mind flashed to my mother and how similar we were. I didn't like the mental comparison, but as I grew older and more reflective about my life, my parents, and my situation, it was hard to avoid the truth.

My mother, Cynthia Pomeroy, had been one of those types of women who always found someone to blame for her situation. She had been beautiful. Tall. Sleek. Like a tigress. Long hair. Long nails. Long legs. My older sister, Zoe, had some of that in her. The sophistication I lacked, she'd gotten in spades.

But then my mother, in a fit of melodrama, announced her affair with my birth father, Buck...oh, and then later she abandoned me, my older sister, Zoe, and my stepfather and was never heard from again, leaving the household enveloped in a cloud of emotional turbulence.

Did I have the same volatile tendencies as my mother? Was that why I fought so hard against the easy relationship I'd found with Ben? I'd dated many guys before him, and none of them stuck. Well, I didn't stick with them, that is. Usually, my relationships lasted only a few months before I got cold feet or found a flaw or something else about the guy and quit on him.

If I ended a relationship before the other person did, I could control how it ended, when it ended, and be the decision maker rather than the one who failed to live up to expectations. It had been a safe way for me to have a relationship without feeling like a failure.

Kyle Stroup, my previous boyfriend, was the longest relationship I'd ever had. One year. He'd been "safe" in my book. My father had worked with him and thought he was a good guy, so I thought so too.

Boy, was I wrong, and I'd almost lost my life making that assumption.

Ben was the opposite of Kyle in every way that mattered. When he kissed me, I felt whole. When we were in bed together, I was able to forget everything weighing me down and focus only on the present—Ben and me. Nothing else mattered but the two of us.

A pang of remorse gripped me. I wished I hadn't snapped at him. When my dive was over I'd apologize, make amends for my rude words.

I looked down at the suction hose. I'd been sucking up gold and dirt without even hardly paying attention, like driving on autopilot. Sometimes that happened down here. The quiet and insular nature of the work made me go so deep inside myself, I lost track of time and space. I hoped subconsciously I'd been doing a good job.

My fingers cramped from the tight grip on the handle and the cold that had seeped into my extremities. The farther I got from the hole, the more the hot water in the tube lost heat on its way to keep me warm.

I took a breath and shook out one hand and then the other to get the blood flowing again. But when I sucked in air, only a trickle came in through my regulator.

Shit.

Panic surged as I realized it had frozen up on me. A sharp, desperate cry escaped my lips, a visceral sound. Desperation clawed at me, urging me to breathe, but the frozen regulator denied me air. A primal instinct for survival kicked in. The world around me blurred as a cold numbness crept over my face.

"Rory?" Ben's voice sounded distant and weak. "Are you okay?"

Stars appeared in my vision. I was losing consciousness.

Then I felt a hard tug on the umbilical of hoses that connected me to the surface. My body accelerated away from the suction hose and toward the distant hole in the ice.

CHAPTER 7

The next thing I remember was Ben's worried face hovering above mine. "Breathe, Rory, breathe."

I gasped and coughed. My lungs filled with pure, sweet air.

He rested his forehead against mine. "Thank God you're okay." Then he kissed my cheek, his lips warm against my cool skin.

"I'll be fine." Despite my brush with suffocation, I skillfully buried any traces of fear and maintained a composed exterior. If he thought there was too much risk involved, he might shut everything down. To me, that was not an option. I was a gold dredger, like my dad, and always would be. As I reassured him, a casual curiosity took over: "How's the gold looking in the box?"

Ben's eyes brightened at my question, and he smiled tentatively. "The gold in the sluice looks pretty good so far." Then he sobered. "What happened down there?"

I attempted to sit up. He helped me, and I reached for the zipper on my suit. "My regulator iced up. I wasn't controlling my breathing very well. Rookie mistake." I didn't want to think too deeply about it. That would only make things worse. Better to continue as if nothing had happened. From what I remembered from previous winters, the regulator problem was a common one for first timers under the ice. I should've been more cautious. My dad would've reamed me if I'd been under his watch.

"Ours don't have insulated components?" Ben snatched up the regulator and dive mask I'd discarded.

"Beggars can't be choosers, remember?" Since we were running our dive operation on a shoestring, we repurposed things. No budget existed to purchase separate winter gear. "If you control your breathing, the moisture in your exhaled breath shouldn't have time to accumulate on the metal. I must've lost my concentration." I didn't tell him it was likely because our verbal sparring had stressed me out.

"I guess the Navy spoiled me." He set the regulator on a folding chair next to our dive hole. "We had a whole separate kit for cold diving."

"When it's your turn, think about consistent breathing—slow and steady." I moved away from the hole and headed toward the sluice box. I had to know if we'd found a lucrative spot to dredge. "Let's check the riffles." A good accumulation of gold would make up for almost suffocating on my very first winter dive. I tried to shake off the lingering jitters with thoughts of nuggets and gold dust clogging up our trough.

Gold fever had gripped Ben hard last summer. It was an easy fever to catch. The minute you saw that first small nugget in your hand, it was hard to stop diving and sucking up the ocean bottom for more.

I inspected the sluice box. Gold twinkled in the black sand.

"Not bad." To have gold in the box on the first day was a relief. My mind flashed back to the harrowing moment when my oxygen supply was abruptly cut off and the overwhelming surge of panic and helplessness that had swept over me. My whole body shivered, as if I were shaking off the last vestiges of dread that clung to me. Compared to summer diving, ice diving was a whole other beast.

"I think we found our spot." Ben ran a hand through the gold and smiled at the glistening flakes between his fingers. "But the regulator is a new thing to worry about." He was a great scuba diver, but the air lines used in gold diving instead of a pressurized tank was a different ball game.

As I took a few deep breaths of fresh air, regret came to the forefront of my mind. "Hey, Ben, I'm sorry about earlier. If you hadn't bought this equipment, we wouldn't even be diving. I didn't mean to snap at you down there."

"We were both stressed out. I get it. But I appreciate the apology."

A renewed sense of connection flowed like a soothing current through my body. Any lingering guilt I had about my unkind comment disappeared. "Then let's make the most of this dive, shall we?"

"Agreed."

"The suction hose is not too far east of here." I finished unzipping my suit and toweled off in the frigid air. The equipment heated our shack some, but not enough to provide balmy conditions. Goose bumps rose on my arms, and I scrambled to don a sweatshirt and thick leggings over my damp swimsuit. "If you're game to keep going, you should be able to pick up where I left off."

Ben was not one to back down from a challenge. "Absolutely. I'm stoked."

After we took a few minutes to do a diagnostic check of the hoses, generator, and pump to ensure we didn't have any issues, he suited up and clapped his hands together. "Let's get this party started."

"Let me know if you see something more substantial than fine stuff." I continued drying my hair with a towel. "I didn't see a ton of big gold, but I also couldn't find those bigger rocks we'd hoped for." Bigger rocks meant larger gold nuggets trapped beneath.

"Too bad we can't mine the spot where we were last summer."

I nodded and thought about the orange cones blocking access to the area I'd marked on my phone's mapping app—we could suck up an ounce of gold or more an hour if only it wasn't off limits. "This new site looked virgin to me. No signs of disturbance. I mean, it's a good spot to dredge regardless." He'd spoken of little else than returning to our hot spot during the winter whenever conversation turned to our plans.

Shivering, I hooked him to the air and water lines. Even dressed in dry clothes, the cold bit into me. Where was my parka? I tapped him on the back to let him know he was good to go. He put the regulator in his mouth and slipped into the water, and I leaned over the edge to make sure his lines unwound smoothly. As his shape disappeared into the dark murky water, a sliver of fear pricked me. I don't know why. Ben was incredibly experienced as a diver and probably had done dives in the Navy under much more stressful circumstances than this. I shook it off as a leftover from my iced up regulator and stood next to the sluice so I could tell when he'd reached the end of the suction hose.

***

Before I hunkered down in front of the comms, I took a walk around the small space to warm myself up and stretch my legs. I zipped open a duffel bag and plucked out Ben's carving—the one he'd given me last August—a pair of owls sitting together on a branch and set it on the makeshift counter for our communications station. It had become my good luck charm over the months, and it made me feel warm inside to see it perched where I could see it from anywhere in the shelter. As I passed by our partially opened 'door'—a piece of tarp held open by a chunk of duct tape to help circulate fresh air inside—I caught sight of movement near my father's ice shack.

The door flap of his shelter fluttered in the cold breeze. For Buck to leave his shack open to the elements and his gear exposed was highly unusual. I scanned the site for vehicles, but saw none. Then I saw a shadow pass by the opening. My stomach turned over. What if someone was stealing Buck's equipment? It had been known to happen out here, but it would be unusual in the middle of the day.

Although my dad and I were at odds, my gut told me to check on his stuff. No matter our differences, I couldn't help but look out for him.

I glanced at the comms. I shouldn't leave Ben hanging. But it would only take me a few minutes to hop on the snow machine, scare off anyone lurking around, check on my father's equipment, and return. If it were my stuff, I'd hope my dad would have my back.

I picked up the handset. "Ben, you doing all right down there?"

Loud static erupted and then I heard Ben's deep voice. "I made it to the hose. Everything's golden."

"Awesome." I zipped up my parka then launched into my speech, "Hey, I'm going to zip out to the snow machine and grab my other gloves." He didn't need to know what I was about to do. He'd only worry anyway. "So I might be away from the comms for a minute or two."

"No prob, babe."

"Cool. Be back in a sec." Although I was breaking the safety rules our very first day, he'd understand. Wouldn't he? After all, he'd stepped away from the comms to grab a sandwich. I ran my hand through my damp hair and pulled a wool cap on my head. My heart beat unevenly.

I glanced at the unattended comms. He'd only been under the ice for ten minutes. Ben would be okay.

I trotted to the snow machine, started it up, and zipped across the ice toward my father's shack. As I approached, it appeared as if one of the ties, which kept the shack shuttered overnight, had come loose. Did I really see someone in there? Or had it been a figment of my overactive imagination?

I slid off the snow machine and did a walk around the whole set up to make sure everything was as it should be.

As I made my way around to the seaward side, a truck pulled up next to my sled. "Hey, what do you think you're doing?"

"Kyle?" My mouth hung open in sheer astonishment. There he was—out in the world when he should've been in jail.

It took me a few seconds to find my voice. "I saw the shack door flapped open. Wanted to make sure everything was okay." Over my initial shock, I stood next to the sled as it idled. "I didn't know you'd be out so soon." Kyle had a four-month sentence for aggravated assault, and I had been his victim. He'd only just started his time down state in late January. I'd also heard a rumor—probably from Stella—that he'd planned to leave Nome and go back to his parents' place in Texas.

As Kyle got out of his truck, I went around the sled to the other side, putting it between him and me. My ex had, after all, knocked me out and put me in the hospital.

We stood there silently, staring at one another, wondering who would act first.

A whistling wind caused me to shiver in my boots and parka.

"Got out early. Overcrowded jails. They were looking to release as many of us as they could with minor convictions," he explained.

"Minor?" I scoffed. I wished I never noticed the open flap. "So why are you here?" Was Kyle going to rip off my dad as vengeance for him stealing his great uncle's gold map? Maybe he'd already taken some gear and was coming back for more.

He casually put his bare hands in his parka pockets and leaned up against the door of his truck. "I work here."

I laughed nervously. "My dad hired you? To work for him?"

"You have a problem with that?" Kyle rubbed his nose and then slowly pulled on some waterproof mittens.

I was sure my irritation radiated off me in invisible waves. I wanted to say something nasty to Kyle, put him in his place, but swallowed the words. "I'm just surprised is all."

He must've been the mysterious third figure I'd seen yesterday. I knew there had been something familiar.

"Unlike some people around here, Buck didn't blame me for his accident."

"But you admitted it in court." I wanted to say so much more to him. I wanted to unload everything I'd been thinking since his arrest and the truth about what had happened last summer—he'd broken into my dad's apartment, ransacked the place before I showed up unexpectedly, and then hit me over the head. "Forget it. Just forget it. Look, I thought someone had been messing with my dad's gear. That's it. I have my own work to do."

I climbed on the sled and revved it up. The whine of the motor drowned out any other noise.

Kyle shook his head and went to the back of his truck to grab his diving gear.

As I pulled away, Buck and Nate drove up.

I had no idea why my father had cobbled together such a team of misfits. Although I didn't want to care, didn't want to worry, I couldn't help it. I did.

An hour after eating some lunch and trying to put some mental distance between me and my ex, I reached for the comms to ask Ben how it was going. Before I could say two words, Buck Darling lifted the flap of our shelter and walked right in.

My heart seized. I wasn't mentally prepared for this after last night's blow out. Had Kyle told him something about my visit? Maybe made up a story about why I was there?

"How's it going?" My father looked around the space, his gaze lingering on our rusted generator. He wore the same navy blue parka with the rip in the shoulder that he'd worn for as long as I could remember.

When he spied my dive suit, I braced for impact.

"You're diving?"

"Why wouldn't I be diving?" I crossed my arms as if that could fend off what was about to come flying at me.

"Dammit, Rory. What do you think you're doing?" He picked up the coil of patched up hoses that supplied Ben with hot water and air and then threw them down in disgust. "You know it's dangerous to use shitty equipment like this. Especially for someone without any ice diving experience." This time the harshness in his voice reminded me of the father I used to know—not the one who'd snapped at me in Miner's. The tone was the same one he'd used when I ended up with a black eye playing a pickup hockey game on the iced up Nome River—concerned, worried.

But I wasn't having it. "Talk to Nate about the state of our equipment." I crossed my arms. "He's the one who left us with nothing but the leftovers at the sale."

Buck's eyes bugged out.

"Yes, your partner hung your daughter out to dry. Ben had it all arranged to buy the quality stuff listed in the ad, but Nate swooped in and talked Ben into buying this crap." I fingered the ancient wiring that kept the comms functioning. "Some friend, huh?"

My father's face turned bright red. He apparently had no idea that Nate had suckered Ben. "Look, I know you want to have your own little 'thing' going on over here." He talked over me, which wasn't unusual for him, but when we'd had a better relationship I hadn't minded as much. "And I don't know anything about Nate and what he may or may not have said to Ben." He shrugged as if my accusation had been a lie. "But this is reckless. I know last summer you had to sort of take over when I was in the hospital. But you failed because you didn't have the experience to know what to do."

"I have plenty of experience." But the wavering quality in my voice revealed my worries. My dad had no idea about my regulator freeze up, which had rattled me more than I wanted to admit. "And as for failure, I found enough gold to pay for your surgery and keep you afloat all these months, didn't I?" I reached for the handset before Buck could zero in on my anxiousness . "I need to keep an eye on Ben if you don't mind—"

"I'm sure he'll be okay for a few minutes."

I bristled. "You're the one who taught me to always stay in comms with your diver. "

Buck nodded and then wandered over to our equipment, probably to make note of every repair we'd done that didn't meet his standards. He made sure to peek in the sluice box. "This Ben guy who's your partner—who is he exactly? Is he the one making you dive using this junk? Can you really trust him to have your best interests at heart? After all, he's not family."

"*Making* me dive?" My dad had lost his mind. Did he think I was really that helpless and stupid? "What about you hiring Kyle?"

My father's face blanched ever so slightly.

"How can you trust the person who attacked your own daughter? Who left you to die last summer?" It was hard to believe my dad couldn't see the hypocrisy in his work arrangement.

"I didn't have a choice, Rory. After getting back from Anchorage I had to pull something together within a few weeks." My dad leaned against the sluice box, and his brows knitted together forming a pronounced V-shape. "No one else was available so late in the game. How else was I going to have a winter season without an experienced diver? Besides, he did his time, he's sorry."

"Did he tell you that?" I stalked toward him leaving the comms unattended. "Because he never told me he was sorry."

He waved a mittened hand. "Oh, come on, it wasn't that bad."

I remembered how disorienting and scary it was to wake up in the hospital and not know what had happened to me. "Are you kidding me right now?"

"Just a knock on the head. Not even a concussion." My dad snorted. "He was more scared than anything."

I stared at my father in disbelief. "Kyle hates you so much he lashed out at me to get back at you. Are you so sure he's over that?" How could he dismiss so easily how my ex had harmed us both? It made zero logical sense, which made me wonder if my dad truly had fully recovered from his surgery. Maybe he was on some kind of medication that was messing with his decision-making abilities. Or was he just loathe to have his perfect image shattered? My dad, always yearning to be loved and admired by everyone, had a tendency to overlook faults in those he desperately wanted to see in a positive light. I couldn't shake the feeling that my dad's fondness for Kyle might be veering into dangerous territory.

Ben's voice came strong across the mic at that very moment. "Rory, how's it looking in the box? I have one more section I want to finish before I come up."

I kept one eye on my father, who rocked on his scuffed winter boots with a mottled face, picked up the headset, and answered, "Give me a sec."

"Okay," Ben said.

I walked to the other side of the sluice box to avoid my dad and observed the gold flakes and tiny nuggets filing in the riffles. I did my best to push my father, Kyle, and every other stressor out of my mind to focus on the work at hand.

I returned to the handset. "Looks good." My answer was brusquer than I would've liked, and I wanted to tell Ben he'd found a lucrative spot, but with my father only a few feet away, I was hamstrung.

"Have you told him you've never done any winter diving?" My father pointed at our hole in the ice. "Does he know what to look out for?"

"Who's that?" Ben asked, alarm in his voice.

At that point my anger boiled over. "How dare you come over here and tell me how to run my operation or who to hire or who to partner up with. You talk to me about trust?" I wanted to list the litany of things my father had lied to me about the theft of the gold map, him pretending he'd found all those rich gold deposits on his own. Lies I had uncovered, while he lay in a hospital bed hundreds of miles away.

In the background I could hear static on the comms and knew Ben was speaking, but I tuned it out.

My dad threw up his hands and looked heavenward. "You don't know the whole story, Rory. You don't know everything."

"What in God's name is your problem?" I clenched my fists. "Why did you come over here in the first place?"

"I only came over here because I'm worried about you." He brushed over a messy weld on a section of the sluice. "Looks as if that worry was justified."

"I didn't ask for your opinion," I said. "And I sure as hell am not happy to find out you're here in Nome mining again when I thought you had another month of post-surgical recovery in Anchorage."

"I'm fine. I'm healthy." He pounded on his chest like a gorilla. "I needed to go back to work. Did you really expect me to stay in Anchorage and never come back?" He raised his eyebrows.

My heart raced, and my palms grew sweaty. A thready pulse in my neck made me realize my blood pressure had probably gone through the roof. "I'm glad you're well. Of course I didn't expect you to stay in Anchorage, but you never communicated any of this with me, so I was caught off-guard yesterday. And when I saw Kyle earlier—"

"You cut off all communication with me last August, if you recall," my father said in a quieter tone laced with hurt.

"Because you were a liar and a thief." I felt a pinch of regret when I said those words. I knew it would hurt him.

"Wait until you're a parent someday. Then you'll understand. You don't know what it's like to be responsible for another human being and a little girl at that. You think I just knew what to do?"

"Nobody asked you to take responsibility."

"You did, Rory. You did when you showed up in the airport," he said almost in an accusatory fashion. "How was I going to say 'no'?"

My gut soured.

Ben popped up in our hole. He ripped off his mask and stood on the ice in seconds. He'd read the hurt on my face from across the room. "What are you doing here, Buck?"

CHAPTER 9

My father took a step back from the black neoprened devil that had appeared. "Hey, I'm only here to talk to my daughter."

My boyfriend made a threatening move forward. "You need to leave."

Buck glanced at me.

Not the best way for my father to get to know my new boyfriend.

"Now." Ben stated the word with such quiet intensity, even I quivered inside.

"If you want to talk, you know where to find me," my father said as he made his exit.

Ben followed him to the shelter opening and watched as he left in his truck.

Then he shook out his mane of damp hair. "Are you okay?"

I crossed my arms, scowling at him. "I wish you hadn't done that."

"Done what?" Ben unzipped his suit, exposing his well-muscled chest. "Gotten rid of him?"

My gaze flicked to his exposed skin and then back up to his face. "I don't need you to protect me all the time. He's my father. I know how to handle him." Deep down, I knew I was upset because we'd been in a middle of a fight, and nobody had landed the final punch. But right now, all I could feel was my guilt and anger, and Ben was the closest target. "Why couldn't you have stayed out of it?" I turned my back to him and stomped off to see the results of our work.

"I heard another voice, and I thought something had gone wrong up here, especially since you were ignoring me on comms."

"God, I don't need to hear it right now." I let out a huge breath and tried to shake off my annoyance. "First my dad, now you. Yeah, yeah, yeah. I don't know what I'm doing, I get it. I'm a royal screw up."

"Is it true you've never done any ice diving before?" He frowned. "Why didn't you tell me?"

His questions hit me hard. I'd lied to him—the man I trusted the most—and I had no good reason for it except my stupid pride. The same self-doubt I'd felt last summer came roaring back. Buck was right. What did I know about ice diving? My first dive I'd barely made it out of the water with an iced up regulator. I thought I could copy what I'd seen my father do and wing the rest. That was idiotic and dangerous, especially with subpar equipment that could fail us at any moment. My face flamed hot in embarrassment. "I thought I could do it. I'm sorry."

"Rory, you can't keep something that important from me."

I turned away from him. "I didn't want you to lose faith in me."

Ben came up behind me and touched me on the shoulder. "I've always believed in you. Why do you think I'm here? If I didn't have faith in you, do you think I'd dive in that frickin' freezing water and spend hours on a suction hose?"

I faced him.

He gave me a sideways smile and gently squeezed my upper arms. "We're in this together: me and you."

"I don't know. This is so different. I thought I could handle it." I hadn't even told him about Kyle.

"You *are* handling it. We set up all of our equipment, we cut the hole, we're getting gold. I call that a success. But we need to be honest with each other and be safe."

Honesty. Yes, we both had to learn more about how to open up to each other and not be so scared of the truth. I considered telling him about my ex mining gold only a hundred yards away, but the topic needed to be approached lightly. For now, I'd keep that news to myself. "We should probably call it a day." Although we had some good gold in the box, it worried me that our new spot didn't seem to be as lucrative as I'd hoped. I wanted to think through how we were going to come up with the funds we'd need before the summer season started up again.

He paused before answering. "All right." Ben unzipped his suit and headed for his dry clothes piled on a makeshift bench we'd put together. "But let's add some additional safety rules for tomorrow when you're diving."

"Right." I didn't like the sound of that, but what else could I say? I began shutting down our equipment for the night. "Then we can jump back on our plan." But deep down I worried that our plan would fail, and it would all be because of me.

———

On the ride back to our yurt, I worked hard to find calm and peace. Seeing Kyle had rattled me. How could my father have done that to me? Didn't he understand that I was the victim in all of this—his theft of the gold map, Kyle's attack on me? Why had my own father chosen to support my assailant? Did he hate me that much after I'd sold the *Alaska Darling* to save his life? I leaned into Ben and kissed the back of his parka. I didn't know if he could feel it, but he deserved it. He'd backed me almost since we'd first met. Sure, he'd had his doubts about me, but by the end of the summer, our bond was as strong as forged steel, and his unwavering support had become an anchor in my life.

What would I do without Ben?

He patted my thigh with one of his mitts and then left his hand there the rest of the ride. The reassurance it gave me overwhelmed my senses. I wanted to hold onto that feeling.

I would have to learn to work with my father, Nate, and Kyle on the same ice shelf. That was the truth of it. As much as I wanted to have this one winter for myself, that was wishful thinking. Even without my dad in town, I faced some of the same competition as last summer. All the dredgers probably were thinking the same exact things my father was: that I couldn't hack it out on the ice and that I'd bitten off more than I could chew.

Once we reached the shoreline, he fishtailed the sled—a tricky maneuver—and zoomed around the other yurts that had popped up for the short ice season until he reached ours.

I climbed off the sled and grabbed hold of his arm and squeezed. When I'd first met Ben, I'd thought of him as The Beast. Tall, wide, intimidating. His hair wild and his eyes dark. But he'd shown me a gentle, loving man existed inside. The man I'd fallen in love with. The man who had stood by my side against all obstacles and impossibilities.

He looked down at me, and a slow smile spread across his face. In a flash he scooped me up in his arms and carried me inside. As the door shut behind us, he bent his head down for a kiss. His lips were dry and wind-chapped, but I didn't mind.

Gently, he set me on the ground, and we quickly stripped out of our winter gear.

The minute I took off my parka and got down to my underwear, the temperature of the yurt hit me. Too cold. "Brr."

"Allow me." Ben grabbed his sleeping bag from the nearest cot. "Climb inside, and I'll get the fire going. And don't change a thing about how you look right now."

I touched my hair and rubbed at my cheek, feeling a bit of sand from the sluice that had settled there. Ben was crazy. I probably looked a mess. But I took the sleeping bag, gladly zipped it up to my chin, and sat on one of the cots while he restarted the fire.

Ben's massive frame knelt in front of the small wood stove. His body dwarfed it. "Give me a few minutes, and I'll have this place as hot as Honolulu."

I laughed at his comparison and waited in the sleeping bag, knowing soon enough our bodies would be intertwined, and I'd feel safe again. His again. My old self again. The Rory that Ben had discovered last summer and had made love to all winter. My father had shaken my confidence and made me doubt myself. It amazed me how easily he'd done that. How quickly he'd knocked me down.

I only ever remembered my dad being my champion, encouraging me, asking me to do things that no other girl in my grade was doing. I'd been proud of that. I was Buck Darling's daughter. Could it be that he was only worried about me?

Ben got the fire raging quickly. He was an expert fire maker. In a matter of minutes the small interior of the yurt began to warm, and then Ben warmed me with expert kisses and intimate touches. I left all of my worries and concerns about my day behind and sank into his arms. This is where I wanted to be. Nowhere else.

Later that night, after the fire died down and Ben had fallen asleep, I ventured out to the public toilets near the road. It was bitterly cold, but putting on my parka and boots to use the outhouse at Ben's cabin was my routine. Except instead of the quiet isolation and privacy of the tundra surrounding us, now we were surrounded by a dozen yurts full of our competition. As I trudged past a few, I wondered if Kyle could be sleeping in one them.

Why did I care?

The shock of seeing him back in Nome and working for my father had worn off. I needed to put him out of my mind, trust Ben had my back, hope our equipment kept working, and find the gold. Distractions would only add to my stress and interrupt my focus, and I needed to focus as much as possible down there under the ice.

As I approached the dimly lit restrooms, two shadowy figures appeared between the yurts. I sucked in a breath. As they emerged from between the canvas-covered structures, I recognized one of them—Lola Chang, notorious small-time drug dealer and petty thief. Her long black hair had been stuffed under a gray wool cap, but her neck tattoo, three yellow stars under her jawline, made her instantly recognizable. Although Lola Chang appeared harmless— five-foot-two, skinny as an icicle—the local news stories had explained more than once she ran a gang of dealers who were rough characters.

She lurked in Ernie's Pub most nights, so what was she doing out here in the cold? Her partner was a tall, beefy guy. He sort of looked familiar, but I couldn't place him. Probably just one of the sleazoids I'd seen around Lola before.

Her gaze landed on me, and I shifted my eyes in a different

direction. The last thing I needed was to be on her radar. Most of us in Nome were hard-working responsible citizens, but every town had its sleazy underbelly, even small towns...and especially small, isolated towns in Alaska. Sadly, drug and alcohol problems ran rampant in some parts of our state, and Lola didn't mind taking advantage.

"Hey, you," she called out to me. "I'm looking for someone. Maybe you can help me. You livin' out here?"

Dammit.

I thought of Ben sound asleep in our yurt and wished I'd woken him up to be my escort. But I was a grown woman for God's sake. I shouldn't need assistance to go to the bathroom. Besides, I'd faced rougher situations on out on the Bering Sea fighting over the best dredging areas.

I paused, shoved my mittened hands in my pockets, and nodded.

"You know a guy named Kyle Stroup?"

My gut twisted. Why would Lola be looking for Kyle? He never messed around with her or her cronies as far as I knew. Then again, I didn't think he'd assault me either. I shrugged. "Maybe. Why?"

She gestured at the rows of yurts that dotted the beach. "Do you know where he's staying? Someone told me he was down here."

I shivered. The cold crept into my body despite the thick long underwear I wore as my pajama bottoms. "I didn't even know he was back in town until this afternoon. You think I know where he's staying?" My answer came out sharper than I intended.

Lola raised a brow and frowned. "Well, if you see him, tell him I'm looking for him."

I nodded

Her bodyguard scratched his unshaven cheek.

My gaze flicked to him—he weighed two-fifty at least, probably the same height as Ben. Wonder why Lola brought him along? Didn't bode well for Kyle. What had he gotten himself into since he'd been out of jail?

"Come on, Declan. We'll catch up to him another time." Lola scanned me from head to toe. "You better not be covering for him."

"Why would I cover for him? He attacked me." Better make it clear to her I wasn't a source of Kyle information. I wanted no part of whatever this was. "He's no friend of mine."

A dog howled in the distance and cut the tension.

"What's your name?" she asked.

"Rory," I said, and immediately wanted to kick myself. A drug dealer knowing my name didn't seem like a good thing. Great.

"You Buck Darling's kid?"

I nodded. Even the criminals in Nome knew my father. Fabulous.

"Thought so." She elbowed her companion. "She's tough shit. Ran a dredge operation all by herself last summer. Impressive."

"Is it all right if I use the bathroom now?" I gestured at my destination twenty yards away.

She cracked a smile. "Sure."

"Thanks." As I walked away from the drug dealer and her thug, an uneasy feeling settled inside me. Kyle could be in some serious trouble.

CHAPTER 10

As we rode to our dredging spot the next morning, my father stood near the entrance to his shack, holding a steaming beverage in an insulated cup. Probably the overly sweetened coffee he preferred.

Ben waved as we went by.

Interesting. Did that mean he'd moved past his overprotective reaction yesterday? Or maybe the wave was a thanks for my dad revealing my winter diving inexperience. Either way, I didn't like it. Ben and I were a team. My father had nothing to do with what we were trying to achieve.

To tamp down my feelings, I focused on the ice shelf in the distance. I wished we could be farther out beyond the stupid orange cones that were supposed to be there for 'safety' concerns. Our coordinates from last summer were located well past our current set up. The gold we'd sucked up yesterday wasn't going to be enough. It got under my skin that due to some stupid federal rule changes our winter season was being regulated to death. The gold out there was ours. We'd worked hard to find it last summer, and we needed the money now more than ever. Finding virgin cobble in the public mining area was like stumbling upon an uncharted world beneath the earth's surface.

If only we'd get a few extra cold nights, maybe the ice would thicken up and extend the safe zone closer to our hot spot from last summer. My mind turned over the possibility, and I made a mental note to check the weather. It would take us a day to relocate and cut a new hole, but we could ask Matt and Stella to help us again. This winter we had to succeed or our mining days were over. The specter of failure gripped me, as I gambled on the hope of colder nights to save our mining venture.

Ben slowed as we neared our shack. The door was still securely fastened shut by duct tape and a few zip ties through some grommets in the canvas we'd used. Flimsy, but we had no choice. We didn't have enough crew or equipment to set someone up overnight as a guard. We relied on the cold and dark to repel would-be thieves. Once the sun disappeared, danger lurked. The dark hid weak spots in the ice, abandoned holes, and even newly formed ice heaves from the motion of the water beneath.

Inside our shack we went to work without talking. Ben took charge of the generator. I had the responsibility of refueling. Until the generator produced some heat, the interior of our shelter was not much warmer than outside—the only thing that made it seem warmer was the lack of wind.

After topping off the fuel tank, I eyeballed our remaining containers of diesel. We only had enough for two, maybe three days, at most. We needed an influx of cash soon, or we'd have to dig into our meager savings to fund our operation.

The generator sputtered to life.

"We should schedule a clean-up with Jerry. We need to buy some fuel soon," I said, my breath misting in the crisp winter air. Although the owner of the *Goldfinger* was our rival in summer, he didn't participate in winter mining. Instead, he rented out his clean-up equipment to make a few bucks in the off-season.

Ben nodded and joined me at the sluice. "Have you looked at the weather?" he asked as he smoothed his finger across the gold-bearing material.

"Not yet." Even in the dim light of our shelter, the gold glinted. But I knew it wouldn't be enough to fulfill our plans.

He brushed his hands together over the sluice to make sure every little bit of fine gold was captured for the clean-up. "At least try for a day when the conditions might not be the greatest out here."

"Agreed." I opened my weather app. Although the days appeared clear and sunny, I dug deeper to inspect wind conditions. "Wednesday there's going to be some strong gusts. Fifteen to twenty miles per hour. Could make it treacherous down there."

Strong enough wind would create large waves farther out to sea, which could not only crack and shift the ice shelf, but could disturb visibility under water. That would definitely be a good day to clean.

"I'll give Jerry a call later today," Ben offered.

"Sounds good." I'd known Jerry for years. What did it matter if I called and made the arrangements or Ben? We were a team. But I was already feeling the sting of my agreeing to reduced diving time now that Ben knew I'd never dived under the ice before, and this felt like another small cut to my ego. Maybe I should let Ben know I'd rather make the call?

But he'd moved on to check the heat exchanger for the hot water lines.

I kept my mouth shut. I was about to close my weather app when I noticed a shift in temperature heading into next week. Brutally cold. Cold enough to maybe thicken the ice on the outer edge and put us closer to our hot spot from last year as I'd hoped? If I let Ben win a few this week by accepting his new safety protocols, could I convince him to shift our location next week? If my dad knew what I was thinking, he'd be wagging his finger in my face and reminding me of the one time some dredger set up his operation too close to the edge of the ice shelf and drifted out to sea on a broken piece of ice. But Ben knew the kind of gold we'd found last year, and I knew he wanted that as much as I did. I'd find a way to win him over, even if it meant fudging the truth about how safe my idea was. To succeed, we had to take some risks.

Two days later, we dragged our makeshift trailer behind our Polaris and headed to Jerry's warehouse. Ben drove more slowly toward shore than usual. The gold-weighted dirt we towed filled three five-gallon buckets, and the last thing we needed was to spill them out over the ice and lose a weeks' worth of dredging.

Ben drove us past our yurt, up onto the main road, and made a left to the airport. Near the airport stood a number of warehouse-sized buildings for storage in the off-season. Because residents in Nome lived far away from everywhere, we held onto everything. To fly or ship things to Nome was expensive. What normally might be thrown away or sent to the dump in the Lower 48 usually was stored or kept for repurposing at some point in the future...and then repurposing of the repurposing.

A few businessmen with room to spare and empty buildings in the evenings would rent a corner of their shop for miners to clean their concentrates in above-freezing temperatures. It also was handy they had running water, as gold panning and clean-up required it.

As we curved our way around the airport fence line toward Jerry's warehouse, I saw a familiar vehicle in front of us: Matt's GMC Jimmy. Seemed odd he'd be driving toward the airport.

A shadow of a figure in the passenger seat caught my eye as I watched him make a right away from the warehouses.

Did he have someone else in his truck? Who?

I frowned. Stella was at work. His sister spent all her free time with her sled and her dogs. My best friend would've told me if someone was flying in for a visit—like her married cousin from Talkeetna. Matt's life consisted mostly of working at the gas station and being the best boyfriend ever. Ben came a close second.

In a small town, you noticed when things were out of the ordinary, and this was out of the ordinary.

I shook off the odd feeling that came over me as Ben pulled off the road to park in front of Jerry's warehouse. But I made a mental note to ask Stella about him the next time I saw her.

"You have the code?" I asked Ben. He'd written it on a scrap of paper when he'd made the phone call. "It's cold out here." My nose had lost all feeling ten minutes ago.

"Got it." Ben slipped a hand in his parka pocket to retrieve the code. "4321." He read it with a smile.

I laughed. "You had to write that down?" I flipped up the alarm box and typed in the world's easiest pass code. "Someone should change that." The door clicked, and I pushed on the handle. The chemical scent of motor oil hit my nose, along with a mustiness that settled on everything in Nome after a while—a mix of damp tarps and deteriorating car upholstery.

I flipped on the lights and navigated between boxes, car parts, snow machines, and rusty dredge equipment to reach the thermostat. It would take time to heat up the warehouse. Since we'd be paying for the space, plus the heat, might as well get our money's worth.

Ben came up behind me carrying two heavy buckets of concentrates. I never ceased to marvel at his brute strength. "Where do you want these?" Although the two buckets probably weighed more than thirty pounds apiece, his voice didn't sound strained at all.

I pointed toward an open area about five yards from me against the north wall. "By the sink."

A gust of bitter cold wind rushed through the open door. I squinted at the thermostat, cranked it up another ten degrees, and then hurried to close the door.

"We've got another bucket out there," he said.

"Just trying to keep what little heat we have inside."

He shrugged and set down the heavy buckets where instructed.

"Aren't you cold?" I hugged myself to recapture what body heat I could.

"I've been in worse weather."

"Worse than a Nome winter?" I challenged. "Worse than above the Arctic Circle?"

"We're not above the Arctic Circle."

I rolled my eyes. His exactness was killing me. "We're only a few miles away...give me that much."

"Fine. Yes, worse than a Nome winter."

We made our final trip outside to bring in the rest of our supplies and the last bucket.

"I don't know if I believe you, Ben Abel," I teased.

Ben lugged the bucket, and I pulled a tarp onto which we'd stacked all the smaller bits and pieces we'd need to clean out our gold.

"The Navy made us train in all kinds of weather. All types of dives." He set the bucket next to the other two. "And we didn't get to call it quits if the weather looked bad."

I sighed and shook my head. "I guess you win." I dragged the tarps as close as I could to our set up. Then, I filled up an empty three-gallon bucket with clean, cold water.

"I think a Navy diver always wins, sweetheart." He tipped up my chin and kissed me gently on the lips.

My fingers and toes tingled, and it wasn't only due to the temperature of the warehouse. More than anything, I wanted to warm up with him, skin to skin.

When he pulled away, I dropped the hose into the bucket and directed his mouth back to mine. He welcomed the invitation and slipped his hands over the curve of my ass, and I threaded my fingers through his long, thick locks. His muscular arms engulfed me, making me feel safe and protected.

For a moment I forgot about the crappy equipment Ben had purchased, the fact we needed to find a lot more gold than we had in the last week to cement our future, and the mess of having my dad and my ex as my competition. I knew winter diving wouldn't be easy, but the added pressures didn't help.

Ben unzipped my parka, and I kicked off my boots. Then I helped tug down his jeans and long underwear. As I stripped off my layers, I shivered in the cool warehouse.

"At least it's warmer than the yurt," he said when my skin broke out in goose bumps.

I smiled in agreement and then pressed my naked skin against his exposed chest. As the temperature dropped, our connection seemed to ignite. A shared warmth enveloped us, and the warehouse became a backdrop to a different kind of exploration.

The thought of refining our buckets of concentrates down to the gold we needed to build our business left my head. I wanted to be in the moment and not right back where we usually were: talking about gold dredging.

His lips brushed against mine, so soft and delicate. It was hard to believe my Beast could be so gentle, but he'd proven time and again that he could. The kiss carried the warmth of countless conversations we'd had over the last few months…we'd shared our dreams for the future, and both us of wanted the other to be there for those dreams. The world faded away, and all I could feel was the rhythmic cadence of our shared breaths.

He cupped my face in his hands and stared into my eyes. "I love you, Rory."

A pair of worn, back-to-back seats pulled from a Bayliner boat had been stored against one wall. Ben nudged me in that direction. The softest surface available in a warehouse full of odds and ends. In the heat of passion, we surrendered to the moment, our world gracefully fading to black.

"Should we get to work?" I could feel Ben's voice rumbling beneath my cheek as I lay on top of him awhile later.

His practical words brought me back to our purpose for being in the warehouse.

He leaned over, which slid me off him and onto the seat, and handed me my clothes. I quickly dressed before the heat of our lovemaking faded away. "Wonder if anyone's done that before?" I asked as I zipped my jeans.

"Done what?" Ben pulled his shirt down over his wild mass of hair.

"Had sex in the warehouse." I gestured at the boat paraphernalia, mining gear, and tools that filled the space. Not exactly the most romantic place for a rendezvous.

He grinned at me. "I won't tell, if you won't."

I tossed his jacket at him. "We need to get back to work, Romeo." Water spilled out over the top of the bucket. "Crap." I'd forgotten I'd left the water running while we were busy having fun. Luckily, there was a drain in the floor, which prevented a larger mess.

"Ready to perfect your gold panning?" I asked, picking up two hard black plastic pans from our small pile of equipment. "I know you didn't have much opportunity last summer." We'd mostly relied on my dad's spiral machine to separate the gold from the finer materials—the machine we no longer had access to.

He cocked a half smile, taking a pan from me. "Sure, let's do this."

Across the room, he spied a stack of cheap patio folding chairs. He grabbed two in one hand, carried them over to our work area, and whipped them open one at a time. "Madame," he said in a fake French accent and bowed.

"Oh, *merci beaucoup*," I said and accepted the unfolded chair, which had a strap missing from the back.

The concentrates sat between us with the bucket of fresh water in front. "I should've taught you how to do this last summer." I took a trowel of gold-bearing sand and rock we'd sucked up from the bottom of the ocean, dumped it into the gold pan, scooped up some water from the bucket and then swirled the contents of the pan over the bucket to let the lighter dirt and gravel float out of it. "You have to be careful not to swish things around too much or you might dump the whole pan into the bucket. Do it like this." I showed him my style of panning: swirling the water and dirt in a counterclockwise direction with the ridges along one side of the pan facing the bucket, then tilting slightly so the dirt flowed out and the heavier material remained.

As I worked, he peered into my pan. "I don't see any gold."

"Patience. Watch." I continued to swirl and swirl and more dirt and gravel cleared from the pan. Eventually, after a few minutes of swirling and adding more clean water, flakes of gold glinted at the bottom. "Then you keep going until all you have left in the pan is gold." I showed him the result. A decent collection of gold dust and a few larger pieces sat in it with a bare dusting of black sand remaining. "We'll have to cook that off back at the yurt and use a magnet to get rid of the black sand." I carefully poured the gold into an empty plastic peanut butter jar. "Now you try."

He took the trowel and matched my movements with the pan and the water. At first, he was a little sloppy. I had more finesse with my smaller hands and years of practice. Ben had trouble finding a good grip on the edge of the pan. He was used to manhandling difficult loads, not creating gentle swirls of dirt, gold, and water.

"There, I think you're getting it." I scooped more concentrates into my gold pan and continued working. We had a lot of material to get through.

Ben dumped his first completed pan into the jar and scooped up a second load.

The water was bitterly cold, and the temperature inside the

building hadn't changed much. "After we're done here, we should stop in town and grab some burgers."

"Polar Cafe?" He knew we'd get special favors from Stella if she was working—a few extra French fries, maybe a slice of bacon slipped onto our cheeseburgers.

"Absolutely." I smiled at him. He'd learned a lot about my relationship with Stella. He'd buried the hatchet with her after she mistakenly believed he was a murderer who'd run away to Nome to escape the authorities. "I wonder if Matt's ever going to pop the question."

He raised his brows. "You said they've been dating since high school, right?"

"Yeah. I don't know, it's been six years. I thought they'd be married by now." I shrugged and continued panning, focusing on my work.

"Maybe Matt doesn't want to get married."

"That's all Matt has ever talked about since they met. And why not? Stella's sweet and kind and cute." I imagined Stella's cherub-like round face with pink cheeks and her curly black hair.

Ben chuckled. "Maybe things have changed. There's a lot more to a serious relationship than that."

"I know—" My mind drifted to my stepfather and mother and their horrible disaster of a marriage. "But it's Stel." Somehow my friend was different than every other woman out there, including myself.

"Well, I'll be sure to tell Matt that the next time I see him."

"Would you?" I asked half joking, half serious. "I just don't see Matt wanting to be with anyone else. They're perfect. Maybe he needs a nudge."

"A nudge? From me?" He sat back in his patio chair, set his empty gold pan in his lap, and stared at me. "I'm not doing that. I barely know the guy."

I dumped more recovered gold into our jar. So far our week of work wasn't looking too good. With the short winter dredging season, we needed ten ounces a week to stay on track with our must-reach goal. I didn't want to be too discouraged, but we would be lucky to have three or four ounces based on how the panning was going.

"I guess you're right." Just because I thought I knew everything about Stella and Matt's relationship didn't mean I actually did. "I want to believe some couples were meant to be. That not everything in the world is crap, you know?"

Ben let out a sigh. "I know." He scooped up more dirt and returned to panning, improving his technique with each attempt. "I'm glad I've got you, Rory," he said quietly. "I don't know what I'd do if I didn't have you."

His words settled over me like a warm blanket, but I didn't know how to respond. It had been so easy for him to say the words 'I love you' only a little while ago. But I knew I had thrown them away on Kyle before, and look how that had turned out. I wished I could be so secure in our relationship to reassure him that I loved him back.

I picked up our jar of gold to show him our progress. "If I didn't have you, there's no way I could've done this on my own." Although I knew we'd fallen well short of expectations, I didn't want to be discouraging our first week out. "Best partner ever."

He nodded, and the room seemed to cool slightly. I knew avoiding his attempt at a deeper conversation had hurt his feelings, but I wasn't ready to think about the long-term and where our relationship was going. I'd failed before, and really didn't want to face the reality of probably failing again.

CHAPTER 11

After several hours of clean-up, we were wet, cold, and hungry. We'd dredged for five days, but the gold haul was disappointingly small. A cold unease settled over me, akin to a sudden Arctic breeze which left a lingering shiver. With probably only three or four weeks left to dive, we were way off track to meet our goal.

"This isn't a bad start." I held out the peanut butter jar for Ben to weigh in his hands. "But I'm not sure we found a good enough streak to last us through the season. But it might be enough to attract unwanted attention to our location once we turn it in at the assayers." The minute we took our gold in to turn into cash, desperate divers would hear about it and come crowding in on our spot.

"Maybe we could hold back some of it until the end of the season? Cash in just enough to buy what we need to keep diving."

"Now there's an idea. But where would we stash it? The cabin is too far away, and the yurt isn't exactly secure enough to leave all that gold sitting in it."

"Let me think it over." When it came to safety and security, he always had good ideas. A few months ago he'd come up with a contraption outside the cabin made up of wire and extra pots, pans, and silverware to alarm us if any wild animals were within a fifty-yard perimeter. Good for both security and hunting purposes. "I'll think of something."

"I'll bet you will." I liked the idea of keeping our full gold haul a secret. The last thing we needed was a crowd of winter dredges parking themselves nearby and stealing what little may remain of our find. Especially my father. When it came to locating gold, he was ruthless. Nothing would get in his way...not even breaking the law, as I had found out. "For now, let's weigh out half-an-ounce so we have spending money for fuel, food, and all of that. We can think about how we want to handle the rest later."

I turned my attentions to my rumbling stomach next. "I'm going to order us up those cheeseburgers." As I was about to call Stella at the Polar Café, I noted the time. "I'll have to call Ernie's. The cafe is closed."

"That's fine. I'll take a double, please."

I gave the mountain of a man a once over. "Are you sure that's enough?"

"And a double order of fries."

"Okay." I dialed up Ernie's Pub. After hours they were a good source for cheap eats. "After we pack up this stuff, I'll drop you at the yurt on my way to pick up the food so you can start up the stove. And I'll call Stella to ask if we can clean up at her place. I haven't taken a shower in days." I pulled my parka away from my body, took a sniff, and grimaced at the less-than-fresh scent.

"Yeah, I was about to tell you earlier." He pinched his nose closed with his forefinger and thumb. "But didn't want to be rude." He couldn't hold back a smile.

"You jerk." I jabbed him with my elbow. "You don't smell much better."

He grabbed my arm and twisted it behind my back playfully while his other arm wrapped across my middle and pulled me against him. "Is that right?" he growled against my ear.

I pressed back against him without thought. He had my whole body on fire all over again. My voice trembled with desire as I breathed out, "Yes."

He kissed my neck. "Do I disgust you?"

I shivered at the feel of his lips on my bare skin. "Terribly. I don't know how much longer I can stand here."

"I know how difficult this must be for you."

"Mmmm." I couldn't speak, too focused on his hand inching its way toward my breasts.

He let go of me and spun me around, his blue eyes darkening. "We'll continue this later."

I let out a deep sigh, frustrated that there was still so much to do before we got to the yurt. "Most definitely."

Twenty minutes later we had cleaned up the warehouse, loaded our trailer, and shut off the heat and lights. One successful clean out was under our belts. Only a few more to go and our first ice season would be in the books.

But a heaviness settled in my stomach as we rode back toward town. I'd managed to make it through a rough first week of diving under the ice. My nerves were on edge now that I knew our dive spot wouldn't be enough. We needed more and better gold. My thoughts shifted to the marked location on my phone—a spot too distant to be legal. The known gold there could secure our goal, but it meant contemplating something risky. If the temperatures didn't cooperate and the ice didn't thicken, it would be a precarious gamble.

———

After dropping off Ben, I parked our snow machine outside Ernie's. The wooden facade, battered by harsh Arctic winters, had taken on a faded appearance, hinting at countless summers under the midnight sun. A neon sign, its colors now somewhat muted by time, announced "Ernie's" with a faint flicker that defied the elements. The establishment's windows, with their aged wooden frames, were adorned with a collection of quirky, hand-painted signs advertising drink specials and upcoming events. The bar exuded a certain charm that drew in both locals and adventurous travelers, promising a no-frills, authentic Alaskan experience within its weathered doors. But in the late night hours, a different crowd occupied the bar—one not so welcome in the rest of Nome's establishments.

My stomach growled in anticipation of the greasy burgers and fries we'd ordered, and I walked in to see a half-empty room and

Bobby Sykes working the bar. The juke box played some 80s one-hit wonder a little bit too loudly.

"Hi, Bobby." I walked up to him. "I'm here to pick up an order."

"Right." He touched his forehead with the tips of his fingers and closed his eyes. "Two cheeseburgers—one with no pickles—and a couple orders of fries. Whoever doesn't like pickles on a burger is a moron." He opened one twinkling eye to assess my reaction.

I crossed my arms. "A moron? Really?" Bobby knew I hated pickles.

He grinned. "Let me go check and see if it's ready."

I handed him an empty growler. "And could you fill this with that IPA Ben likes?" I took a seat on one of the bar stools.

The juke box rolled into a new tune—something slow and sexy. Maybe one of the half-drunk men near the pool table was hoping to coax one of the single gals to dance with him.

"Hey, are you Aurora Darling?" The voice that reached my ears carried a subtle lilt.

Ninety-eight percent of the people in town knew who I was. Nome is a small town. I mean, you don't live here for more than five minutes without your name, description, and relationship status getting around to everyone via word of mouth or Facebook community posts. I swiveled my stool to face the person attached to the voice and scanned the male figure in front of me.

"Um, yeah?"

Orange and black parka, shearling style hat in his hands, medium height and thin. This must be Stella's mystery man who'd been asking about me. I knew she'd be fit to bursting if I told her I'd run into him.

Bobby, holding a brown paper bag in his hand, caught my eye and lifted his eyebrows in a silent question.

I raised my hand discreetly so he would know things were okay.

It got rough sometimes in Ernie's, and Bobby—a former college hockey player—had no qualms about jumping into the fray.

For now my curiosity kept me interested in talking to the guy. "Can I ask why a total stranger has been asking around town about me?"

"Sorry, I guess I should've introduced myself." He put a hand to his chest. "I'm Jonah Tanaka."

I looked at him still a little wary. "Am I supposed to know who you are?"

He turned red.

Wow. This guy blushed easily.

"I wanted to know if you'd let me interview you."

I let out a choking laugh. "Interview me? Is this a joke?" I scanned the dark interior of the bar, wondering when someone would jump out, point a finger, and tell me I'd been punked. "Bobby?" I gave the bartender a hard stare.

The bartender set my bag on the bar next to me. "Hey, I've got nothing to do with this."

Jonah took a deep breath. "Can we sit down over there for a minute?" He pointed at a table away from the bar. Was that so Bobby couldn't overhear us? Then, he mumbled something I couldn't understand.

I bit my lip. "I don't know how you know my name or what you want to interview me about—" Different thoughts ran through my head—Kyle's attack on me last summer, the gossip that rocketed around Nome when Ben came to town, my dad's involvement in a theft. I couldn't think of another newsworthy item that involved me. "But I'm sort of busy right now. This isn't exactly the best time." I picked up my bag of food. "Someone's waiting on me to bring dinner."

"It'll only take a minute. I promise."

Although my stomach growled at the delay and I knew Ben was expecting me, curiosity took over. What did he want to ask me? Maybe it was another fluff piece about Nome after the Iditarod. Sometimes *National Geographic* or one of those other adventure-type magazines would feature Nome from time to time. It crossed my mind that Alisha Childress, Matt's sled-crazy younger sister, would've been a better choice. I shrugged. "Okay, I can give you a minute, I guess."

"Great." His brown eyes shone behind black-rimmed glasses. After moving a few chairs out of my way, he led me to a table near the jukebox.

I looked at my cell phone to check the time. Ten-thirty. I'd give him five minutes and then beg off. Shouldn't take more than that to find out what he wanted. Besides, I was sure Stella wanted to know more about this guy. And now I might be able to get the scoop for her for once.

As I sat down, I imagined the look on Stel's face when I told her I'd actually met the guy, knew his name, and found out he was a reporter. She'd be jealous. I smiled at the thought. It was a rare moment when I had news before she did.

"Thanks again for taking the time to talk to me." Jonah scratched the back of his neck.

I could see why. He wore a wool sweater under his jacket that looked as if it had seen better days. Old wool equaled scratchy wool, and leaving the cold outside for the warm inside only made the itchiness intensify.

"Sure." I found myself checking the time again. When I glanced back up from my phone, Jonah stared.

Guilt washed over me. I put my phone face down on the table and gave him my full attention. "Okay, you had some questions."

He set a laptop bag in front of him. I hadn't even noticed it had been slung across his torso. "Give me just a sec."

I swallowed the sigh that threatened to come out. Five minutes didn't seem like five minutes anymore. "Sure."

He slid out a yellow legal pad that was already covered in blue ink pen.

"What publication did you say you were with?" It was awkward sitting there in silence, so I wanted to fill in the quiet.

Half focused on his notes and half focused on me, he answered in a distracted fashion, "I didn't." He scribbled on the legal pad a few times. "I'm a pretty fast note taker."

"Hey." I touched his arm to get his attention.

He looked at my hand then looked at me.

"I'm curious enough to sit here for a little bit, but if you aren't going to give me some idea of how you got my name and why you want to talk to me, I'm going to walk out the door." The only thing keeping me in that chair was knowing Stella would go out of her mind once she heard. I'd disappeared for most of the winter and left her stranded without me, so figuring out what this guy wanted so Stella had the latest gossip was the least I could do. I had to make it up to her somehow. I'd even let her spread the news around. That's how nice I was ready to be. So I'd have to tolerate sitting here with Mr. Nerd Boy and his legal pad for a few minutes.

"Please don't do that." He dug into a little zippered pocket on the outside of his laptop bag. "I'm a freelance reporter." He handed me a business card.

I took it from him and stared at its shiny surface.

Jonah Tanaka, Freelance Reporter, Seattle, WA

That was it. I flipped it over and on the back was an email address and a phone number.

"I wanted to interview you about your dredging operation. Gold mining. The business. The risks. The culture. All of it." He smiled, and his whole face changed in an instant from nerdy, goofy glasses man to somewhat attractive nerdy guy with potential.

He should really smile more.

"Um, okay." I was surprised he chose dredging for an article. "But why me? There's plenty of other people in Nome who've been doing it longer than I have."

"Yeah, but you're the only woman in Nome who runs a dredging operation. That's the story I want to tell."

"Where did you hear that?" I could hear the guarded quality in my own voice.

"From a source."

"What source outside of Nome would even know or care?'"

"I told her I wouldn't say anything." His face flushed. "She'll kill me," he said under his breath.

"Who said she'd kill you?" I waited a few seconds for an answer, and when he didn't offer one, I pulled the pin. "I won't give you even a two minute interview unless you tell me who your source is."

His mouth drooped. "Zoe," he mumbled. "She was only trying to help me out." His voice rose a couple of notches. "She knew I needed a good story. Something different."

"My sister told you to come interview me?" My older sister had a way of playing 'mom' and checking up on me. But this was a new one. Usually, it was phone calls where she guilted me into things. "I should've guessed."

"Please don't tell her I told you, Aurora."

Anyone that desperate I stay silent must have the hots for my sister. Considering she didn't have too much luck with men, I probably shouldn't upset the apple cart for my own comfort. She had been very supportive of my choices last year, when I knew she would've rather had me abandon Nome and come back home to my stepfather and her in Washington. As much as I didn't really enjoy the thought of talking about my private life and business with Jonah, I knew it would please her.

I sighed. "I won't tell her. And please call me Rory."

Jonah's worried look melted. "Rory, right." He pressed his lips together. "Zoe told me you hated it when she called you 'Aurora.' Guess I was nervous."

Wait. Zoe knew I hated it, and she *still* did it? I'd have to ask her about that next time she called. "It's all right. I'd prefer you use that name in your article, if you don't mind."

"Not a problem. The full interview shouldn't take much time. I only want to learn a little bit more about what you do. Then maybe I can take some photos?"

My insides twisted uncomfortably at the idea of having my face splashed all over some magazine. But I thought again of how much it would please Zoe, and maybe she and my stepfather would finally understand how serious I was about dredging and staying in Nome. "Okay. Only a few, though, and nothing too dopey."

Jonah reassured me, "No, nothing too fake. I'm looking for real. A real story about a real woman. That's what I'm trying to achieve here."

I sneaked a peek at my phone. Ben would be wondering what was taking me so long. "You did really catch me at a bad time. Can we set something up for later?"

"I'm only going to be in town for a few more days. Did you know that a big storm might be coming?"

"Really?" That was the first I'd heard of it.

He nodded. "I don't want to be stuck here any longer than I have to."

"I don't blame you." I gestured at the bar's interior—the space was dimly lit, with only a few flickering lights casting a feeble glow over the worn furnishings. The laughter was sparse and the patrons rather rough.

"Oh, I didn't mean—" His eyebrows arched, and he offered an

awkward smile. "I need to go back to Seattle and work on the story. Deadlines, that kind of thing."

"It's okay, Jonah, I know what you mean. Being stuck in Nome in the middle of winter is not exactly a vacation." I laughed, hoping he'd lighten up a little bit. He thought he'd been insulting me, as if we didn't know what people in the Lower 48 thought about us Alaskans. "Let's meet tomorrow. After I'm done mining for the day. But not here." I scanned the room double checking nobody I knew saw me sitting in a dark corner with Jonah. It was one thing to stop by and pick up some food, but entirely different if I spent an hour late at night in the place with a strange man. Rumors had a way of becoming truth in this town. "How about over at Miner's Bar and Grill down the street?" Sure, I might be recognized, but at least I knew the crowd was mostly regular folk and not people looking to score easy sex or illicit drugs. "Ernie's can sometimes be a little wild." I didn't want to explain Ernie's reputation had really started to go downhill. Some locals had been arrested here for dealing drugs. Jonah didn't need another reason to report to my sister why Nome wasn't the place for me.

"Miner's. Okay. I can do that. Say around six? Then maybe we can take some photos afterward? The light should still be okay."

I hadn't had a shower for two days, and I knew my hair was probably going to be a fright. I needed that key to Stella's place. And what did someone wear for a photo shoot anyway? "Sure, six will work."

"Oh, and don't change anything. I want you looking just like you do right now."

I lifted up my arms and looked down at myself. "Like this?" He couldn't be serious.

"I want real, remember?"

I thought about Zoe and how much she was going to owe me after this. "Real. Right." But I was at least was going to take a shower and run a brush through my hair after diving. Unless that would make things worse.

"Okay, six at Miner's." Jonah pointed at the business card on the table in front of me. "Call if you have any trouble."

I picked up the card. "Sure thing." My mind grew numb.

What did I just do?

CHAPTER 12

As I left Ernie's, I wondered how I was going to sneak away to do an interview. Maybe I could think of some way to introduce the topic to Ben, but the whole thing made me instantly uncomfortable. I knew how Ben felt about reporters, newspapers, the media in general. He'd been railroaded for months following his arrest for the murder of his fiancée. Even after he'd been cleared when the autopsy showed a drug overdose, he'd continued being harassed by not only the local news, but Laura Snow's parents and family who believed their stories, which caused him additional grief. That was the reason he'd fled Idaho and started over in Nome. Before me, Laura had been the only other woman he'd loved, and reporters had tried to tarnish that feeling. I felt a bit stuck between wanting to help my sister, who certainly would call me up and annoy me if I didn't do the interview, and wanting to please Ben, who would balk at the very mention of someone poking around our business.

I set the appointment aside in my mind and thought about the good meal waiting for me in the brown bag, the shower possibilities at Stella's, and a warm, cozy night with Ben in the yurt. I'd think of something. Eventually.

A shouting match interrupted my thoughts.

"You owe me."

I turned to see Lola Chang and her massive partner, Declan, confronting someone on the icy sidewalk.

The last thing I needed was Lola noticing me a second time in a week, so I kept my attention on the paper bag as I stowed it safely in the under-the-seat compartment. Whatever was happening wasn't my business. A few more minutes, and I'd be zipping out of there.

"I told you I'd pay you when I get paid."

I straightened up instantly, recognizing the voice. *Kyle.* My gaze zeroed in on the three people arguing.

His lanky body and that stupid Coors Light baseball cap were unmistakeable.

Our eyes locked. He looked away quickly, took off his cap, and ran a hand through his dirty blond hair.

But it was too late—Lola had noticed.

She turned to look at me. "You. I know you." She nodded to her man. "Bring her over."

The big guy headed straight for me.

I froze.

"She doesn't have anything to do with this." At least my ex tried to keep me out of whatever it was he'd gotten himself into. "I only need a few days." His lip twitched.

This did not look good.

Before the scary big guy could reach me, I swung a leg over my snow machine and sped out into the street, racing toward home— and Ben. I needed to tell him about what happened the other night and now tonight. This could turn into something dangerous.

As I moved farther away, my heart slowed. Instead of fearing for my own safety, my thoughts shifted to my ex. Although my anger toward Kyle still burned hot, I didn't want anything bad to happen to him. I only wanted him out of my life. And now I'd somehow drawn Lola's attention to the fact I knew Kyle. That didn't bode well.

It made sense now why she had been hanging out around the yurts looking for him. He owed her money. Why, I didn't really want to know—for drugs?

He'd never been into anything like that before, but maybe a few months in prison had twisted his perspective. I'd seen it happen with Nate. A drug addiction had changed him—he couldn't seem to stop, made decisions completely out of character, and ended up losing almost everything. If he hadn't gone to rehab last year, it could've been him on the sidewalk in the middle of winter being strong armed for cash.

Or was the reason more sinister? Did Kyle still harbor ill feelings toward my father or me? What else could cash buy someone?

An ache hit the back of my throat.

I needed to tell Ben what I'd seen.

I arrived at our yurt with the burgers and the growler of beer from Ernie's, the only one in town who carried such a bizarre IPA from Boise. I wanted to surprise Ben with his favorite beer, but now all I had on my mind was the encounter with Kyle and Lola.

"Hey," Ben said as I opened the door laden with food and drink. "I'm starving. What took you so long?" He stoked the fire in the wood stove a few times and threw something in it before grabbing the paper bag stuffed with cheeseburgers and fries.

"What was that?" What he'd tossed in the fire looked like a thick envelope full of papers.

"Just some junk mail from the box Nate dropped off." He shuffled his feet and avoided direct eye contact.

I let the strange explanation slide, as I hadn't yet figured out how to describe what I'd witnessed on the sidewalk, or how to tell him that I ran into Lola just outside our yurt the other night. I was glad it was overly warm, as I felt my face heat. Why couldn't I just tell him? What was I so afraid of?

Ben's beatific smile as he scooped out his double cheeseburger in its greasy wrapping stilled my thoughts. He took a huge bite and rolled his eyes heavenward. "Divine." He passed the bag to me.

"I got you some of that Roundhouse IPA you love." I gave the growler a little shake. I wanted to stay here in a happy place with Ben. I didn't want to ruin it by bringing up anything negative.

"What?" His eyes lit up...blue as a cloudless sky. "No way. Here in Nome?"

"I may have special ordered some last fall," I dug a red plastic cup out of our kitchen supplies and poured him a drink, "when I ran to town for some more supplies before the big snow." It had been on a whim. We'd discussed our favorite things, and he kept coming back around to this single IPA repeatedly. Ernie's usually special ordered some beers before the Iditarod, so I knew I might be able to convince Bobby to add that one to the list.

"You are the best girlfriend in all of Alaska."

"Yes," I said. "Yes, I am."

He slugged down a large swallow and let out a satisfied sigh. "That's the stuff."

I shoved my fears about Kyle, Lola, and the big scary guy to the back of my mind, along with my curiosity about the strange bit of mail Ben had burned. It could all wait until later. "Bobby not only gave us extra slices of cheese on our burgers, but he managed to slip in an order of onion rings. Someone changed their mind, and they were just going to throw them out." I took out my burger and then set the fries and onion rings on our cooler.

"Nice." He grabbed a few onion rings and made them disappear in short order. "So, I've been thinking."

I perked up, figuring he found a place to stash our gold.

"What's up with Nate do you think?"

I popped open a soda I'd grabbed from the cooler, wondering if he was still hung up on Nate sabotaging our equipment. "You have to let it go, Ben. There's nothing we can really do about any of it now. We're stuck with the junk he convinced you to buy." I bit into an amazingly greasy, cheesy burger that tasted absolutely divine.

His face turned red. "It pisses me off, Rory. I don't like being made a fool of."

"It can happen to the best of us." I shrugged.

"That doesn't help." He guzzled down his beer and then wiped his mouth with the back of his hand. "Maybe you would've been better off without me."

"What are you talking about?"

"I fucked up, Rory. Me. I'm the one who messed this up for us. How many times do I need to say it?"

"I'm over it—the equipment thing. We have to deal with it and arguing won't help that." How did things suddenly go so wrong?

When I'd dropped him at the yurt, he'd been in a jovial mood. Why the strange change in demeanor? "I need you."

I lightly squeezed his arm, and he seemed to deflate. "I'm sorry. It's been a bad day." He touched my cheek and gave me a sad smile. "You're right. We need to deal with the situation we're in, and I'm here for the long haul."

"Nate's a jerk." I wanted him to think about who really was at fault, and it wasn't him. "Rehab can't fix a personality problem."

"Plus, long-time drug use can really mess someone up." His lips pinched together for a split second.

"Laura." The name came out of my mouth without warning.

Ben looked away.

Dammit.

I didn't want his dead fiancée to come between us. Why couldn't I keep my mouth shut?

He crumpled up the paper bag that had held our food and tossed it next to the wood stove.

Was the memory of Laura fading? Or was I still competing with a dead woman?

Ben avoided the topic. "Last summer Nate was a selfish prick. Guess nothing has changed there."

"He and my dad were close. Really close. I think when my dad fired him, he let those feelings build and build. I don't know." I crunched down on one of the onion rings. Nate and I hadn't exactly been the best of buddies even before the firing, but I respected the relationship he had with my father. "I'm not surprised he acted in his own best interest when you showed up at the equipment sale. Just Nate being Nate."

"Maybe." Ben shrugged and kept his face neutral. "I'm never going to trust him ever again."

"I don't blame you." My mind flashed to the moment Nate tried to attack me during a clean-out, and Ben had come to my rescue. His first real encounter with the guy hadn't been a positive one. "Better to let it go and not let it drag you down. We don't have time for that. And he's not worth it."

"True." He thoughtfully chewed for another thirty seconds.

Should I bring up Kyle and Lola? This seemed like the perfect opportunity. From a recovering drug addict to a possible new one —and both working with my dad.

The fire crackled in the wood stove, and the wind whistled outside.

Did I want to open the door to a brand new worry? It would be so much easier to eat, relax, and forget. I decided to let it go. If I had another run-in with Lola, I'd let Ben know.

"What bothers me more is Nate giving up what was left of his half of the dredge sale to get back in business with my dad," I said. "He just cleaned himself up—seems like a risky venture for a man trying to get back on his feet."

"Well, it's his money to spend how he wants." Ben took another huge bite of his burger.

"The whole situation is so uncomfortable." My mind filled up with so many negative emotions about last summer, I couldn't think straight. "Let's talk about *our* gold instead, and then we can head over to Stella's and use her shower tonight."

Ben's eyes gleamed. "Yes, the gold. Let me show you." He popped the last piece of burger in his mouth and pushed aside one of our plastic container boxes.

I was glad to see he had left behind the anger that had burst out of him earlier.

"You hid it under the yurt?" I knelt on the floor next to him. "Genius."

The floor was made up of scrap lumber—rudimentary, but it kept us off the frozen ground. Ben had loosened a floor board and dug a small depression in the packed sand below. Our three little ounces safely sat in it.

He picked up the plastic peanut butter jar that held our first clean-out, worth maybe six grand. "I don't think anybody would think to look under here.'

"I can't wait to add more to it."

Ben placed the jar back in its hole, covered it with a little bit of sand, and then replaced the flooring and slid the box back into place. "Think we can double it this week?"

We'd need to more than double our first week's clean out, but that wouldn't be possible at our current location with the gold-bearing cobble drying up. If we wanted to meet our goal for ice season, we'd have to make a change. "I think there's a way we can do that." But we would have to take a big risk—one probably even my risk-taking father would pass up. But if my gut was correct, our current output was about to disappear, and we didn't have time to waste.

"Sweet."

He looked me up and down. I probably looked about as bad as he did...lank hair, dirt smudges on his face from the clean out, and grime under his nails. "So this shower you mentioned. Do you want to save some time and share?" He smiled at me and my insides heated up instantly.

He'd seen right past my mess, but with Stella present it wasn't exactly the most opportune moment. "Maybe next time," I said in an optimistic tone as I sent Stella a text:

We're coming over, if that's still okay.

She texted me a thumbs up. I showed my screen to Ben. "Shower is a go."

***

Stella's apartment, cozy but cluttered, looked the same as always—too many people living in one small space. Alisha's passion for sled dogs and sled racing stood out more than anything. Stacks of racing memorabilia and training books claimed every available surface, and bags of dog food had been piled in one corner. Blankets adorned with sled dog prints, posters of renowned racers, and a motley assortment of sled dog-themed decorations added to the congestion. I knew in the single bedroom at the back of the apartment Stella's and Matt's belongings had been stuffed into the small space to make room for Alisha. They could barely move in their ten-by-twelve room with one closet to share between the two of them.

Ben had been in the shower for what felt like an eternity. The sound of water and the steam seeping out from under the bathroom door reminded me if I wanted a private conversation with my best friend, I didn't have much time left.

Stella and I huddled on the couch, catching up on the week. Her eyes sparkled with that familiar curiosity, ready to delve into every detail of my life.

"Stel," I began, eager to give her some gossip to latch onto, "I think I've met the mysterious stranger you mentioned the other day. He's a reporter from Seattle—Jonah Tanaka."

She leaned in, curiosity piqued. "A reporter? Why was he looking for you?"

I suppressed a smile. "He's here to interview me for some story about dredging, if you can believe it."

"What? No way!" Stella's mouth dropped open. "That's amazing."

I shushed her, worried that Ben might hear. Although I wanted Stel to have the latest news and beat the other local gossip queens to the punch, I had to find a way to keep my involvement with Jonah on the down-low. "Ben doesn't know, and I'd like to keep it that way."

Her brows drew together.

I explained before she could say anything. "He's hated reporters ever since what happened in Boise—you know." I didn't want to elaborate. Thinking about Laura Snow and the fact she could've ended up as Ben's wife if things had been different still made me feel uncertain about the strength of his feelings for me. "My sister was the one that sent Jonah up here, so I feel sort of obligated, you know?"

"Zoe knows this guy?" My friend pursed her lips together.

"Yeah." I squeezed Stella's hand. "So go ahead and spill the beans about who our mysterious visitor is, but leave my name out of it."

She nodded. Her brown eyes held a snap to them I hadn't seen in a while. Letting her be the one to reveal Jonah's identity to the various customers at the Polar Café had made her day, and that warmed my heart. Anything to make my best friend happy. She'd stuck by me all these years when other friends drifted away for different reasons. No matter how ridiculous I had acted in the past, her friendship had never wavered.

I changed the subject, reflecting on something Jonah had told me at Ernie's. "Have you heard anything about a storm headed our way? I keep checking my weather app, but don't see any prediction like that." If I'd somehow missed an important change in the weather, I wanted to know before I firmed up the fledgling idea I had about how to up our gold take.

"A storm?" She shook her head. "Who told you that?"

"The reporter guy said something about wanting to leave Nome before the storm." I shrugged. "Maybe it was something he saw on the TV in the Seattle airport or something."

"Maybe." A thoughtful look came across Stella's face. "Hey, can I ask you something?"

"Sure."

Her round, red-cheeked face, usually radiant with warmth, had taken on a slightly paler hue, as if a cloud of concern had temporarily dimmed her usual vibrant complexion. "Has Matt ever said anything to you about wanting to take flying lessons?"

My mind flashed to seeing Matt driving toward the airport with a mystery passenger. I'd intended to ask her about it, but now seeing the look on her face, I changed my mind. Did I want to be the one to confirm something that clearly upset her? "No," I answered honestly.

Before Stella could tell me more about her concerns, the bathroom door creaked open, and out walked Ben dressed in clean clothes with hair still damp from the shower. Just seeing him made my heart skip a beat.

"Your turn, Rory," he said, flashing a charming grin. "Wish you'd taken me up on my offer, though."

My face heated.

Stella glanced from me to Ben, reading the between the lines, then gave a cheeky grin. "I can leave, if you want."

"Don't mind him," I said. My heartbeat quickened, and a heavy shroud of self-consciousness settled over me.

Stella's eyes again snapped with warmth and humor. Her worries about Matt took a back seat now that we were no longer alone. I'd have to find another time to talk to her and maybe 'fess up to what I'd seen, though I couldn't help the relief I felt that that time wasn't now.

I headed into the bathroom and hoped Ben could behave himself in my absence.

CHAPTER 13

The next morning, I woke up snuggled next to Ben on a single cot—each of us in our own sleeping bag. I did remember waking up feeling cramped at one point in the middle of the night, but I liked the feel of his large, hard body next to mine. Instead of moving to my own cot, I found a way to get comfortable and went back to sleep. A part of me missed being in Ben's cabin with the snow all around us, a fire burning in the wood stove, and the real world far, far away.

But we had gold to get, so I slipped my feet into my wool clogs and rose to stoke the fire.

Ben noticed my absence, rolled over, and woke with a grunt. "Hey, come back to bed," he mumbled.

I opened the stove door and tossed in another log from the diminishing pile. We'd have to grab some firewood in town next time we bought more diesel. "We don't have time to waste." I stripped out of my long underwear, pulled a hoodie over my head, and stepped into a pair of insulated snow pants.

"You sound as if you have something in mind." Ben's tousled hair revealed signs of a deep slumber. "Care to clue me in?"

Even though the space was small, the temperature must've dropped considerably over night. I shivered as I dressed. "We have to reposition ourselves."

"What? Why?" He unzipped the sleeping bag; as the cold air met his skin goose bumps appeared. Ben donned his clothes one layer at a time, his breath forming small clouds in the chill of the yurt.

"My last dive, I wasn't seeing as much gold. I think it's starting to play out." Without looking at him, I grabbed a protein bar and started some water boiling to make instant coffee. I knew he wouldn't like this change of plans. "We don't have time to waste out there."

"So you want to spend time moving our operation?"

"I think we have to." I sat in one of our fold-up chairs.

His face clouded, and his eyes grew dark. "Dig a new hole?"

"Yes. We can do it ourselves this time." Didn't he understand our pathetic gold total from our first week of diving wasn't going to cut it? If we wanted the big gold, we had to take risks, and we only had a few weeks left. "Sure, it was nice to have Matt helping with the truck, but if we chop the ice into several chunks, we should be able to haul it out with our snow machine."

"A whole day lost?" His brow furrowed, and doubt settled into the lines of his face.

"I'd rather have a whole day lost moving closer to our summer spot than working ground that someone else already has." I'd seen the signs—instead of undisturbed cobble, I had started to encounter an obvious line of tailings. Proof positive we'd reached the end of virgin ground. "I have to go with my gut, and that's what my gut is telling me."

"I thought our old spot was too far out to be viable." His eyes, typically bright blue and full of certainty, now held a distant and questioning look.

My stomach tightened. He was right. It was dangerous, it was risky, but it would be the only way for us to achieve our goal. "I think it's been cold enough these last few nights that maybe the ice shelf has been extended." I pulled out my phone to show him the spot on the map where we thought our big gold from last summer was located. I pointed to a new spot I'd placed on the map—our current hole. "See? Not much farther. All we need is to find one little piece of that gold run...and then we can chase it. We don't need our hole to be right over it."

His mouth set in a line. "I thought the powers that be didn't like dredgers setting up on the edge of the ice."

"They don't. But let them come tell us we're too far out. Even if we can only dredge there for a single day, I'll guarantee we'll get more gold per hour than we did all last week." I blew at my boiling hot coffee to cool it down so I could take a sip and warm myself up. "Plus, what else are we going to do? The longer we stay on our original hole and hope it improves, the less time we'll have on the ice. Three ounces isn't going to cut it, Ben. You know we need around forty."

"Shit. You're right." He clicked his tongue.

Ben had been so excited about the gold we had been sucking up, he had forgotten that we needed enough to fund our summer operation, and that meant a lot more cash. "I know we lose dredging time when we relocate, but it'll be worth it. I promise."

I handed him a thermos cup of instant coffee and then poured another for myself.

"I'm in." He flashed me a smile and shook out his long mane of hair.

I glanced around the yurt. We'd put so much into this, we couldn't give up yet. In the end, it had to be worth it. Didn't it? But a chill of doubt crept its way up my back and had me questioning my rash decision. What if this was the wrong move?

Ben and I rode on the snow machine pulling our equipment behind us. It had taken a couple of hours to break down everything, leaving plenty of daylight for us to set up a new site. Maybe we'd even have time to dive for a bit. If the wind remained still and the gold looked good, why not?

As for the supposed storm Jonah had claimed was headed our way, I didn't see it. The sky was clear and nothing on my weather app indicated it. Perhaps it had been a false alarm. I held my phone in my hands and kept an eye on the map as we neared last summer's hot streak. And I had been right: the ice had grown thicker due to a few extra cold nights, and the ice shelf had extended farther out into Norton Sound.

Ben pointed to a series of orange cones set in a long line a few yards in front of us and stopped.

Stupid government.

What did they know about safety out here?

I'd participated in winter dredging with my dad for years before the government decided to step in and ruin everything. They didn't understand how quickly ice could build up, how much thicker the ice could be after only a few nights of below zero temperatures. And who was coming out here every day to check? They just set the boundaries the first day and left it that way.

I poked Ben in the back and pointed toward our spot. About thirty feet from the cones, I estimated by the look of it. Plenty of ice extended beyond that. I'm sure once we cut out our new hole, we'd find the right thickness. We'd be safe.

I could see the ocean beyond the ice shelf. From our original location, the water had appeared like a black line on the horizon. Now it was a seething, living thing.

My gut soured.

I ignored it.

If we set our hut as far distant as we could from the edge and on the thicker ice, we'd still be able to mine safely and follow our gold streak from last summer. We'd mine as far as our hoses would go— just like summer dredging. Same water, same ground.

Ben turned to look at me. The weak winter sun glinted off his mirrored sunglasses. I nodded.

He throttled up the engine and moved us past the cones.

The ice felt solid beneath us.

See? I wanted to tell him. *See how much I know? We'll be safe here. Trust me.*

He stopped about halfway between the cones and the edge of the ice.

I climbed off, knelt down, and swept off the snow with my mittened hand. Our hole would be here. I checked my phone one more time. The coordinates were slightly east of our position, but this would be a safe base of operations. Plus, the weather showed more cold nights, so if I followed the logic, the ice should thicken and extend even farther. Our position would become safer.

I looked over my shoulder at the other dredgers who were sprinkled closer to shore, but I didn't see any authority headed our way. The Alaska Department of Natural Resources didn't really have time to pay attention. They set the limits of the winter mining area at the beginning of the season, and that was it. By the time they realized anyone was out this far, ice diving would be over, and Ben and I would be flush with gold. Even if we had to pay a fine, what did it matter if we could reach our forty ounce minimum goal?

My dad would probably notice, though. But I'd seen him do worse things for a better gold position. Would he really have the guts to rat me out and further ruin our already fragile relationship?

Ben carried the auger and rested it tip down on the ice. "You worried about your dad?"

I shrugged. "I don't care what he thinks. This is our operation, and we're making the decisions, not him."

He scanned the ice. "I don't see anyone else out this far, Rory. Should I be worried?"

"No." But I left out the part about the potential for ice breakage if the weather made a bad turn. The authorities decided to put out the cones for a good reason. To my way of thinking, though, we had no choice. We couldn't find enough gold unless we took this path. Besides, odds were low that would happen. I only remembered it once or twice over the last ten years. I pointed to the spot I'd cleared. "Right here. Make your starter hole, and then we can cut the rest with the chainsaw."

If we could pull this off, we'd be set for the summer.

Ben augered through the ice, which turned out to be about eighteen inches in thickness. "See? Plenty thick." A slimmer margin than I'd hoped for, but still safe in my experience.

He smiled. "I'll try to remember that next time you come up with a crazy idea."

"Crazy?" I snorted. "This is the sanest idea I've had in a while. We thought we wouldn't be able to mine out here, and Mother Nature provided. It must be destiny."

While I unhooked our rickety trailer, Ben began to cut out a rectangular hole with the chainsaw. I worried the noise might attract attention, but the distance between us and the rest of the miners was farther than I'd originally thought.

Good. Less snooping by the competition—and my father.

Once he completed the hole, he went about chopping the large chunk of ice into more manageable pieces. I grabbed a long strap out of our supplies and secured one end to the snow machine. Then I tossed it to Ben who slipped a loop around one chunk of ice.

He hopped on the snow machine, throttled it up, and pulled. The ice got hung up on the edge of the hole.

"More power!" I yelled.

Ben complied.

The engine whined, but eventually the chunk came free of the hole and landed on the ice. Within a few minutes, we'd cleared the rest of the chunks and were ready to go back for our shelter.

I stared out at the horizon once more. Was that a dark line of clouds in the distance? Maybe Jonah had been right about a storm rolling in soon. The desire to take advantage of our new spot stalked me.

Jonah. The interview later today. I'd almost forgotten.

I glanced at Ben. I hated to lie to him, but it was only a little interview with the wanna-be boyfriend of my older sister. It was a favor. It would be over within a few minutes. He wouldn't even have to know.

"Come on, let's go grab our shelter," I said.

After Ben returned to our old hole to retrieve our shelter, my cell phone rang. It was my sister, Zoe. Although I wanted to organize our supplies and equipment before Ben returned, I'd recently repaired my relationship with my older sister and wanted to keep it that way. Plus, I had a feeling I knew why she was calling.

"Hey, sis. What's up? Something important?"

"Oh, I just wanted to talk to my little sister." Zoe's voice had a practical and no-nonsense quality to it that cut through the clutter, conveying information with clarity and efficiency. "It's been awhile. How have you been?"

My older sister was not known for her casual phone calls. She always had an agenda. "I've been fine. Ben and I have our winter dredge operation set up," I scanned the heap of stuff next to our brand new hole, "and it looks like it's going to be a good season."

"Oh, great." Her voice was laced with boredom.

Inwardly, I smiled. She wanted me to bring up the topic. Rather than keep her dangling, I helped her out. "Oh, and I set up an interview with some reporter yesterday."

"A reporter?"

"Mmm-hmm. So random. He was wandering around town looking for me, apparently. Somehow he'd heard about me and wanted to do an article about gold dredging in Nome."

"Is that so?" Zoe voice immediately shifted from bored to pumped up. "Tell me more. I'm dying to hear all about it."

"Zoe," I said, and a grin pulled at my lips. "I know it was you who sent him. Jonah. He's your friend."

"He didn't tell you that, did he?"

I could hear the blush on the other end of the line.

"No, I figured it out. Not so easy to pull one over on your little sister." I laughed. "He's cute, by the way."

"We're just friends."

"Right. 'Just friends,' it is." Six years my senior, my sister was a notorious serial dater. Seems we both were gun shy of long-term relationships—a product of our mother's abandonment, I'm sure. "I'm meeting with him tonight." I looked over my shoulder at the sound of our snow machine approaching.

"Great. I know you don't think of your life as anything that special, but when I told Jonah about what you do, he was really interested. Made him realize other people might be, too. Hard to think about my little sister as an adult with a work ethic."

I rolled my eyes. Zoe had never approved of the work I did with Buck, but now that it was of use to her newest boy toy, she suddenly found some respect for me. "If he thinks it's interesting, I suppose I don't mind spending a couple of hours with him. It's not that big of a deal." I was sure nobody would read his article anyway, and Ben would never find out about it. At the same time, I would be doing something nice for my sister.

I tucked my free hand deep inside my parka pocket. The cold was starting to creep up on me.

"Jonah's thinking this piece might be 'the one' that gets him noticed, so I'm really grateful for your willingness to do it."

"So how did you meet him?" Since she was suddenly so talkative, I thought it was my chance to learn dirt on Jonah before the interview. It might make me feel a little more comfortable talking about myself if I knew some personal details about him.

"At some goofy wine tasting in Yakima Valley for work. One of those corporate weekend retreats."

Zoe acted as if I knew all about fancy work events. My work events consisted of diving under water for hours and trying to stay warm.

We were sisters, but we lived totally different lives.

"Jonah was there to do an exposé on the wine industry and their use of illegal labor," Zoe said with a note of pride in her voice. "We got to talking in the tasting room. He thought I worked there." She laughed. "So cute. I had to set him straight, but by the end of the night, we found out we had a lot in common."

"Plus, he's not bad looking."

She sighed. "Yeah, there's that, too."

"Well, I'm glad for you. He seems like a nice guy. I'll do my best to behave."

"Yes, please, Aurora," she said. "I really do think you'd make an interesting story for his kind of journalism."

I didn't know much about journalism or what she meant by her comment. And I was too afraid to ask. "I'll give you a call in a day or two and let you know how it went."

"Oh, would you? That'd be great."

I glanced over my shoulder again and saw Ben rapidly closing in on my position. "Well, I gotta get going, Zoe. It's freezing out here, and we have a busy day."

"Jonah mentioned some storm blowing in?"

"Maybe," I said, looking at the horizon. No change.

"He said he might have to stay a day or two later than he planned if the weather doesn't hold." Zoe sighed. "Which sucks because I'd carved out a whole chunk of time in the middle of my day to pick him up. Now he'll have to Uber it home."

Yep. Zoe was serious about Jonah. Altering anything about her enormously busy corporate CPA career definitely meant she saw Jonah as something more than a passing fancy. I'd have to tuck that bit of info away for later.

A strong gust of bitterly cold wind blasted my body. "I really have to go, Zoe. I'm about to turn into a block of ice."

"Okay. Talk to you soon."

"Sounds good. And tell Dad I love him." My stepfather, Henry, and I had worked through some things last summer, and I said those words with true feeling.

"Absolutely."

Ben buzzed past the orange cones and pulled up to a stop.

My body tensed.

How was I going to meet Jonah that evening without Ben knowing about it?

CHAPTER 14

With our new location established and equipment set up in record time, Ben and I ended up with several hours of daylight left to dive and find out if we'd found our secret summer streak. I shoved aside my worries about the hose repairs I'd had to do for a third time, the strange clanking noise that signaled potential mechanical issues with the generator, and the thermal fatigue cracks I could see forming on our heat exchanger and focused on the possibility of better gold.

"Who was that on the phone earlier?" Ben asked as he munched on a ham sandwich.

We were taking a well-deserved lunch break, but my excitement on the gold potential just under our feet overcame any hunger pangs. I picked at the crust of my sandwich, wondering if I should use the phone call to create a reason for being gone later. Before I could change my mind, I said, "It was Stella." My face tingled. I didn't want to lie to him, but I felt torn between pleasing my sister and avoiding unnecessary conflict regarding his history with reporters. We'd only just found a way forward after the equipment disaster got between us. Ben didn't need one more thing to worry about. "She wanted to know if I was free tonight for some girl talk."

He nodded. "Trouble in paradise?"

I swallowed a small bite of sandwich I'd forced myself to eat. "You mean Matt?"

"He's a hard one to read."

Ben's words surprised me. I hadn't thought Matt's demeanor indicated anything negative. Matt was just Matt. He'd always been that way. "I think she wants to dish tonight about whatever gossip I missed in the last few months. We didn't have enough time yesterday to have a really good chat. She's used to having me in town all winter." It wasn't far from the truth—Stella had told me she missed seeing me in town and wanted to find time to catch up.

"That's fine," he said. Despite his casual response, Ben's eyes held a hint of something guarded, as if there were more to his response that he wasn't sharing.

The subtle tell in his gaze made me feel even worse. Did he know I was lying? Or was it something else? I couldn't be sure. But something about his reaction was unsettling.

"I'd like to dive first," I blurted out. The weight of my lie was uncomfortable. Being under the water and focusing on gold would maybe free me of it.

He popped the last piece of sandwich into his mouth and headed toward the comms. "Did we double check the equipment? No problems?"

"Everything seems to be holding together," I reassured Ben. With the equipment troubles sorted out for now, my focus shifted, and the only thing on my mind was getting back in the water and diving for that elusive gold. "Our gold is out there waiting for us." A shiver of excitement ran through me. I knew it was there—the big nuggets, the riches hidden among the sand and rock.

"The generator's been making a weird noise. Didn't you hear it?" he asked. "And we're pretty far out if something goes wrong."

I'd heard the same sound and had to shrug it off. Who knew if it was a signal of a major problem that might mean our only power source conked out at the wrong moment? Did we have the luxury to worry? "It's nothing." I didn't believe my own words, but we had to start diving to make up for lost time moving ourselves to a new hole.

I stripped off my oversize sweatshirt and headed for the line we'd strung across one end of the shelter where we'd hung up our suits. "I'll take the first dive. That way you can baby the generator."

Before I could reach them, he touched my shoulder. "Let me

dive first, Rory. I've been through a lot of specialized training, you haven't." The last sentence came out harshly. A darkness flickered in his eyes. "Things can go wrong when you least expect it."

"I know," I said quietly. "But I'd rather have you up top to keep an eye on the equipment." I drank the last of my soda and picked up my cold water suit. I didn't want to argue with him. He was right, though. I'd only dived here in Nome, and not under the same kind of pressure he experienced in the Navy. He ran through some safety checks on our comms and other systems.

As I stepped into my suit, I conjured up how the scheduled interview might go that evening with Jonah to soothe my nerves. Some questions about underwater gold dredging, a few about living in Nome, and then probably some personal questions. If he brought up Ben, I'd have to let him know he couldn't be included in the story. After the harassment he took from local news and Laura's family, Nome had been a refuge for Ben—with many good memories of his grandfather and his cabin. Our successes with gold dredging only added to the positive feelings. No, I wouldn't allow Jonah to intrude on that.

"Everything looks good," Ben said.

I nodded and stepped up to the edge of our new ice hole. The dark blue depths called to me. Our gold was right beneath us, I could feel it.

My heart hammered in my chest, and I stepped up to the edge of our new ice hole. As I stared into the darkness below, my excitement grew and overcame my thoughts about the coming interview. Our gold was right beneath us. I imagined a box full of gold at the end of our day.

Ben helped me attached the hot water and air lines. "You ready?"

"Absolutely." I jumped into the water and emptied my head of all thoughts except one: finding the gold.

<hr>

The moment I leaped in, my confidence surged. I followed the suction hose down to the bottom, just like always, but the water was deeper than I remembered, and the thick ice above blocked out most of the light. Normally, the anticipation of striking gold would send a rush of excitement through me, pushing all doubts aside. This time was different. The added depth felt like a personal challenge to overcome, and the darkness added an air of mystery. My heart raced with exhilaration. I wanted to be here, fully embracing the adventure. Mind over matter? For sure.

"How's it looking?" Ben's voice sounded in my ear. "Did we find our spot?"

I slowed my breathing. I couldn't let the thrill that ran through me overtake my judgment, that could lead to some bad outcomes—number one being another iced up regulator. "I just reached the bottom. Hold on." My blood hummed in my veins as I approached the fuzzy, distant line of ground that marked the end of the sandy bottom.

I grabbed the end of the hose to center myself on something familiar and solid. Panning the light attached to the side of my diving mask, I took in the terrain surrounding me. "Cobble. Lots of untouched cobble." My adrenaline spiked. "I think we're right on top of it."

"That's awesome, babe. I'll start the clock. You've got ninety minutes, and then you have to come up."

Our agreed upon safety plan after my regulator freeze had annoyed me, but I knew Ben's concerns were realistic ones. I had to learn how to temper my desire to go all out when the gold was good—that's how mistakes happened. "Go ahead and turn on the suction." I had to make the most of my short dive and fill our sluice in record time. Our future dredging operation depended on it. No time to waste. I clutched the handles on the hose as tightly as I could and waited for the powerful suction to begin.

"You got it."

The hose jumped in my hands. I straddled it and began sweeping it from left to right. Gold bearing material disappeared inside the six-inch opening, and I tried to keep my focus on my work and not let my excitement run away with me. I needed to keep a level head. The streak went eastward—the same direction as last summer. "It's looking really good down here." Much better than our original ice hole. Maybe an ounce or two ounces of gold an hour. At that pace, we could hit our goal in a few weeks of steady diving. The weight of my anxiety over our pocketbook lifted some.

"I can hardly wait to take a turn," Ben said.

My mind wandered back to the coming storm Jonah had mentioned. The distant bank of clouds on the horizon made me think that maybe the predictions had changed. Our new position should be able to handle a bit of rough seas, shouldn't it? Although we were closer to the end of the ice shelf, we'd had to cut through a good foot-and-a-half of ice. But even if our position was solid, the clarity under water could change if the winds picked up and the waves grew turbulent. Even more pressure to move quickly and make as big a dent as possible in the mass of material that lay in front of me.

As I found my rhythm, I grew accustomed to the dark waters around me and the bumpy ice ceiling above. No longer a novice ice diver, I couldn't help but wish my dad could witness my progress. If Buck had been here, I knew he'd be proud of me, and part of me longed for him to share in my success.

When I was in high school, I'd begged my dad to let me learn how to dive. For three years I'd watched him and Nate dive for hours and heard them talk about the sights they saw below the surface. I wanted to experience it for myself. My dad had been proud of my courage, but protective. He made me take it slow. But when he'd finally let me do my first solo dive, I'd loved it. So freeing. In that silent, weightless realm, I'd discovered an unspoken connection with the vast, enigmatic depths below, and for the first time since my arrival in Nome, I truly felt like I belonged somewhere.

Although the basic work was the same, I felt as though I leveled up in this winter environment. I'd had to master a new set of challenges that I hadn't encountered before—the reliance on my head lamp, keeping track of the location of the dive hole, watching out for my hoses so they didn't get hung up on the uneven ice ceiling above me. I had a newfound comfort and confidence in navigating the demanding conditions.

"How much time before I have to come up?" I wished I could stay down here all day.

"Thirty minutes." The quality of Ben's voice shifted from light to serious. "Is everything okay?"

I smiled to myself. "I'm fine." I followed the path of the gold and got so lost in it that I barely remembered I was underwater. Gold glistened in a swirl of pebbles and sand as the hose made quick work of the cobble. Running into a large rock, I flipped it over only to see visible nuggets hiding there for me. "I'm so glad we made the move. The gold here is incredible."

"Glad to hear it was worth it."

"Wait until you see it for yourself."

"Twenty more minutes, and I'll be taking over."

"I think we've got this in the bag, Ben. We'll be able to replace the worst of the junk you bought and even afford a decent dredge boat."

"Right," Ben said in a clipped tone.

Dammit. I'd poked his sore spot. Me and my big mouth.

Before I could apologize, the suction died in my hose.

"Shit. The pump crapped out."

Now I felt even worse for mentioning how crummy our equipment was. He'd take the pump problem as his own personal failing.

"I'm coming up," I said, grabbing hold of the suction hose and working my way back to the hole. No point in waiting in the cold and dark without being able to work. "We'll fix it together."

"I think we have to take it all apart—could be a worn out gasket, a bad hose."

"We'll figure it out," I said in a soothing tone. "No worries." To calm him down, I brought up a happier topic as I climbed the hose toward the surface. "How's the gold looking?" I knew what I'd seen down there had been good, but the proof would be in the box.

"I don't care about the gold right now," Ben said, the annoyance in his voice unmistakable. "This pump could shut us down if we can't fix it. What a fucking mess I put us in."

"We'll fix it," I said quietly. "Don't worry."

"You don't know that," Ben bellowed. "I spent every last dime I had on this shitty equipment. If I can't figure this out, I'm screwed."

My ears rang at the force of his words. I'd never heard him so angry. This was also the first time I'd heard him talk about himself as a one-man team, rather than the both of us being in this together. Was he pulling away from me?

As the hole grew closer, a heavy knot formed in the pit of my stomach. Would our relationship weather the challenges of the ice season?

CHAPTER 15

"Once again, thanks for taking the time to let me interview you," Jonah Tanaka said, setting up a legal pad and his phone, set to record, in front of him.

"No problem." I sounded normal, but my heart was thumping. I felt as if I were cheating on Ben somehow, especially with Marla's curious gaze on us. I should've told Ben what I was doing. Why did I believe I needed to keep him in the dark to spare his feelings about reporters? It seemed stupid now. My eyes darted around the room for anyone I might recognize.

Jonah and I sat huddled in our dimly lit corner of Miner's Bar & Grill, our conversation an island amidst the raucous sea of noise and activity. A couple of miners well past sobriety hooted and hollered from the bar while watching an NCAA basketball game. An old couple sat in the corner near the bathrooms quietly eating their dinner. A clutch of women in their 30s gathered around the pool table and shared a game and a basket of peanuts.

And Marla surreptitiously watched us from across the room. With each glance from her, my nerves lit up. I could tell she was dying to ask me about my dining companion. Miner's may not have been the best choice for a meet-up.

Ben, still seething over the broken pump, had bought into my lie about heading to Stella's for a girls' night out. The usual gossip, pizza, and rom coms on Netflix. He'd been so quick to say 'no problem' I wondered if he'd even heard me. When I'd come up out of the water, defeat was etched into his face. Although he was able to temporarily fix the pump problems and made it possible to dive the rest of the day with weaker suction, for a more permanent fix we'd have to find some replacement gaskets. Ben's usual positive demeanor had disappeared after that. I think he was relieved I'd be with Stella to give him some space to sulk. But if he knew what I was really doing, would he have been so eager to see me ride into town?

"Interview with Aurora Darling. Nome, Alaska." Jonah clicked his ballpoint pen, bringing me back from my wandering thoughts. "Tell me about growing up in Nome."

Easy answer. "I came here when I was twelve, and everyone was super welcoming. I made friends in five seconds flat." The image of pre-teen Stella popped into my head. Pink-cheeked and friendly. Eager to meet the 'new girl' from the Lower 48. I was an exotic creature for a few months anyway. The most popular kid in class until I wasn't. "My dad was a dredger—is a dredger—so he taught me the family business. I helped him out every summer until his accident. Winters too when I was a little older. Harder to keep an eye on a kid when you're ice diving. More details to worry about. More dangers. Plus, the cold."

"And the dredging." Amidst the clamor, Jonah leaned closer to me, raising his voice to be heard over the commotion. "Are there many women doing that kind of work on the Bering Sea?"

I furrowed my brow and scanned the bustling establishment for any faces I knew. "A few. Tenders. An occasional diver, I've seen some over the years. But they don't usually come back."

"Why not?" he asked, his curiosity cutting through the bar's cacophony.

I took a sip of my drink, my response tinged with a hint of resignation. "The culture is different here. Men and women compete on an even playing field. I don't know if you've ever heard about Alaskan women, but we are a different breed. If you've got the skills, they'll welcome you in the door. It's about what you can do, not who you are."

"But I heard last summer the guys gave you a hard time when you had to take over your father's dredge."

Marla dropped off our drinks. "Food'll be up in a few minutes. Can I getcha anything?" She smiled broadly, noticed the phone recording in the middle to the table, and let her grin melt away. "Oh, sorry," she whispered.

Jonah smiled. "It's okay."

Marla skulked away with her tray.

"So to get back to my question—the guys gave you a hard time?"

"True." I'd overcome so much last summer, the razzing I got from my fellow dredgers sat at the bottom of my pile of worries. "I think that was more about my capabilities as a dredge owner and how much I knew about the business. Some may have thought I didn't earn my place."

Jonah's inquisitive eyes focused on me, the bar's dim lighting casting shadows across his face. "Did you?"

"I like to think I did," I replied, the memory of my competition last summer and how roughly they'd treated me surfacing in my mind. "I really didn't have much of a choice. It was either take up the reins or fail. And I couldn't fail."

Jonah nodded, his expression thoughtful. "How does a woman run things differently from a man out there?" he asked.

"A woman doesn't run anything differently than a man. We are the same exact person out there: worried about our crew, making sure our machinery is in tip-top shape, and then fairly distributing the daily take."

"The gold," he said with a bit of reverence in his voice.

"Yes, the gold," I acknowledged, a wistful quality to my voice as I recalled the glint of treasure beneath the Bering Sea. "We work on percentage agreements around here. If you don't pull your weight, your percentage might get cut. Another responsibility of the dredge owner."

Jonah raised an eyebrow, his curiosity evident. "Job performance?"

"I suppose that's what you could call it."

The bar's atmosphere seemed to fade into the background as our conversation took center stage. Jonah leaned in, seeking more from my experiences. "Have you ever had to fire someone?"

The memories of past decisions weighed on me, and I fidgeted in my seat. "Yes," I admitted. "I really don't want to talk about that." Kyle had been the one and only person I'd ever fired. It had been in a moment of fear for my father's life and anger thinking Kyle had slacked off while tending, which caused his near-drowning. A busted air hose needing replacement had been overlooked. Although later it had been revealed the accident may have been more purposeful in nature. Only my father and Kyle knew that one for sure.

"You don't have to name names or anything. Just wanted to get the full picture of what you encounter on a day-to-day basis."

I cleared my throat. "You have to do what's right by the business. Set aside your feelings and take the hard road. People make mistakes, sure, but some mistakes are unforgivable." I didn't know exactly what had happened the day of my father's accident, but I couldn't help but be worried that Kyle still harbored ill will toward my dad. And now he was back to working with him. Despite our rift, I still cared about my dad. And now that Kyle seemed to be involved with Lola somehow, I wondered if there was more to worry about than I knew.

"Who had the burger?" Marla swept in like a fresh breeze and set our plates on the table. "Anyone need ketchup?"

"Please," said Jonah. He lifted the top bun off his burger. "Are these homemade buns?"

Marla blushed. "Yep. I make 'em every morning along with the cinnamon rolls and donuts."

"Donuts? At a bar?" he asked.

"Hell, yes, honey, and I make the best donuts in town. You should stop by during our breakfast service." She winked and set the tab on the table. "I can take that up at the bar when you're ready. Need a refill?" She pointed at my empty glass.

"Please." I could drink a gallon of iced tea if she'd bring it.

"You got it. Oh, and I'll bring that ketchup, too."

"Great." Jonah smiled and then switched back to reporter mode. "I hear last summer was pretty rough for you."

"You could say that." I looked down at my hands.

"You had to hire someone on the spot—a stranger. New to town."

Ben. I didn't want to bring Ben into this. "I did. But that's not uncommon. A lot of thrillseekers show up here in the summer looking to make a quick buck. Gold does that to people."

"Does what to people?" He tapped his pen on his legal pad.

"Encourages rash decisions. Gold Fever. It's real. I've seen it up close." A panoply of faces stirred in my memory. Summer miners who didn't last. Who couldn't take the danger or didn't like the company. The job was hard, and most people weren't prepared for that. But Ben hadn't quit. Even when I'd made it less than pleasant for him to stay.

"So your partner, Ben Abel, had gold fever?" Jonah scribbled on his legal pad.

I frowned. "I'd prefer it if you'd leave Ben out of your article."

Jonah paused, looked up from his notes and, after a moment, set down his pen. "I only wanted some background information about your team to show the parallels between a woman captaining a dredge boat and women in other leadership roles in the corporate world."

I chewed my lip, thought about wanting to help out my sister, and then answered, "No, he only wanted a job. Any job. And that was his background: diving."

"A Navy diver, I hear. With war experience."

"He was military, yes." My brow furrowed. I didn't like where this was going.

From a bag on the seat next to him, Jonah pulled out a manila folder. He opened it. "Six years in the Navy. Was a decorated sailor. Had a tour during the Iraq War in the Gulf."

As close as Ben and I were, I knew next to nothing about his time in the Navy. He hadn't wanted me to ask, so I'd avoided the topic. Just like he avoided the topic of my mother who'd run off when I was twelve never to be seen again. "If that's what your papers say, then I guess it's true." I picked at my French fries. The piping hot battered fish sitting on my plate turned my stomach suddenly.

"He was awarded the Purple Heart."

The scar on his back. The story he wouldn't tell. The dark look in his eyes when I asked. I wanted to grab the folder and read for myself. Find out all the hurts and secrets Ben carried. Even after I'd told him I loved him and didn't need to know any more about his past, my curiosity grew like a weed. Every time I tried to poison it, it would grow back stronger and harder to kill.

Then I said the words I wish I hadn't: "What happened?"

"Did you want to read the report?" Jonah offered me the folder.

I lifted my hand to reach for it. I wanted so much to see the words on the page bringing Ben's past to life. The mystery of his time across the globe when something had damaged him so badly that he couldn't tell me anything about it. The story others could know, but I could not.

"Here's the ketchup and that refill, Rory," Marla said.

I averted my gaze from the older woman. I didn't want her to know what I was about to do. "Thanks." I snatched the folder and set it in front of me, hands trembling. I eagerly scanned the two typed pages. My heart had settled in my throat. A thready pulse fluttered at my wrist. This was wrong. So wrong. But I didn't care. I wanted to know. I needed to know.

"Looks like he was doing some underwater recon in the shipping lanes near Iraq and Iran...he and his partner, Ian Kilgore."

I skimmed the straightforward report. Something from a military source. "How did you get a hold of this?"

"His fiancée's family entered it as evidence in a civil case against him...didn't he tell you that?" He took a French fry and dipped it in ketchup. "They're suing him for wrongful death." He munched casually as if he were giving me the weather report.

"Oh." My face heated. I lifted a hand to my cheek. The coolness soothed. I blanked. Words wouldn't come. I picked up my glass and chugged a third of the iced tea in the glass. I'd never been so parched after a day of dredging.

"Anyway, they think he has PTSD and some anger management problems." He shrugged and took a bite of his burger.

Then I remembered the thick envelope full of papers Ben had tossed into the fire the other night. Was that what he was hiding from me?

The direction of the interview reminded me of taking a wrong turn in downtown Seattle and ending up in South Park. Dangerous. Dark. No easy way out. "He is an excellent worker," I blurted. Anything to change the topic. I slammed the folder shut and pushed it toward Jonah. "But he wouldn't want to be mentioned in the article, so please don't name him."

I wished I'd never opened that folder. Never read a word on the page. Ben trusted me. When he was ready to tell me about that part of his life, he would. My stomach twisted painfully. I bit my lip. No way was I going to cry. Not here in front of the intrepid reporter. It would end up in his article: *Local Dredger Weeps Over Fried Fish*. No thanks.

"Right. Sure." I frowned as Jonah scribbled some more in a notebook. "I have a few more questions about dredging. Some stuff might seem kind of basic to you, but readers would really like to understand the work better."

I cleared my throat and crossed my legs. I could do this. I could move on with grace and without Jonah ever suspecting I was two steps from the edge of cry town. "No problem. What do you want to know?"

For the next twenty minutes we chatted about dredging techniques, gold prices, and the future of dredging in Nome due to new rules put in place as a result of a few accidents in recent years. All the while in the back of my mind, I wished I'd read the full report on Ben.

CHAPTER 16

"Can you move a little closer to the monument, please?" Jonah asked.

The wind played with my hair. Beyond the carved wood monument on the outskirts of town, storm clouds gathered. Guess Jonah's predictions had been accurate. "How about this?" I sidled up to the gold miner carved at one end.

"Great. Now you aren't blocking the words." Jonah held his phone steady as he snapped photos. "The light this time of day is amazing."

My smile wavered. "How much longer?" I said without moving my lips. "It's a little cold out here." I'd stripped off my heavy parka to reveal my best pair of blue jeans and my yellow sweater underneath. What passed for 'nice' in Nome.

"Just a few more."

A truck passed by very slowly. I didn't even want to look at who was behind the wheel. So much for my interview 'secret.' "I still don't know why you didn't want to take pictures at the gold pan in town. World's Largest Gold Pan? Usually people can't resist," I said. Plus, it was in Anvil City Square. Nobody would've noticed me there. But standing right off a main road? Impossible to hide.

"Too cliche." He snapped a few more. "Done. Torture session over."

Why did I agree to do this? Was my relationship with my half-sister really worth it? I sighed. Yes, it was. I'd find a way to tell Ben...eventually. Or was it too late?

"Great." I scooped up my parka and zipped it up, clapping my chilled hands to get the circulation going before shoving them in my pockets. "Brr."

"I appreciate it, Rory. The time you took with me, the photos, everything. This is shaping into a really great piece."

I nodded, not really caring where the story ended up. Lost to the many blogs and news sites online that nobody read and nobody cared about. "No problem. Guess I never saw anything I did as unique or different."

"What?" He swept his arm to take in the Bering Sea beyond the monument of two Swedish gold miners from 1898. "You think this isn't unique?"

"Nome?" The darkening clouds worried me. What would a storm do to our equipment and our newly relocated shelter? Had I made a mistake in my eagerness to chase good gold?

"Not just the location, but what you do. It's so dangerous." He made his way back to his rental car. He'd given me a lift to the photo shoot rather than have me follow him on the snow machine.

I didn't look forward to making small talk all the way back to town. "I guess." I shrugged. "I've been doing it so long, I don't think about it being that unique or different. A lot of jobs in Alaska are dangerous: crab fishing, bush pilot. There's a thousand ways to die up here that don't even exist in the Lower 48."

"Can I quote that?" Eagerly, he grabbed his legal pad out of his backpack and scribbled down my words before I could say anything.

"Sure." My dad would be flattered one of his sayings would make it into the article. A lump formed in my throat. My dad. He would've been thrilled a reporter wanted to write a story about me. Too bad he'd ruined our relationship. I missed the closeness we used to have. It would've been so much easier if he stayed in Anchorage.

"That's almost the perfect opening line."

I climbed into his rental and shivered. My body hadn't recovered from the exposure to the rapidly dropping temperature. Nate would've made fun of me for not wanting to be pictured in my parka. To him and many other dredgers, femininity was a sign of weakness. My mind skipped to my mother. My beautiful absent mother who liked to wear yellow...

"Can we get out of here?" I asked. "It's been a long day."

"Sure," said Jonah. He started up the car and drove me back to town.

When Jonah dropped me off near my snow machine, I breathed a sigh of relief. The whole ride I'd been tense waiting for more penetrating questions, but he'd been quiet most of the drive back. We said our goodbyes, and he mentioned he hoped his flight back to Seattle wouldn't be cancelled tomorrow so he could beat the storm, and I thought nothing of it when he drove away.

Now that he was gone, I thought over the shocking details about Ben brought to light during the interview. Why had he tried to hide the civil suit from me? As I reflected on his actions, I couldn't shake the realization that I, too, was keeping parts of my past from him. It unsettled me that both of us were hiding things. We were supposed to love and trust each other, yet the revelation Ben withheld information made me question the strength of our relationship. I didn't like the feeling of secrets between us, and the interview had laid bare the need for open and honest communication that, sadly, seemed lacking in our partnership. Even my little white lie to Ben about being at Stella's caused my stomach to sour. How much did I love Ben if I couldn't be honest with him?

My cell phone rang, interrupting my uncomfortable thoughts. It was Stella. I'd rather have a friendly conversation with my best friend than delve too deeply into the weakness in my relationship with Ben. It hurt my heart to analyze how I'd treated him, and I wasn't sure how to fix it. Maybe I needed to get over being afraid of his reaction to the truth and just 'fess up.

"Rory, I'm so glad you picked up." Her voice had a strained quality to it that immediately grabbed my attention.

"What's going on?" Something was wrong.

"Can I come over?" Her voice trembled.

I looked at the snow machine covered in a thin dusting of the white stuff. The storm might not arrive in Nome before tomorrow morning, but already the precipitation had begun. "I'm in town. I could come to your place." I'd rarely heard Stella sound this upset. She was the epitome of a sunny personality.

"No. That wouldn't work." She cut me off abruptly. "How about we meet at Miner's?"

I mulled over the likelihood that Marla would mention to Stella my earlier visit with Jonah before I could confess everything to Ben. But there weren't many places to meet in Nome where two girlfriends could gab without being bothered, and Stella needed me. "Sure. I'll grab us a table."

"Thanks, Rory."

Fifteen minutes later Stella and I shared a small table in a quiet corner of the bar. Marla hadn't even blinked an eye when I showed up for a second time that night. Maybe she was too busy serving drinks to a group of rowdy miners to even notice me.

"I need some advice, Rory." Stella sat across from me.

My friend was usually the one wanting to sling out the advice, so the request threw me for a second. "About work or—?"

She bit her lip. "Relationship advice."

My mind flashed to the litter of failed relationships I'd left in my wake before Ben came into my life. Stella was the stable, normal person with the stable, normal relationship. What could I possibly say that she'd find useful? "Are you sure?"

"I trust you, and I know that you've been wary of long-term stuff, so I think you might have the point-of-view I'm lacking right now."

I scratched the side of my neck, my cowl neck sweater suddenly itchy and too warm. "I'll do my best." I silently prayed I'd be able to give her the support she was looking for without being crass or insulting.

"Matt and I got into an argument last night."

"Over what?" I'd never seen the two of them argue before, so to hear Stella bring this up made me think it must've been something serious.

"He told me he never wanted to work at the gas station and only did that to make me happy. To bring in some money to pay the rent." She swallowed. "And that I've been standing in the way of his dreams." Her eyes grew wet, and her voice went all sideways and squeaky.

"What?" I grabbed her by the hand. "What dreams?"

Stella's face fell. "I mentioned it to you the other night—flying lessons. He wants to be a pilot. I'm freaking out."

Matt had always seemed content in his quiet-yet-manly sort of way. He'd make sure Stella's car was warmed up and ready for her before she started an early shift at the Polar Cafe. He'd run out for more of her favorite diet soda even in the middle of a winter gale and minus thirty windchill. To me, he'd appeared to be so in love with Stella she could do no wrong.

But he'd never been a superstar in the classroom. Average kid, average grades. College hadn't been a consideration. Higher ambitions didn't seem like Matt.

Was that what he'd been up to? Could he have been taking flying lessons behind her back?

Maybe the other figure I'd seen in the truck with him had been his instructor.

"Did you tell him your feelings about it?"

"A long time ago when we first were dating, he talked about being a pilot. I mentioned how I could never do that—all those accidents you read about all the time. But I thought it was just kids talking, you know? We were seniors in high school. I wanted to be a travel writer. Remember that?"

A sharp pang hit my belly. "Yeah, I do." I tried to keep my voice even. I should've told Stella about when I saw Matt at the airport when Ben and I had done our gold clean out.

"Until I figured out I had to have the money to travel in the first place." Stella sniffled.

I grabbed a paper napkin and handed it to her. "Here."

"Thanks." She wiped her nose. "I guess Matt was serious about the pilot thing. We've been together for six years and not once has he brought this up beyond some random one-time conversation all those years ago. I didn't know this was a 'dream.' And now he says that I'm the one in the way of him achieving it."

"Why would he say something like that?"

She sighed. "I guess I said something about how dangerous it was. You know how I feel about those little planes. Not a week goes by without another story of a bush pilot crashing."

"You may have mentioned that a time or two." Actually, more than that. "The wedding comes to mind." Stella hadn't left Nome ever since she had a bad experience at eleven years old in a Kodiak on a trip to Talkeetna for a cousin's wedding.

"That's what Matt said: I told him about that awful trip. He took it to mean I didn't want him learning how to fly a plane. But I never said that. I'm just worried, you know?"

"He probably inferred that you wouldn't be open minded about him pursuing a job like that."

"I suppose he's not wrong there. But I never said the words, and now he's mad at me." She wiped at her nose with the napkin. "I can't stand it, Rory. We never fight. I couldn't sleep last night after he blew up at me. Then his sister came home in the middle of it all, took his side. God, I wish she would just get her own place already."

"So you'd really keep Matt from becoming a pilot because of your own fears about flying?"

"It's so dangerous, Rory." Her brown eyes shone with unshed tears. "When he brought up the idea of doing it for a living, I panicked. Learning how to fly is one thing, but flying every day in all kinds of weather? I don't know how I could mentally handle that all the time."

I didn't blame Stella for being so fearful. Most planes in Alaska were small and could be dangerous in the changeable weather. Every year there were a dozen or more small plane crashes in our state. People killed. People crashing in the middle of nowhere. But it was also how mail, food, animals, people, repair parts made it from one isolated location to another.

Carefully, I thought about my statement. I didn't want to make things worse. "A lot of jobs come with danger attached."

"But a lot of jobs don't." Stella grabbed another napkin and dabbed at her watery eyes.

"True, but I'm sure Matt is also thinking about the income he could generate with a job like that. Better pay than the gas station. A lot better pay. I'm sure he's only thinking about taking care of you."

Stella's pink cheeks grew pinker, and the tears threatened to spill. "I don't know, Rory. I want him to be happy, but this would make me so *un*happy."

I squeezed her hand. "Give it some time. Maybe with the truth out there, it was a shock, and you just need time to adjust to the idea."

Stella looked down at the table. "Maybe."

She didn't sound convinced.

"You could try talking to one of the pilots and asking them about the experience." Should I tell her what I knew? That Matt was already spending money on pursuing his dream? "Maybe it's just a matter of asking the right questions and finding out more."

Stella nodded.

"Oh, Stel, I hate to see you like this."

At that moment, Marla approached our table, but stopped when she noticed Stella almost in tears. "I can come back later."

My friend looked up and tried to smile. "It's okay. I need to go. It's getting late, and I really just needed to unload." She stood and let out a breath. "Thanks, Rory."

"Of course." Now was not the time to ask her to cover for me if Ben asked about tonight. It could wait. I left a ten on the table to cover our drinks and walked my friend to the door. "We should probably get together one of these nights for pizza, no?"

Stella smiled. "I'd like that."

"Great. I'll text you later."

After Stella left, Marla handed me my change and said, "So who was that good looking guy you were here with earlier?"

My stomach dropped.

Marla waited for my answer. She wasn't the gossipy type, so I knew her question wasn't asked with mean intent. She truly was curious about Jonah as not much happened in Nome in the middle of winter after the Iditarod. I also knew she had a single twenty-something daughter. So maybe her question had an ulterior motive.

I attempted a smile. "He's a friend of my sister's." Better to stay within the limits of the truth than make up some story I might have to dredge up later. Plus, if word did get back to Ben I'd have my story down pretty well.

"Oh?" Marla wiped her hands on a towel she'd tucked into an apron pocket. "Is your sister visiting?"

"No." I didn't elaborate.

"Hm." She scanned my face. "Well, I hope he had a nice visit and manages to leave before the surprise storm hits tomorrow."

I nodded. "So what's the latest forecast?" Even though I knew the edge of the storm had reached us, I hoped by some miracle the wind had shifted.

"You know, I haven't looked." The older woman adjusted her red framed glasses. "But last I heard, it was going to dump snow on us, and there was a prediction for some pretty bad storm surge."

Great. "Then I'd better go. Ben and I need to batten down the hatches if that's the case." I didn't want to think about how likely it might be the storm surge could destroy the ice shelf and put our whole operation at risk. A heavy lump settled in my chest.

"You're staying at those yurts, right?"

"Yeah. The cabin's too far from town to run back and forth every day."

"Not the most secure things in a storm," Marla said. "Make sure you watch for flooding, since you're so close to shore."

That hadn't even crossed my mind. My worries had been focused exclusively on our dredge set up. How far were we from the water line? I'd have to inspect in the morning.

"I'll keep that in mind. We're near the last row of yurts, so we should be okay." But I didn't know for certain that was true.

Marla smiled broadly at me. "Well, say hello to Ben for me. He's been a nice addition to the community."

"Oh?"

"I've got a soft spot for vets." She twisted the towel in her hands. "My dad fought in the Korean War. Did I ever tell you that?"

"No, I didn't realize." Was she about to regale me with war stories? I needed to head back to Ben before it grew too late.

"Marla!" The rowdy crowd of miners around the bar signaled they needed refills of their pint glasses.

"Looks like I have to play serving wench for a few more hours."

Marla smiled and threw the towel over her shoulder. "But you bring that Ben back any time. I'll even buy him a beer."

"Thanks, Marla. See you around." I froze when I saw who was in that crowd of men: Lola's heavy, Declan. His black gaze connected with mine.

I needed to leave.

By the time I'd opened the door, Marla was doling out beers and topping off shots to the hollering miners. Declan's dark look shifted from me to his glass. He downed the shot in one swallow. I hurried out of the bar, just wanting to be back in the yurt with Ben.

Kyle was pulling me into something sinister. I could feel it.

After brushing an inch of white stuff off the seat, I started up our snow machine. Before I could make my getaway, a heavy hand rested on my shoulder.

My insides loosened.

I knew it was Declan before I even looked up.

"Where's Kyle?" His deep voice rumbled like a freight train barreling through a tunnel. "He promised he'd pay."

"Kyle's problems have nothing to do with me." My voice came out a lot more confident than I felt. Should I gun it and make a run for it?

"Aren't you his girlfriend?"

My mind lit up like a forest fire when it hit dry brush. *Dammit, Kyle, what did you do?* "No, I'm not. Did Kyle tell you that?"

His grip tightened on my shoulder almost to the point of pain. "I saw you two together last summer."

"We broke up. You didn't hear why he was in jail?" Why did I come to town by myself? The interview had been a mistake. I looked around, hoping someone would come out the bar and see us, but of course when I wanted to be seen, no one was around. "He attacked me."

"Lola thinks you know something. I think you better come with me."

Oh God.

This was not good. I never should've gotten involved with Kyle.

I bucked away from the burly man looming over me, but he grabbed me around my waist and effortlessly threw me over one shoulder as I screamed. My cell phone fell out of my pocket and landed in the snow.

I pounded my fists against his back, but Declan only cuffed me in the side of the head as a response. Pain exploded in my right cheek.

Automatically, I stilled. Self-preservation move. He outweighed me by at least a hundred pounds.

Where was Marla? Where was anyone?

He tossed me in a pickup truck. As he pulled away from Miner's and drove us far away from everyone and everything I knew, I thought of only one thing: Ben.

CHAPTER 17

As we rode in silence down a gravel road, I'd never felt so helpless.

My face throbbed where he'd hit me. I touched my cheekbone and felt the swelling already. That was going to be one ugly bruise.

I wish he'd knocked me unconscious so at least the surge of fear wouldn't be so nauseating. I wanted to act. I wanted to scream. But some part of my brain kept me quiet, docile.

Wait for the right opportunity, it said.

Flinging myself out of a truck in the dark on a lonely, empty road was not a good strategy. What would Ben do? The tough Navy man would probably have already taken control of the situation and pummeled this guy into a bloody mess with one hand and commandeered the truck with the other.

Lola's heavy gave me the side eye. "I wouldn't think of jumping."

"I'm not." My oddly confident voice outside Miner's had disappeared and had been replaced with a quavering, squeaky one. "I don't know anything about Kyle or any money."

"Shut up."

I bit my lip. I didn't want that massive fist hitting me for a second time.

Why hadn't I told Ben about Lola and her thug? Now there was no chance of him knowing I'd been taken.

Ben wasn't going to save me. I had to save myself.

The headlights lit up a few single-wide trailers that appeared abandoned.

How far out of town were we going to go? And how was I going to get back?

My body grew numb.

Maybe I wouldn't be going back.

"Have you looked at my dad's place?" I didn't like the idea of some drug dealer's bodyguard crashing my dad's apartment, but if Kyle wasn't at the yurts it was a possibility. And maybe it would be a way to make him take me back to town.

"He was supposed to meet me with the cash tonight. He didn't show. He ain't at his place, and he ain't at Buck's."

He'd been to his place already?

My mouth went dry.

He slowed the truck to take a sharp turn to the left. "Lola wouldn't like that, see? So you're the next best thing I've got."

I was the consolation prize. He must've known without Kyle and without the money, returning to Lola empty-handed would be a mistake. Seeing me in Miner's must've been a relief to him. Grab the 'girlfriend' and save his own ass.

So big, scary Declan was afraid of Lola? Interesting. Maybe he wasn't nearly as tough as he looked.

"How much cash?" I asked.

"Twenty grand."

I coughed at the amount. No wonder Lola was so angry at him. "What? Kyle doesn't have money like that."

"He said he would."

"From mining?" Is that why my father offered him a job? Out of pity for some financial bind Kyle had found himself in? Maybe Buck did feel responsible for Kyle's problems after stealing the map from the Stroup family. Had this been my father's sloppy attempt at reconciliation?

"Buck's a good miner," Declan said. "Everyone in town knows it."

I nodded. Knowing Kyle's debts only made me feel worse about my current situation. "How come Kyle owes Lola so much?" Could he really have used twenty thousand dollars' worth of drugs in the few months he'd been in jail?

"Here we are." He drove down a long snowy driveway that hadn't been cleared all winter. Deep tire ruts in the snow made driving difficult. If the coming storm was as bad as Jonah thought, we could get trapped by new snow if we stayed too long. I'd say and do almost anything to make sure I was back in town before that happened. There had to be some offer I could make that would satisfy these criminals.

We pulled up to a modern-looking house on stilts with a set of steps up to a deck that surrounded the main floor. Not at all what I was expecting after passing so many dilapidated trailers. Guess Lola wasn't as small-time as I thought.

"Get out."

I obeyed the bodyguard. He had no weapon, but I knew the power in those hands. I was no match against them, and he had no qualms about using them on a woman.

"Up there." He pointed at the stairs. "Let me do the talking."

I climbed the stairs to the snow-covered deck.

Lola opened the front door and grimaced. "What the fuck, Declan? Why'd you bring her?"

My knees buckled under me.

Declan lifted me off the deck by my arm.

Lola stepped back. "Put her on the couch." She flipped her long black hair over one shoulder and let a breath out through her nose like a bull readying to run down a matador. "Jeez, what'd you do to her face?"

He shoved me onto a couch that looked fresh off the showroom floor but already smelled of cigarette smoke and cat pee. "She wouldn't shut up."

"You kidnapped me." Although fear surged through me like a riptide, I couldn't let him get away with such a massive lie. "What did you expect?"

He narrowed his eyes at me.

Lola smirked then hardened her face almost instantly to hide her bemused reaction to my comment. "Where's Stroup? I want my money."

"Don't know, boss." He jerked his chin in my direction. "But this is his girlfriend. He'll want her back."

"What am I supposed to do with her?" She eyed me with disgust.

"And if you can't find the guy, how is he supposed to know she's even here?"

Declan may be strong and intimidating, but he sure wasn't very smart. I shifted my gaze from the drug boss to my captor. Now it made sense why this lunkhead ended up working as the muscle for a small town drug dealer.

He shrugged and headed to the kitchen. "Got any beer?"

She zipped up her red puffer vest and stuck her hands in the pockets. "No beer until you bring me either the money I'm owed or the deadbeat."

"Why does Kyle owe you so much money?" I asked.

"You told her?" She swung her head around. "What the fuck, Declan?"

He paused with his hands on the refrigerator door handle. "Shit, boss, I told you she wouldn't shut up."

"Does that mean you need to tell her everything?" She had a severe mouth, like an arrowhead, pointy and sharp. "Get your damned beer. I can't think with your stupid ass staring at me."

"I didn't think Kyle did drugs—" I mumbled.

"You think all I do is deal, huh?" Lola paced in front of me, her thin arms turned out at the elbows.

Although her heavy had punched me in the head, for some reason, I didn't fear the slim Asian woman in front of me. We were both business women, trying to keep our heads above water in a place where that was very hard to do. Half the town scraped by and took on odd jobs—sometimes illegal ones—to get by. I could sort of understand how she'd ended up doing such work.

"No." But I didn't really believe it when I said it. What else could leave Kyle with such a huge debt?

Lola quirked a smile and shook her head. "Yeah, you do. All the papers tell you that."

"You mean the *Nome Nugget*?" That was the only paper in town. I couldn't imagine a low-level drug dealer's fifth arrest would make it into the papers downstate. Possession charges were a dime a dozen. The cops had never managed to tie her to anything larger...yet. Was that the reason she was so upset Declan had brought me here?

Lola ignored me and joined Declan in the kitchen. "I want you back out there. You'd better not find out Stroup left town with my money."

"He didn't." As much as I wanted to run out the front door while they weren't looking, I knew I needed these criminals to make it to Ben and our yurt. I really didn't want to help these two find Kyle, but they were my only way back to civilization before the storm hit.

"I thought you said you didn't know where he is," said Declan.

"I don't, but I know where he likes to hang out," I said quickly. I had to get them to trust me if I was going to get out of here. "If he knows you're out looking for him, he might hide. But if he thinks it's only me—"

Lola nodded. "Good thinking. Everyone sees you coming from a mile away," the drug dealer said to Declan. "Stroup wouldn't suspect his girlfriend of double crossing him."

I didn't correct the lie a second time. Who knew what they'd do if they found out Kyle hated my guts? They'd never trust I could convince him to hand over the money he owed.

"And don't even think about fucking me over or I'll make sure Declan gets some one on one time with both of you." Lola let the words hang in the air for several moments.

He finished his beer, his eyes on me like he wouldn't mind having to beat the hell out of us one bit.

I nodded and prayed that my plan would work.

Kyle, where are you?

CHAPTER 18

The ride back to town was treacherous. The snow had begun
to fall in earnest, and the truck slid around several curves
and almost off the road more than once. Even though Declan drove
in four-wheel drive, the tires must've been bald because it felt as if
they had no traction whatsoever.

Lola turned around in the passenger's seat to look at me.
"Where to?"

My mind raced through the possibilities. Declan indicated
earlier he'd stopped by my dad's place, and both he and Lola had
been seen around the yurts, so he'd probably checked there, too.
His stop at Miner's maybe had two goals: a drink and locating Kyle.

"The old Quonset hut on the east side of town." I didn't know if
he'd be there, but it was a start—Kyle's old place. The one he rented
from the retired miner who lived in Florida. If he knew Lola was
out looking for him, maybe he'd hunker down there. It had been for
sale since Kyle's arrest.

"On Nugget Alley?" he asked.

"That's the one." The anemic heat from the front blowers didn't
quite reach the back seat, and I shivered even in my zipped up
parka. "But drop me a couple blocks away or he'll probably run
again. He knows this town like the back of his hand."

Mr. Muscles gave his boss a glance.

"She knows what happens if she can't pull this off," Lola said to him. "Would you rather get me my money or spend an arm and a leg on a hospital bill?" She scanned me up and down as if she were judging how hard it would be to put me on a stretcher.

"I'm not going to screw you over," I said as confidently as I could, although I had no idea how Kyle would put that much money together. In my head I called out to Ben to find me. By now someone would've noticed the idling snow machine outside Miner's, wouldn't they? "I know what's at stake."

"Good." She pulled her knitted wool hat lower on her head, its bright pink and white striping at odds with her menacing demeanor. "I'll give you twenty-four hours to get me my money. Kyle has my number. You better convince him it's in his best interest to set up a meet. This is his last chance."

I swallowed.

Declan drove us through Nome. As we approached the section of town close to Kyle's old place, I recognized his little gray Toyota truck parked up the street. My instincts had worked in my favor. A warm rush of relief flooded me. At least I'd found him. Now all I had to do was convince him to cough up the cash.

"Stop." I pointed at the corner, about a block away from the truck. "Drop me right here."

The vehicle slowed, fishtailing in the soft snow. When it came to a complete stop, I reached for the door handle. Lola's slim hand gripped my forearm.

"I want my money, you understand?" Her words had an undertone of anxiety that hadn't been there earlier.

I nodded. Maybe Lola owed money to someone else far scarier than she or Declan.

She let go. Declan stared me down in the rearview mirror as if he would enjoy following through on Lola's threat. He didn't care who I was or why I was in this mess, he only wanted some payback for the trouble Kyle had caused him.

As I stepped into the snow, goose bumps rose on my skin, and not only because of the cold. When my captors drove off, I let out a ragged breath. All I had to do was convince Kyle, a man I hated, to come up with twenty thousand dollars before time ran out.

I wrapped my arms around my body and trudged through the deepening snow toward the Quonset hut. Kyle had better be in there, or I was going to be in a world of hurt.

M y feet slipped in the deep snow that had built up since I'd been driven out of town, and I looked over my shoulder to make sure that Lola and Declan had lived up to their end of the deal and were long gone. A shiver ran through me. Was it because of the cold or because I'd somehow succeeded in temporarily talking my way out of a dangerous situation? Guess they'd rather give me a chance to locate the money owed then draw more attention to themselves with more brutish tactics.

I scanned the Quonset hut across the street. The interior was dark. Usually the light above the door was turned on, but not tonight. However, if it was up for sale, maybe the electricity had been shut off. Was Kyle even in there? My stomach fluttered. This was not a smart plan. Except for running into him on the ice, I hadn't talked to Kyle alone in months. If he was in there, would he even listen to me? I had to find a way. Lola already thought I was involved. If I didn't resolve this money issue between her and Kyle, I'd be blamed.

No one was going to help me. Only I could solve this problem.

Even though there were no lights on, I circled around to the back to make sure the neighbors didn't see me and think someone was trying to rob the place. Plus, there was a window back there that had never been sealed properly. It always leaked in the spring when the snow began to melt and throughout the summer rains. The wood frame had warped over time, causing the lock mechanism to fail. More than once, we'd climbed in through the back window when one of us forgot our keys.

I smiled at the memory. Kyle would boost me up and into the kitchen, and I'd let him in the back door. Things had been good for a little while with him. Too bad it had all turned sour.

He could've broken into the place using that window, and I wanted to check if it was open.

A weak light emanated from inside the hut. Maybe a lantern?

My heart pounded.

Kyle was there.

I stepped up to the back door and knocked.

The light went out.

I knocked harder. "Kyle, it's me. Let me in, it's freezing out here."

The seconds ticked by. Snow fell down the back of my parka. I jumped at the cold precipitation on my hot skin.

The door opened a crack. "What are you doing here?"

"Lola dropped me off." I pushed on the door. "Open up. You don't have a lot of choices. If she doesn't get her money in twenty-four hours, you're toast." I didn't tell him so was I.

"She told you?" Kyle's hold on the door eased.

"Everything." I pushed harder. "Get out of the way."

The door opened, and I was inside before he could think of doing anything stupid. "I'm not a threat to you."

"What happened to your face?" He touched my cheek.

I flinched and backed up a couple of steps. "Lola's buddy Declan thought I talked too much."

"Shit. I'm sorry, Rory. They think we're still together."

I crossed my arms. "Who gave them that idea?"

He shrugged and put his hands in his jacket pockets. "I was just shooting the shit. They knew I was working for Buck; they wondered how I got the job. Told 'em we were dating. They seemed to buy it."

"Was that so they thought you'd be good for the money?"

"I screwed up. I thought this would be over by now." He didn't elaborate why he'd dug himself such a deep financial hole.

"Well, I'm the only one who can help you." It was a lie, but it was all I had. I certainly didn't have the kind of cash he needed to get out of trouble with Lola.

"Is that right?" His voice dripped with a mixture of skepticism and disdain.

It was too dim inside the hut to read his expression. Everything inside me said to run, to leave this place and never look back. I could figure out another way.

With the threat of Lola and Declan no longer present, my brain began to function again. This was a mistake. Why did I need to make Kyle's problem mine? I looked at the back door. Only a few feet away.

He pointed a gun at me. "Don't even think it, Rory."

CHAPTER 19

My limbs shook as I stared at the gun pointed at me. "Where did you get that?" This was not the Kyle I knew. Sure, he had attacked me last summer, but he wasn't the type to threaten to shoot someone, to shoot me.

"It was Uncle Arthur's." He shrugged. "I hid it in here a long time ago. Never know when you might need extra protection. When I saw this place up for sale, I was worried that maybe they'd found it." He waved it at me. "But looks like I'm good at hiding things."

Kyle lifted the gun, and the air in the room seemed to thicken. Was this real?

"It's too late to change your mind." He knew I was going to bolt. "You're going to help me with my problem." He leaned in closer, his eyes locking onto mine with a predatory intensity. "We're going to fix this once and for all. You and your father owe me, Rory."

I glanced at him and then toward the door and back again. I wanted to run so badly. Would he really shoot me if I tried?

I squeezed my eyes shut so I could think. I didn't want to be shot, but I didn't know how I was going to help Kyle out of his trouble. I don't know why I thought I could. I guess having Declan punch me in the face and threaten me with worse was a motivator to make ridiculous promises. I'd escaped one scary guy only to have another take his place.

"How?" I asked.

"You're Buck Darling's daughter. Rumors say you had a pretty good clean-out the other day. I know you have some gold lying around," he said. "If you don't hand it over, sounds like Lola's gonna come back for us both. Think how upset Ben would be if a second woman dies on him?"

Hot tears threatened to spill.

Before I could respond to his demand, he spun me around, hooked an arm across my throat, and pressed the cold barrel of the gun against my temple. "Where's the gold, Rory?"

My body froze and a cold sweat broke out across my skin. As much as I didn't want to give up our gold, with a gun to my head, the choice became an obvious one. Did I really want to be shot over a few thousand dollars? Ben and I still had a few weeks left in ice season, we'd just moved to a better location, and the gold we had in the box after one day of work probably would replace what I'd be giving up to stay alive.

When he pressed his arm harder against my larynx, I choked out, "Okay, okay. Just don't shoot." The gun was by far scarier than Declan's fists. "You can have it."

He lowered the gun and pushed me away from him. "How much?"

My muscles dissolved into jelly as the threat disappeared. "Maybe six grand."

His eyes were two pitch black holes in the darkened room. "Where did you stash it?"

"In our yurt—but Ben is there." My mind scrambled. How to make this work without Ben getting drawn into it? "You could call him. Tell him I'm hurt or need his help. Maybe tell him the snow machine stalled at Miner's." At least Ben would know I was okay.

"He wouldn't listen to me." He paced in front of me. "He hates my guts."

Even though the Quonset hut took us out of the cold and snow, it wasn't heated. My hands and toes were beginning to grow numb.

"What about Stella?" Everyone in town had a soft spot for the cheerful young woman who served coffee and pancakes with a smile. I hoped Kyle was no different. "You could call her, and she could call Ben. We could park down by the yurts and wait until he leaves."

He nodded his head, his gun hand dropping to his side. "That could work." I let out a sigh of relief, both that he was listening to me and that the gun wasn't staring me in the face.

I saw his cell phone on the kitchen counter to my left and grabbed it. "Here, call her. I have her number memorized."

"No, I have it." He took it and scrolled through his contacts with a thumb. "Matt gave it to me once in case of emergency."

Matt?

I puzzled over that one but didn't have time to process why Kyle and Matt would ever have crossed paths.

I held my breath while we both waited for Stella to answer. I didn't want to give Kyle our hard-earned gold, but if I could maneuver a way out of this by distracting him with our clean-out, I had to do it.

"Hey, Stella. It's Kyle." He launched into a long rambling story about why Ben needed to meet me at Miner's and how my phone had run out of battery power. By the end, he had her agreeing to call Ben.

What would Ben think when Stella told him Kyle had called her on my behalf? One thing I knew, he wouldn't be happy about it.

Kyle tucked his phone in the back pocket of his jeans and then pointed the gun at me. "Let's go. We have some gold to grab." A wicked smile lit up his boyish face.

For a moment I pitied him. His downfall began the minute my father had stolen his family's gold map. I couldn't help but feel partially responsible for what had happened after that.

As we left the protection of the hut and headed to his truck, I hoped he'd forget about all the rest of the debt he owed once he saw our hidden cache. I had nothing left to offer and once he found that out, he might end up pulling the trigger.

Kyle parked his truck on the road above the beach where the yurts stood. With the snow falling steadily and the wind blowing to remind everyone a storm was on its way, no movement could be seen. The only indication of life visible in the anemic street light's glow were drifts of smoke from the individual wood stoves that cranked out heat for the occupants.

Ours was noticeably absent of smoke. Snow had drifted up against the walls of the all the yurts, but ours showed signs that someone had opened the door recently.

"Do you see him?" Kyle turned his ball cap backwards, his gun resting in his lap.

I could sense his eagerness to take ownership of our hard-won gold to partially solve his money problems. My stomach burned at the thought of losing it. But the barrel of the gun pointed in my direction reminded me my life wasn't worth a few thousand bucks.

"I think he's already gone," I said.

"Think or know? I don't want to run into that monster." Then he rubbed his hand along the black barrel of his handgun and smiled. "But if I had to—"

"Why do you owe Lola so much money?" I didn't want to think about the possibility of Ben being shot, bleeding out at my feet, while my ex-boyfriend stood there and watched. But for all my troubles tonight with Lola, Declan, and now giving up my gold, at the very least Kyle owed me an explanation. "Twenty grand? It doesn't make any sense."

Kyle shifted his gaze from the yurts to my profile. The weight of his stare was as heavy as a full bucket of concentrates after a few days of dredging. "I did what I had to do."

I bit the inside of my cheek. "What do you mean? You couldn't have spent it all on drugs. I know you, Kyle. You're not a druggie."

"I didn't buy drugs," he ground out. "Is that what you think of me? I hate that shit."

I pressed my back into the seat. The last thing I wanted was to anger him. "I'm sorry. I only want to understand."

He picked up his gun and put it in his pocket.

When it was out of my sight, I could feel my heart rate slow a little.

"Jail is a fucking scary place. When I thought I'd be doing a full six months, well, I'd heard stories about the gangs, the attacks, the violence." He put his hands on the steering wheel and gripped it tightly. "I ran into Declan one night at Ernie's a few days before I was going to start my sentence. He said he had an offer for me. A way to keep me safe in jail, if I'd work for him."

"For Lola."

"Yeah." Kyle nodded. "Said I'd be paid pretty good, too."

"To do what?"

"Sell contraband."

"Sell drugs, you mean." This was not the Kyle I knew. Why would he agree to something so risky?

"Anything a guy wanted in prison. I was going to be the source and I'd get my cut."

"Oh, Kyle," I mumbled.

"I don't want to hear any of your pious crap, Rory. If you were in my shoes, you'd be considering the same deal. I was in debt, my family was thousands of miles away and had no idea I'd been arrested, so I couldn't ask them for help."

"You didn't tell them?" That shocked me.

"How could I, Rory? They were so proud of me when I came to Nome. My dad said I was 'carrying on the family legacy.' He thought I'd come back rich and make up for Uncle Arthur's failures. They don't understand how hard it is to make it here."

He was right. So many people heard the word 'gold' and thought it was an easy way to make big money quickly. For those with little knowledge, it was a hard lesson to show up in Nome and find out there was a lot to learn about underwater dredging before you ever saw a nugget turn up in your sluice.

"So that's what I did. Lola gave me some cash to bribe a guard one of her crew had made a connection with, and he'd look the other way when I received packages every couple of weeks. She charged a huge fee for her services, and I was supposed to make a cut."

Made sense a drug dealer would find other ways to diversify her business. "But I still don't understand why you owe her so much money. Weren't you sending her the profits she was owed?" Then I remembered what he'd said at the beginning—that he'd been in debt. Not broke, but in debt. "Who did you owe money to?"

His shoulders slumped. "My attorney, my landlord, everyone. It kept piling up. I thought I'd come out of prison with nothing. Then what would I do, Rory? I thought I could borrow a little bit here and there. Lola would never know. I only wanted enough to pay my bills. So I didn't end up in more trouble once I'd done my time." He shifted in his seat. "But then they let me out early—I had a delivery that was coming in that week. Plus, I knew how many more deliveries I needed to pay her back. It would've worked out perfectly if only—"

"But twenty grand?" Our gazes met.

He tapped his thumbs on the steering wheel. "You don't know how expensive lawyers are."

I mulled it over. What would I have done if I were in his shoes? Last summer I'd been desperate for cash, in debt, and my dad needed life-saving surgery. Hard to know what anyone would do if her back were against the wall. But I'd been lucky enough to find Ben. He was my savior. Not only a great diver, but a man who'd won my heart. Where would I have ended up without him?

I looked out at the yurts. "I think it's safe for us to go."

"Show me."

Kyle turned off the engine, and we both headed out into the blowing snow.

<hr>

A knot tightened in my abdomen as I opened the door to our yurt. I half expected to see Ben asleep in his sleeping bag. But when I looked inside, it was cold, dark, and empty, as if he'd been gone for a long time. Had he left to search for me before Stella had called him?

"What are you waiting for?" Kyle shoved me, and I fell to the floor. "Where is it?"

I thought if I cooperated with him, he'd treat me better. Seemed as if any kindness he could've spared me had disappeared the minute he knew gold would be in his hands. At this point, I was only a means to an end.

I sat up on my knees, my palms stinging. "Calm down." Then I saw the butt of the gun sticking out of his pocket, and a wave of fear hit me again. "Let me turn on a lantern so I have some light." I reached for the large battery powered one that sat on the floor near our cots.

He grabbed the hood of my parka. "Slowly. A military dude probably stashes all kinds of knives and shit everywhere. We don't want any accidents to happen now, do we?"

That's when I felt the barrel of the gun against my back.

My blood ran cold. He knew the gold was in the yurt somewhere. Did he even need me anymore? I should've kept the location of our stash closer to the vest.

"The gold's over here, but I need to be able to see." I inched forward on my knees toward the plastic container, which marked our hidden cache. "I want to help you, Kyle."

His grip loosened on my parka, and the gun barrel disappeared.

Tears welled up behind my eyes. Why couldn't this night be over already? I wanted to be wrapped up in Ben's arms and feel safe again. I'd thought myself so tough and independent, but right then I wished he were there. Right then I wished he would prevent Kyle from hurting me again. And I didn't care if I had to admit I couldn't handle this all by myself.

"Where is it?" Kyle's usually mellow voice had risen in pitch.

I scrambled across the floor, shoved the container aside, and pulled up the loose floor board. "It's here." Blindly, I dug through the cold sand. Without the lantern light, I was doing it all by feel.

A light snapped on. Kyle's breathing grew heavy.

My body cast a shadow across the hole I was digging. My hand touched the peanut butter jar. I grabbed it, sat back on my heels, and held it out. "Here, here it is. Take it."

Kyle stared at the gold inside the jar, putting his gun away as he took it from me. "Nice." He hefted it as if he would be able to figure out the value without a scale.

"It's almost three ounces. I swear." I sat with my knees against my chest. Would I be free to go now? Would this nightmare be over? I wanted nothing more to do with Kyle, Lola, or Declan. I wanted to pretend as if this night never happened. I could make up some story for Ben. Claim we'd been robbed while both of us were out. Come up with some excuse about where I'd been. Thinking about how many lies I'd have to tell made me feel nauseated. Ben didn't deserve that.

In a fluid movement, Kyle leapt up and offered me a hand.

"Come on. Let's go. You really came through, Rory. Maybe you are a friend after all."

Did he think I gave him our gold because we were friends? Did he not see the imbalance of power—man with a gun, me with nothing? And not even that, either I had to help Kyle repay his debt, or he'd shoot me. I'd had no choice.

"Where are we going?"

"Out on the ice."

"What?"

Kyle held the jar and shook it. "This is a good start, but I know you've got more out there."

I felt the blood drain from my face.

The smile that he wore gave him the appearance of a man who had a screw loose. "I'll bet your sluice box is packed with gold already, and with a few more hours of diving I'll be square with Lola."

"It's almost the middle of the night." The wind picked up at that moment and caused shudders across the skin of the yurt. "And there's a storm coming."

"Not until tomorrow morning. We'll be fine." He picked up an empty five-gallon bucket. "Here." He tossed it at me. "Put that in the truck."

"Kyle, it's dangerous out there." My decision to move our dredging operation seemed like a stupid one now. What had I been thinking? I'd been driven by greed and the fear of not making the goal we'd set for ourselves. Why couldn't I have had some patience? My dad was right: I might know the mechanics of ice diving, but I sure didn't understand all the risks.

"Shut up. I don't want to hear anymore whining." He touched the butt of his gun. "Let's go. We need to be off the ice before dawn —the last thing I need is for you to make a ruckus and attract attention."

I scanned the yurt before Kyle dragged me out. Would Ben come back and see the mess we'd left? Would he know it was me?

As the icy bits of snow stung my face, I prayed Ben would save me.

CHAPTER 20

Kyle drove us across the ice in his pickup. The headlights barely cut through the swirling snow. It was coming down even harder now. The wind blew in gusts—no wind one minute, howling the next. Had the storm predictions changed? To dive under these conditions in the middle of the night was madness. The farther we drove out on the ice, the more deep breathing I had to do to bring my emotions under control.

In the daytime, the lack of light underwater was an annoyance that required patience and a good light. At night? My body shook at the thought. Aside from the small light from my head lamp, it would be complete darkness. I'd never felt this scared to go diving.

My fear came out in my trembling words. "We shouldn't be doing this. This is dangerous."

Kyle laughed. "When hasn't dredging been dangerous? But that never stopped us before."

Us. As if we were a couple, a team who had made this decision together. "We moved our shelter to a new spot today. Closer to the ice shelf." Maybe that would deter him. Would he let go of the greed he had taking over his mind and think for a minute? "If the storm breaks the ice loose—"

"I know." He pressed down on the gas, and the truck slipped on a clean patch of ice near someone's operation. Up ahead I could make out the orange cones marking the end of the safe zone for dredging. "I saw the two of you today moving out here. You think I don't pay attention?"

"No, I just thought that—"

"I remember where you were mining last summer. Heard you found some big gold. I knew you wouldn't be able to resist it, Rory. You're exactly like me—a risk-taker." He drove past the cones and toward our new spot.

Beyond our shelter, I could see nothing but blackness. I shuddered, knowing the dark roiling sea was out there. "I made a mistake. We need to go back." I turned in my seat, taking one last glimpse of Nome. A sprinkling of lights caught my eye. Safety and home looked so far away. Nobody would think to look for me out here. Not even Ben.

Kyle stopped the truck right next to our new spot and then grabbed my arm as quick as a snake bites its prey. "Time to suit up."

I shook my head. What he was asking me to do was madness.

He leaned in and whispered harshly in my ear, "If you don't like it, I'll strip you down, force you into a wetsuit, and keep you underwater until the box is full."

I sucked in a breath at the images running through my mind. "I'll dive."

He released my arm and sat back. "Good." After zipping up his parka, he pointed at the empty bucket. "You grab that. I've got my hands full." He picked up the peanut butter jar and flashed his gun at me as he cocked a half-smile. "This is going to be just like old times, Rory."

As we left the warmth and security of the truck, the wind and snow howled around us. The crashing of waves against the edge of the ice shelf was deafening. How much stronger a surge could the ice take before it began to crumble around us?

Kyle forced me into the shelter, tucked the gun in his pants, and headed straight for the sluice, raking his fingers through the black sand and gold flake caught in the riffles. "I knew you'd have more out here." He snapped his fingers at me. "Bring me the bucket."

I did as he asked. He set the peanut butter jar on the ice and then took apart the sluice so he could roll up our miner's moss and stuff it into the bucket. A feeling of helplessness came over me. All our hard work was being stolen right in front of me, and there was nothing I could do about it.

After he'd finished with the sluice and laid down fresh miner's moss, he eyeballed our worn-out generator.

I prayed it wouldn't start. For the first time, I found myself strangely glad that Ben had invested in somewhat unreliable equipment.

When it roared to life after only a few attempts at starting it up, he whooped.

My heart thudded dully behind my ribcage.

I stared at the black dive hole. If it were a normal day, I'd relish the challenge. But Kyle forcing me into it caused a sense of unease to creep over me. The abyss beneath seemed dark and ominous. The excitement I usually felt before a dive was replaced by an unsettling worry.

The ice creaked beneath us. I imagined cracks forming under our feet, the truck breaking through and plunging into the water, taking us with it.

"Get dressed." Kyle's eyes glittered in the dim light emanating from a single battery-powered lantern. His gaze roved over me.

My stomach heaved.

Sure, he'd seen me in my underwear before, but that had been under completely different circumstances. My mind cried out to Ben, *where are you?* If he knew I was here with Kyle, he'd be furious, a force unleashed, an avenging angel.

"Do it." He pointed the gun at me.

I swallowed and took off my parka.

I sat on the edge of the ice and took a deep breath. Either I was jumping into the black hole or I was facing the barrel of a gun. No good options existed. I dug deep to find the stubborn Rory I knew. The overly confident Rory who believed she knew everything when it came to gold dredging.

"Time's a-wasting." Kyle stood over me.

"Right." I pulled my mask down and popped the regulator into my mouth. Before I could change my mind, I dropped into the water.

I used the suction hose to guide me to the bottom. As I propelled myself downward, I paused to snap on the light attached to the side of my visor. It barely cut through the gloom. As I descended, I could feel the force of the water pushing against me as it surged. It took my breath away, and I clung to the hose as the one thing I could rely on.

My mind drifted to my father, and everything I had learned from him over the years about underwater dredging. I ran through the safety rules, the accidents I'd witnessed, the tips he'd given me. I grabbed onto to anything and everything I could to keep me focused.

When I finally reached the bottom, gold sparkled under my anemic light. I panned my head back and forth, back and forth, and bright pops of metallic yellow lit up in the dark. If I only concentrated on that, I could forget about the threat waiting for me in the shelter above. This was more gold than we'd seen earlier today.

"I was right," I said to myself. Even though I didn't want to be here, the fact I'd seemed to have found our summer hot spot gave me a little bit of satisfaction.

"What?" Kyle's voice assaulted my ears. It unnerved me I was relying on my enemy for life-giving air and hot water.

"Start her up!" I shouted into my headset.

"Got it."

Within moments I felt the kick of the powerful suction hose. Sand and rock swirled up into the six-inch opening. My vision narrowed down to a small window of cobble where my light glinted off the gold flakes. The motion of the water made it difficult for me to keep control of the hose, so I forced my body perpendicular to the ocean floor and straddled it, hoping my weight alone could overcome the force of a whole ocean in the throes of a terrific storm.

"How's it look," Kyle asked.

The faster we collected the gold, the sooner I could be up on dry land. "Great." I attacked the gold-bearing cobble with gusto, thinking again how much I wanted to be done with this night. If I had told Ben what I was doing, if I had never gone to Miner's in the first place, I could be snuggled up in a sleeping bag with a fire roaring in our woodstove and Ben combing his fingers through my hair.

Out of habit, I yanked at the umbilical to gain more distance. Sometimes the hoses would tangle, and I'd need to use some muscle to straighten them out. But the moment I yanked, I knew I'd done the wrong thing. The hose snapped in my hands and the nozzle end flew out of my one-handed grasp, hitting me on the knee.

"Dammit." It hurt, but I wasn't about to cry over it. The hoses had gotten hung up on a tricky piece of ice. The light from my head lamp didn't cut through much of the dark, so it was impossible for me to see where the snag had occurred.

Kyle didn't respond to my choice language. He probably left the comms to check on the gold in the box. He didn't care about me, he cared about himself and the money he needed.

I had to figure this out on my own.

I let the hose settle to the ocean floor and grabbed hold of the umbilical lines taped together. Precious air and warm water flowed through those hoses to keep me alive. The last thing I wanted to do was rip the hoses apart or create a kink and cut off my air or heated water. I shook the bundle of hoses, sending a rapid shockwave down the length. But everything happened more slowly under water. The pulse of energy I'd wanted to send down the umbilical resulted in a weak ripple effect that wasn't strong enough to work the hoses loose.

"The gold's looking good, Rory." Kyle's voice lit up my comms. "If you can keep this up, we should be out of here in no time."

My frustration built to a mild level, but I didn't want to admit it to my captor. He'd probably enjoy it. I could handle this without his help. No problem.

"Have a little hang up I have to work loose," I grunted as I tried whipping the hoses even more strongly. He'd notice soon enough the flow of gold bearing material had stopped.

"Hang up?"

Dammit.

The second attempt did nothing either. The umbilical was still tightly stretched out. "On the ice." I tried whipping the lines from side to side, to see if a different motion would work.

Suddenly, a massive surge of seawater lifted me off my feet, breaking my grip on the suction hose that anchored me in position, and carried me yards farther from the safety of the hole. My stomach churned. Although I was still connected to the pumps up top, I only had so much extra umbilical before it ripped free and I was left without air or heat. I'd drown in seconds. And even if I managed to hold my breath, I'd die from hypothermia before I could ever make it back.

"Shit!" Kyle swore.

I didn't know why he was upset, but I was too busy with preventing a disaster under water. I struggled to find my footing in the rocky ground beneath my feet, but the surge kept coming, pushing me farther and farther. There couldn't be that much slack left in the line. A swell of panic rose in me. I waited for the air line to snap and cold water to rush into my mouth and nose.

Somehow, my toe found a crack on the underside of a boulder. I shoved my foot in as far as it would go. Then I crouched down and wrapped my arms around it and held on as the powerful wave rolled over me and prayed.

CHAPTER 21

I could hear Kyle's voice in my ears, but I couldn't respond. The power of the water frightened me. I imagined being carried farther away under the ice, the air line ripped from my mouth, and my body disappearing never to be found. Kyle could drive away, never tell a soul, and my whereabouts would forever be a mystery.

I'm sure Jonah, the plucky reporter, would love to be the one to write that story. I thought about my family: Zoe, my dad, my stepfather, and Ben.

Oh, Ben, you'd never believe them, would you? That I just disappeared without a trace? You'd come looking for me. You'd track down my last moments. You would find out who was responsible.

I already felt dead. Either I died here under the ice, or I somehow made it out of this alive. But the latter seemed nearly impossible. There was no way out of this one. Everything was stacked against me.

"Rory, answer me," Kyle's words finally broke through my panic. "Did you untangle the umbilical? Why isn't there any more material in the sluice?"

Just when I thought my arms and hands had lost all strength and I'd lose my grip on the boulder, the sea calmed. But for how long?

I sucked in air way too quickly. I knew that the worst thing I could do was hyperventilate and freeze up my regulator. I closed my eyes, tried to imagine I was safe in Ben's cabin with the fire roaring, and forced myself to calm down.

"Rory!" My ex's voice grew demanding. "What's going on?"

"The storm is making it too dangerous down here." With the water calmer, I took the opportunity to walk back toward the one bit of light I could see: our hole in the ice. A faint blue glow, created by the battery powered lantern, emanated from a spot that seemed much farther away than it should've been. "I lost my footing and the surge almost carried me away, and I think the umbilical could still be caught on something."

"I need that gold."

Tears of frustration blurred my vision. I couldn't do this. The storm could send another surge my way any moment, and I might not have the strength to hold on a second time. "I'm exhausted, Kyle." Around me the water traveled in the opposite direction—seaward—we were about to be hit with another blast. I didn't have much time to reach the safety of the hole. "If you want the gold, then you're going to have to get it yourself."

I didn't care if I made him angry. I knew I wouldn't survive a second surge. The ocean was too powerful. Nobody would be strong enough to withstand multiple batterings, and if Kyle thought he could, let him try.

"Get your ass back here."

I'd pissed him off.

"On it." His words no longer bothered me. I'd faced certain death and survived. My only goal now was to reach the hole, get out of the water, and think through the steps to making it out of this situation alive.

I reached the spot where my umbilical had gotten hung up—a massive ice stalactite that had formed on the ceiling above me. I shined my headlamp on it. I never would've shaken the lines free by myself.

The ocean reversed direction. I could feel the slight change. In a few minutes it would be too strong for me to fight against it.

"Kyle, you're going to have to help me," I stammered, my voice trembling with a note of desperation. "Pull on the umbilical. The storm surge is coming."

"Nate was right. You are weak, Rory," he said with disgust.

I ignored his insults and powered forward with all my remaining energy. Suddenly, I felt a tug as my body propelled toward the hole at twice the pace. Thank God Kyle listened to me and decided to help.

When I reached the spot under our ice hole, I took off my weight belt. I jettisoned upward with the change in weight and one final yank from Kyle. Relief flooded through my exhausted body, and I reached the surface moments before the sea rushed toward Norton Sound. It definitely would have taken me with it—all the way—this time.

I pulled off my mask and breathed fresh air. "Get me out of here." I clung to the edge of the ice. I couldn't climb out on my own.

Kyle grabbed my forearms and pulled.

I lay on the ice inside our shelter unable to speak. I'd never been so frightened in my life—and that included having a gun pointed at me by my ex-boyfriend. My father had been right. Diving under the ice was incredibly dangerous. I'd never doubt him again.

"Take off the suit." Kyle stood over me, his face in shadow, but I could see the cloud of his breath escape from his mouth. "We can't stop now."

"It's too dangerous, Kyle." As much as I despised this man, I didn't want him to die. I wouldn't wish such a death on my worst enemy. "Besides the fact that visibility is crap when there's this much motion, I barely made it back here by myself. The storm is worse than you think it is."

"Take off the suit." His words came out clipped.

He'd lost his mind. Was he really that desperate? I shivered in the cold as I slid the suit from my body. "I don't want you to die, Kyle. Please don't do this."

"Shut up." He donned the wet suit and prepped to dive. "The best part about this is, I know you won't screw me over up top. You don't have the guts." With a half-smile, he sat on the edge of the ice and slipped into the dark depths.

CHAPTER 22

Kyle was insane. Certified crazy. I couldn't believe he thought he'd be able to dredge in these conditions. I'd done some radical things to find the gold, but I don't think I'd ever been as desperate as he. Even last summer didn't compare to the situation Kyle had gotten himself into. Declan and Lola were not people you wanted to cross.

He'd left me alone in the shelter with his truck keys and a gun. It was my chance to escape. Did he really think I was too wimpy to save myself? If he wanted the gold, he could have it.

I scanned the interior of our homemade dredging hut. We'd only recently relocated so most of our equipment and other belongings were in large plastic totes. The peanut butter jar was nowhere to be seen.

Where would he put his keys? And where would he hide a gun?

Searching through the pockets of his parka, I came up short. Nothing but a box of mints and a few extra bullets for his pistol. I dumped out his boots. Nothing there either.

Dammit.

Those keys had to be here somewhere.

The comms crackled to life.

"Rory, you there?" Although only minutes ago his words had come out confidently, cruel even, the voice over the handset sounded weak and scared.

Screw him.

He wanted to dive despite my warnings, so whatever happened was his own damn fault.

Instead of answering, I rummaged through totes and boxes.

Outside the wind howled louder than ever. A massive gust pushed so hard against our shelter, I heard two-by-fours crack. A corner of our hut sagged where the wood had snapped in two. I should've predicted that salvaged wood from the dump wouldn't have stood up to the brutality of a Bering Sea winter storm.

How much longer could it withstand the punishment?

I needed to get out of here.

Now.

I lifted the door flap. Snow blew sideways. I couldn't see the lights of Nome anymore. It was whiteout conditions. My stomach rolled. Not good. Could I make it back to shore walking across the ice?

I had to try.

"Rory?" Kyle's voice sounded strained. "I can't breathe."

A weight settled on me.

The training I'd received from my dad when I'd learned to tend a dredge rang in my head: never leave a diver stranded.

Although my ex had threatened me, forced me to dive, and dragged me out in a storm, instead of abandoning him, I felt duty bound to help. I didn't want his death on my hands. Kyle was right. I didn't have the guts.

"Crap." I let the flap fall back into place and manned the comms. "Your regulator's icing up. You need to slow your breathing."

The handset clicked several times.

Was Kyle trying to signal me? Had he lost the ability to speak?

As I ran through the options, a massive heave of the ice beneath my feet made me cling to the stool.

Then I felt a shudder, and a deafening explosion hurt my ears.

A massive wave from the storm surge must have hit the ice shelf. Although Kyle was in desperate need of help, I rushed out of the shelter with my parka unzipped to survey the damage.

As I stepped out into the storm, my thoughts scrambled to comprehend what I saw in front of me. Instead of the white expanse of ice connecting us to shore, I saw a black gap between me and the rest of the ice. Kyle's truck, parked near the orange cones, had fallen part way into the water. When another massive wave hit, I watched helplessly as it tumbled into the sea.

My God.

We'd broken off from the rest of the ice. Within moments we'd be drifting out to the open ocean and any chance of escape would be lost.

The storm raged around me. My hands hurt from the cold. I'd forgotten to put on my gloves. My mind blanked. I couldn't think of what to do next. The last time a diver had been stranded on a chunk of ice, he'd never been found.

"Help me, Rory," Kyle said weakly. "Help me."

If I didn't try to help Kyle reach our hole, the force of the storm water would rip him loose from the lines. I only had minutes to act before it would be too late, and I'd be alone on an ice floe drifting out to sea. All of the advice and training my father had given me over years came rushing back in a flood as I shoved my feelings toward Kyle far to the back of my mind.

The safety of your diver is always first—before your own safety and certainly over and above the gold.

What did I care about gold now? We were going to die out here. No one knew where we were, it was the middle of the night, and the storm had way more power over our fate than we had over it. We had to somehow rescue ourselves, and I'd rather have two brains on that seemingly impossible plan than one.

I lunged for the hoses that sent precious life-giving air and hot water to Kyle and yanked on them with all my might. Although Kyle made it seem easy when he'd helped me back to the ice hole, my arms strained at the force being applied.

The comms clicked again.

Kyle might be suffocating.

I slid my butt across the ice toward the sluice and the generator, still pulling on the lines. I needed somewhere to brace my feet and give me more leverage. I probably weighed forty pounds less than Kyle, and women weren't known for their upper body strength.

The dark maw of the ice hole mocked me.

I trembled at the possibility of losing my strength and tumbling into the ocean beneath me. Without a dive suit. Without air or heat. I'd suffer from hypothermia in minutes.

Raw fear ignited my nerves.

I managed to scoot my way behind the generator just enough to brace my feet. This forced me to pull sideways on the hoses, but at least I felt more secure.

The ice floe under me dipped and rose with the motion of the raging ocean beneath.

All of my focus had to be on helping Kyle or I might slip into a panic.

One thing at a time, Rory.

I clenched my teeth and pulled with everything in me. I screamed at the pain in my elbows and shoulders. My hands hurt, and my grip began to slip.

"Come on, Kyle. You can do it."

But he was like a dead weight on the other end.

I listened for more clicks on the comms, afraid to let go of the lines, but all I heard was silence.

Would Kyle die first and then me? Would we be just another couple of dredgers who were lost while defying the rules in search of gold? Would Ben always wonder why I'd consented to diving in a storm with an ex who'd attacked me? Would anyone know the truth about what happened tonight?

If we drifted out to sea right now, the waves outside of the protection of the Sound would be enormous. Twenty, thirty, forty feet high. As my arms lost strength, my stomach turned over at the death I was facing.

I'd be swept off my ice raft into a bitterly cold ocean and either drown or freeze to death, whichever came first. My body would never be found.

Tears rolled down my cheeks from fear, sorrow, and utter exhaustion.

I couldn't do it anymore.

An odd buzzing sound disrupted my thoughts. Something loud and mechanical. I couldn't wrap my head around what it was. Maybe my ears were playing tricks on me.

As I lost my grip on the hoses that kept Kyle connected to our piece of the ice, a black figure appeared in the doorway, snow swirling in behind him.

I broke out in a sob. "Ben, thank God." Euphoria lightened my limbs. "How did you find us? How did you make it here?"

Without a word, he grabbed his wetsuit.

CHAPTER 23

"Don't let go," Ben said while zipping up his suit. "Is it Kyle down there?"

I'd never seen his eyes so black and so devoid of emotion.

I nodded.

I felt ashamed about where I was, what I was doing, and who I was with. But I didn't have time to explain. I could tell him the details once we were safe and back on dry land. Because one thing I knew: Ben would save us.

"What happened to your face?" Ben's face contorted with a mix of anger and concern as his eyes fixated on the bruise forming on my face. His jaw clenched tight, and the lines on his forehead deepened. "Did Kyle do this?"

I shook my head. "No. I'll fill you in later. We don't have much time." His arrival had invigorated me. I didn't know how he'd made it onto the ice floe, but my task was not so impossible now. I gripped the hoses with all of my remaining strength. "I think his regulator iced up. Then the ice broke."

He grunted.

When he grabbed his mask out of his bag, it dawned on me. "You can't go down there. We don't have a second set of hoses." How could he dive and rescue Kyle without air, without heat? Impossible.

He grabbed the umbilical near the edge of the hole and pulled.

The two of us together were able to haul in about ten feet of hose. But it wasn't happening fast enough. There were no more clicks on the end of the line. Who knew if Kyle was still conscious. We could be recovering a dead body. And was it worth it to risk our lives for that?

A gust of wind battered the half-collapsed shelter. The tarp rippled. I half expected the whole thing to be blown away, leaving us unprotected and at the mercy of the elements.

"We're drifting out to sea." Ben wrapped his meaty hands around the taped together hoses and pulled even harder. "We don't have a lot of time."

"Even if we can save him, how are we going to get back to the ice shelf?" I didn't understand how Ben reached us. To me, it seemed as if he were a superhero with special powers. The whiteout hadn't deterred him, the drifting ice floe had been no obstacle. What couldn't this man do?

"I borrowed a Zodiac." Sweat dripped from his brow as he hauled in ten more feet of hose. "I have to go in, Rory."

"How?" His words confused me. No one could dive in the Bering Sea in the middle of winter with no heated water line, much less no air. And if I lost Ben... "You can't." My arms relaxed as Ben's physical superiority meant I no longer had to prevent the hoses from ripping away from our machinery.

"I can do it," he said between gritted teeth. "He can't be that far away, our hoses aren't that long."

"Free dive in a storm?" He wanted to swim under the ice holding his breath without any connection to our ice floe. The definition of insanity. "You'll be killed. You don't know how strong the storm surge is. I could barely make it back to the hole, and that was with help."

His darkened gaze penetrated me. "You were diving down there? What were you thinking, Rory?" He grimaced. "Why would you do something so dangerous?"

His breathing turned ragged.

"I had no choice." A knot formed in my belly at the idea I'd hurt him, but there was no time for explanations now. "If you dive, you won't come back to me." The weight of my decision that evening—to confront Kyle about the money he owed Lola—sat heavily on me. If I hadn't lied to Ben about the interview, maybe the night would've gone differently and Ben would not be considering doing something so dangerous. "Please don't, Ben, he's not worth it."

In one quick move Ben dropped the hoses, pulled his mask down over his face, and dove straight into the black water.

My body shook in a flash of terror, and I rushed to the hole on my hands and knees, somehow thinking I could stop him from making such a deadly decision.

But Ben had disappeared into the dark depths, and I could no longer see him.

I struggled to my feet as panic suffocated me. "Ben!" I leaned over the edge, desperately hoping Ben would surface. If he didn't make it back to the hole in a couple of minutes, he'd be overcome by hypothermia. He'd lose consciousness. I imagined his muscular body drifting under the ice, his face turning blue, his beautiful eyes clouding over. "Ben!"

Everything in me wanted to dive after him, pull him back to the safety of our little chunk of ice being bounced about in the storm. Any moment, the waves could become monsters. If both Kyle and Ben died—my mind didn't want to go there.

The Zodiac must be tied to the shelter and waiting. What if neither man returned? Did I have the courage to save myself?

"Ben, please come back to me." I collapsed and curled up in a ball. I'd never felt so alone and so frightened.

CHAPTER 24

The wind howled outside as if crying along with me. Ben had disappeared into the stormy freezing ocean to save a man who'd held me at gunpoint, a man I stupidly thought would leave me alone once I gave him our gold stash, and now they both were going to die.

My mind slowed down. What should I do? Ben couldn't help but play the hero. It was a role he was built for. I should've known he'd dive in without even thinking about the risks. I felt useless standing up top; I needed to do something. To help in some way.

The comms clicked again.

Could Kyle still be alive?

Suddenly, my body kicked into motion. I raced to the handset. "Kyle, is that you? Ben is on his way." A wave of nausea churned in my stomach. "Hold on, Kyle."

Maybe there was hope yet.

I searched through our plastic bins and found what I was looking for: a stack of wool blankets and a massive flashlight. One of those big heavy ones with the LEDs that shone brighter than a nuclear explosion. I set the blankets right next to our hole, flicked on the flashlight, and shined it into the water.

Earlier, when I'd been diving, the lantern light guiding me back to the hole had been minimal. With the turbulence of the storm, conditions had probably become even murkier. If Ben had any chance of returning, he'd need the brightest light I could find.

The black water looked like a path to hell as it churned in the storm. I tried not to think about the odds. I knew they weren't good, but if I let myself think too much, I'd break down again. Ben needed me.

Seconds ticked by.

Then a minute.

Then two minutes.

"You have to come back." I stared at the water, willing Ben to return. "You have to." If only my dad were here, he would know what to do. He would've figured out some way to rig up a second air and hot water line out of whatever bits and pieces we had laying around. Or he'd pick up the comms and bring Kyle back to life with his voice alone.

My heart ached for someone else to share this burden with me. I didn't want to be left floating by myself on a chunk of ice with two men lost in the water below. I'd rather throw myself into the freezing sea and join Ben than die alone on the open ocean.

Like some sort of Greek God, Ben erupted from the hole in a shower of spray, one muscular arm looped around a limp and very pale Kyle. He sucked in a massive breath of air and shoved Kyle onto the ice and then managed to claw his way out and collapse onto the ice before I could even move.

My whole body tingled. He'd made it back!

I grabbed a wool blanket out of the pile and threw it over him. He would need more than that to keep from succumbing to hypothermia. What else did we have to warm him up? Could I start a fire with some diesel and wood scraps?

Ben crawled out from under the blanket, his body spent, and dragged himself to Kyle. He ripped off his mask and leaned in close to his mouth to listen for breaths.

Kyle didn't move.

Ben's hands trembled as he picked up a piece of air hose that had split right above a recent repair. It had been a failure of the worn-out gear, not an iced up regulator.

My blood ran cold. Only minutes before Kyle had jumped in, I'd been using those same hoses.

"It's not your fault." I knew what he was thinking. "You need to dry off, dress in dry clothes—" I pulled at Ben's arm. Kyle was gone. No way Ben could do anything for him.

"Shut up!" Ben roared, his face a twisted mask of agony.

I took a step back in surprise. He had never raised his voice to me. Not like this. It sounded like the bellow of a grizzly bear when you wandered into his hunting grounds or the roar from a moose when a mountain lion threatens him—wild and angry and scary.

Ben pushed against Kyle's chest, His thick, muscular arms doing their best to force life back into the limp body of my ex.

I stared at Kyle. His face was so white, his eyes were partially open, and his lips were blue. He still wore his dive suit with the compromised hoses streaming out behind him. I thought about his parents in Texas who had relied on him after they filed for bankruptcy. They'd been so proud of him when he'd come to Nome to follow in his great uncle's footsteps. How would they handle the death of their son? I wondered if they'd blame me for luring him out here, convincing him that gold was the answer to his massive debt problems.

I blinked. The scene was surreal. This couldn't really be happening, could it? I was unable to tear my eyes away from the horrific events playing out in front of me. Ben breathed into Kyle's slack mouth and followed the steps of cardiopulmonary resuscitation. I didn't know he was skilled at it, but he looked like a pro.

Although I knew Kyle was too far gone, I didn't want to speak. The Beast I thought Ben was when I first met him had finally appeared, and it was truly frightening. Something had been triggered in the man I loved when he found out Kyle was in trouble under the ice. A deep dark hurt that I didn't know about. Something worse than the death of his fiancée. I could sense it.

Kyle was dead, and Ben couldn't accept it. He moved into a maniacal mode, speeding up his motions. The strength of each compression less as he frantically attempted to squeeze life into a dead man, a man he didn't even like. But he couldn't seem to stop, and it made my heart ache.

I did the only thing that made sense to me, I knelt next to him and hugged him hard. I wanted to give him as much warmth as I could, as much comfort as I could. "He's gone, Ben."

"No." He pumped at Kyle's chest over and over and over, continuing the rhythm of compressions. "He can make it. They'll be here soon. He can hold on."

"Who will be here soon?"

Ben pressed his fingers to Kyle's carotid artery. "No pulse. Keep going."

"No, Ben, he's gone. There's nothing we can do." I pulled at his arm to keep him from continuing with the CPR. Kyle's half-open gaze and pale face, his lifeless body—no amount of CPR was going to bring him back.

Ben's eyes were watery, and his pupils were tiny pinpoints. He stared blankly at me. "I've killed him. He thought we should go back, and I told him we needed to keep going. I didn't know that he would—" He couldn't seem to complete his thoughts.

I knew then he was lost in a memory—a place he hadn't taken me to. Now I wished I had been able to ask him about the short report Jonah had shared with me, which would've allowed some kind of controlled release of these deep and painful emotions. "Kyle is dead, Ben. We have to get off this ice before we drift too far out to sea. We have to leave."

"I can't, Rory."

I touched my boyfriend gently on his shoulder and said, "That's enough, Ben. You've done enough."

Kyle wasn't coming back.

My gut clenched.

All this for a debt that needed to be repaid. Lola was responsible for this and no one else.

Ben was on his knees, looking down at Kyle, with wide and unseeing eyes. Was it shock? Or the fact he probably was suffering from hypothermia? It was on me to make sure no more tragedy occurred tonight.

Suddenly, I kicked into gear. I grabbed a wool blanket and covered Kyle. The visual of his limp, lifeless body was upsetting—not only to Ben but to me. I shoved what just happened to the back of my mind. I had no choice. If it hadn't been for stupid me, we'd never have relocated on this dangerous slab of ice. So I had to make sure Ben and I made it safely back to shore.

The storm and Lola weren't going to beat me.

My father taught me to be a fighter, a winner. The toughest girl in Nome.

"Ben, we have to make it back to shore." He shivered in his wetsuit. "You said you came by Zodiac. How did you bring it out here?"

"The snow machine," he said between the chatter of teeth.

That's when I knew Stella had followed through on her promise to Kyle. When Ben didn't find me near the Polaris, he probably questioned Stella about where she'd gotten her information. "Who else knows you're out here?" I dried his hair with the edge of the blanket he now clasped around his body.

"Jerry." He took control of it with a trembling hand. "Saw you and Kyle head out. Knew the ice could break up. Told me to take his boat."

Ben needed to be warmed up. Any moment he could slip into a confused state, and I'd be left figuring things out on my own. "We have to get in the Zodiac—now." I looked at our broken down dredging equipment crammed into our small shelter. There was nothing worth saving and no time to collect the bucket filled with the mats to save any gold we'd collected from our new spot. I prayed that Jerry had called for help.

Ben's face was pale, his lips purple. But who cared about gold? He was running out of time.

I grabbed his arm and yanked as hard as I could. "Now!"

He blinked rapidly, glanced up at me, and seemed to understand. With slow grace, he rose to his feet. That's when his body began to violently shiver. I picked up Kyle's parka and stuffed Ben's arms into the too-small jacket and pulled the hood up over his head. Anything to protect him from the raging storm outside. I had no concept of how far away we'd drifted from the main ice shelf that connected to shore. Although I'd never steered a Zodiac before, I knew outboard motors. I'm sure I could figure it out.

We headed for the door and the wind and snow that lay beyond. I stepped around Kyle's body lying on the ice. We had no choice but to leave him there. If Ben had been coherent, he probably could've carried him to the boat, but we had no time to figure out how to make that happen.

I took one last glance around our shelter, battered by the

elements, full of our hopes and dreams. My gaze grew unfocused. How could I lose everything for a second time? It didn't seem fair.

A glint of gold behind the generator caught my eye: our plastic peanut butter jar. The only thing of value that I could save. Kyle had tried to hide it from me before he decided to dive. Maybe he thought I would leave him under water, take back my gold, and find a way to shore on my own.

Ben stumbled on an uneven bit of ice.

"Wait, Ben." I needed to help him into the boat, but if I had a chance to save something out of this nightmare, it would be our hard-won gold. I scooped up the jar. That's when I saw Kyle's gun tucked away under an edge of the tarp that made up our shelter. I grabbed that, too. Lola and Declan were still out there. The weight of the gun in my hand served as a stark reminder that danger lingered.

I joined Ben at the shelter's entrance. He'd hauled the Zodiac onto the ice and tied it to one of our support braces, so I worked the knot loose—one I'd taught him last summer.

Snow blew into my eyes. The storm was as strong as ever. But the dark was so complete, I had no idea how far the main ice was from our location or which direction I should go. The blowing snow obscured any lights we might see from town. But I'd rather be in the boat than on the drifting death trap of ice. Though Ben was in bad shape, he understood the urgency to climb in the boat and return to safety. I tossed the gold and the gun into the water-craft and then climbed in after. When I pushed on the ice with my hands to slide us into the water, Ben helped. It was his strength and his muscle that made it happen even while shivering and exhausted. At last, we slid free. The raging water tossed us around as if we were nothing more than a cotton ball riding on the waves.

Fear threatened to paralyze me. I could feel its cold tendrils seeping into my body and my mind. Telling me to stop, there was nothing I could do, I was too weak, too scared, too stupid to do it.

I pulled with all my might on the cord of the outboard. It came to life on the very first pull. I thanked God for that little miracle, as I didn't think I had the strength to try again. I grasped the tiller and steered us away from our floating dredge. I navigated merely on instinct, not knowing if I was heading us away from safety or out into the open ocean.

Ben lay back in the boat and shivered. He had curled up into a ball. I wasn't even sure he was conscious any longer.

I pointed the bow toward where I thought the main ice shelf should be and prayed.

CHAPTER 25

Two bright lights shone in the distance. These weren't coming from town—no, they were much closer. I steered the Zodiac toward them. Someone must be out on the ice. Was it Jerry or someone else? Either way, I thanked God for whoever decided to come out on the ice in the middle of a storm to guide me in the right direction.

"Ben, are you awake?" I wasn't sure he'd answer me. He needed a doctor. For all I knew, he'd already lost consciousness.

The rough water made it difficult to stay on course, the engine wasn't that powerful. I didn't want to think about what we were up against, so I kept my eyes on the twin white lights growing larger with each passing minute. I ignored my frozen hands, the snow, like ice, stinging my face, and the fact that Kyle was dead.

Soon, a break in the dark water told me we were reaching the ice shelf.

"Almost there." Ben's limp figure worried me, but I thought talking to him might keep him with me. "Someone's coming to help."

I aimed the bow directly at the misty line ahead, uncertain about the distance to the rim at the end of the ice shelf—the dark and the whiteout conditions made it nearly impossible to judge. Without any warning, we hit the edge with a bang. I leapt out, wind and snow blasting me in the face, and pulled the Zodiac up onto the ice as far as I could. Ben's weight meant I needed help to fully beach the watercraft, as I didn't have the strength to accomplish it alone.

While I scrambled to figure out how to keep Ben and the Zodiac from slipping away, two snow machines came toward us, their shapes barely visible in the swirling snow. I drew back, unsure if they were friend or foe. But as they neared, I recognized my father's parka and knew it must be Nate not far behind.

How did they know to find us here? Did Jerry tell them?

My dad leapt from his machine and rushed over; his face contorted with worry. "What happened? Is he okay?"

"He's hypothermic," I replied, gesturing to Ben's limp figure. "He needs a doctor."

"What about you?" he asked getting a glimpse of me in the snow machine headlights. "It looks like you got in a fight."

I touched the painful swelling on the side of my face. I probably looked terrible. "I'll be fine. Ben's the one that needs help."

He nodded. Nate joined us and, together, we hauled the boat and Ben all the way onto the ice.

"Help me hook it up," Buck instructed, handing me a tow line.

Without a word, I did as he asked, clipping the line to the Zodiac. It would have to act as a transport sled for Ben who hadn't stirred since help arrived.

"Do you have some blankets?" Ben's core temperature must be incredibly low after his daring dive. Any warmth we could provide might be the deciding factor in whether he pulled through. The image of Kyle's corpse flashed before me, and I squeezed my eyes shut to force the gruesome picture from my mind. Ben was not going to die tonight. I'd make damned sure of it.

Nate handed me an emergency blanket from the back of his snow machine, and I quickly tucked it around Ben's motionless body, weighing it down with the jar of gold and the pistol.

"Is that a gun?" Nate asked with some surprise.

I didn't answer and, instead, checked Ben's pulse in his neck. The slow thready beat beneath my fingers worried me, but at least he was alive.

"What the hell happened tonight?" Nate stood back and watched my actions. "Where's Kyle? Jerry said he saw Ben take off on the ice after you and Kyle."

"We have to go." I tested the tow line. "I can explain everything later."

"Do we need to call the Coast Guard for a rescue operation, Rory?" my dad asked.

I swallowed, looked him in the eye, and shook my head.

That was all it took to convince them to leave.

My dad and Nate climbed on their snow machines, and I rode on the back of my dad's. He turned the key in the ignition, and we set off back toward town and the emergency room.

As we sped across the frozen water, a deep sadness set in. Kyle had died because of his terrible choices, and Ben might be next.

———

Thirty minutes later I was sitting in the E.R. waiting room with an ice pack pressed to my face provided by a very concerned clerk at the registration desk. My dad gently held my free hand in his stronger, stubbier one. It was as if our big blow out argument had never happened. The intensity of what I'd experienced out on the ice washed away any lingering bitterness. Our father-daughter bond, strained last summer and then intensified during our argument a little over a week ago, suddenly became an unbreakable lifeline, connecting us in a way I had never imagined. I squeezed his hand, and he returned it.

Nate had left to go find us some coffee. We were all chilled to the bone after our ride across the ice as the storm raged.

I peeled the ice pack away from my skin when it grew numb. "Do you think Ben will be okay?" Exhaustion settled in as we waited. I must've been riding on a ton of adrenaline ever since Declan kidnapped me and took me to Lola's. That seemed like ages ago. But the worry I had about Ben remained as strong as it had been when he'd dived into the ice hole and disappeared into the dark, churning water.

He rubbed his free hand down the leg of his jeans. "He'll be fine. The doc said he'd seen worse pull through, remember?"

I nodded. Right. After a quick assessment of Ben's pupil response, reflexes, heart rate, blood pressure, and his body temperature, the doctor informed us he should be okay.

He *had* to be okay.

My dad touched the injured side of my face. "Did Kyle do this to you?"

I shook my head.

His eyebrows furrowed then released. "What were you and Kyle doing out there in the middle of the storm?" His voice thickened. "And why did you have a gun? Help me understand, Rory."

We still hadn't talked about what happened to Kyle. But my dad had called the Coast Guard to let them know a body needed to be recovered once the storm had let up.

"I don't know where to begin." My voice quivered. "You won't believe me."

Buck leaned forward. The waiting room seemed to grow quieter, the only sound being the gentle hum of the coke machine. My fingers fidgeted with the zipper on my unzipped parka.

"Try me," he urged, his voice filled with a quiet intensity, inviting me to share the weight of my burden.

Nate showed up with three Styrofoam cups of coffee, two gripped so hard in one hand, the hot liquid threatened to spill. "Here, I don't know what everybody likes in their coffee, so I just brought three black."

"That's fine," my dad said, taking a cup. "Thanks." His face looked drawn and haggard, and he rubbed a hand across it.

I glanced up at the clock—four in the morning. We were all exhausted.

I took a cup from Nate and sipped the hot coffee, hoping it would re-energize me. Until I knew Lola and Declan wouldn't come looking for me, I'd never be able to sleep well. I gave my father's partner a brief smile that I didn't feel. "I'm sorry you were dragged into this. I never meant for anyone to get hurt."

"We just want to know why you were out there with Kyle, Rory," Nate said. "It doesn't make any sense."

Despite how I'd felt about Nate last summer and his under-handed behavior with Ben over the equipment sale, he really had cleaned up his act in Anchorage. Rehab had really done good things for him. He'd put on weight, he showered regularly, and even had bought some new clothes. I liked this new version of Nate and was thankful for his help.

I stared into my lap. "I guess Kyle owed some bad people some money, and I got dragged into it."

"What people?" my dad asked with a frown.

I scanned the nearly empty waiting room. For a split second I expected Lola or Declan to be looking for me. But why would they? Kyle was dead. There was no money. It was over. I explained to Nate and my dad what had happened after I left Miner's—the kidnapping, Declan and Lola's involvement, and why they were looking for Kyle.

My father's eyes widened. "I can't believe he got into so much trouble and then dragged you into it. I knew he had problems when I hired him, but damn."

"I'm scared for Ben, Dad." Every little bit of fear I felt out on the ice came out in hot messy tears. "And Kyle…I can't believe he's dead."

"Hey, hey." My dad wrapped an arm around me. "It'll be okay, honey." Although he and I had been driven apart by the truth about the gold map, he was still my dad. He could bring me comfort even if I didn't agree with some of the choices he'd made.

At least he hadn't killed anyone.

"Should we call the police?" Nate asked. "Those two thugs need to be rounded up and arrested for what they did."

"Kyle thought he could find enough gold to get them off his back." I stared at the shiny beige flooring beneath my boots. "Or we never would've been out there."

"So the gun was his?" My dad asked.

I nodded. My ex-boyfriend's manic behavior when I'd caught up to him in the Quonset hut, the strange look in his eye when he talked about the gold Ben and I had recovered, and the insistence I take him out to our new spot on the ice ran through my mind. Would anyone question the decisions I'd made?

"I didn't want to go." I stumbled over my words. "I told him it was crazy—that the storm was dangerous. But he wouldn't listen to me. That's when he pulled the gun on me." I rubbed at my wet eyes. I couldn't stop the stupid tears. "I had no choice, Dad. Can't you see I had no choice?"

"If that's what he did, then yes, you had no choice." He swept my long, messy hair away from my face, so I couldn't hide from him. "You did the right thing, and you're alive because of it."

I lifted my head, and the rest of the story poured out. "I didn't want to dive. I begged him not to make me. I've never seen the water like that...and it was so dark...and the storm surge was too powerful. But he wouldn't stop. He thought there would be enough gold down there to fix things. When I surfaced, I told him it was too dangerous, but he didn't listen. He put on a wetsuit and jumped in, some of the hoses failed, and then the ice cracked and we were drifting to sea." Nate flinched. "I couldn't believe it either. He was crazy, Dad. I've never seen him act like that."

"He was desperate, honey." Buck patted my arm. "That's the only explanation."

I nodded. "I thought his regulator iced up. I knew he was going to suffocate if I didn't help him, but I couldn't pull him in." The weird sounds that had come across the comms filled my mind and made my heart flutter irregularly. It could've been me down there when the hose cracked open. "The surge was too strong. That's when Ben showed up. He dove in without any heat or air lines. Freediving with only a suit on."

"Shit." Nate's eyebrow shot up. "He's fucking nuts."

"It was too late, though." I didn't have the energy to describe how I knew Kyle wouldn't make it. His deathly white face floated in my mind's eye, tormenting me.

"Don't worry, honey, Ben will be back on his feet in no time and the police will take care of those criminals." He downed the rest of his coffee in one massive gulp.

A short, dark-haired, familiar-looking nurse clutching a clipboard approached the three of us. "Are you waiting for Ben?"

"Hi, Kathy," I said, remembering the woman who cared for me in the hospital after my attack last summer. "Yes, we're waiting to hear about Ben's condition."

"Oh, hi, Rory," Nurse Kathy smiled. "I didn't even notice it was you."

She didn't need to explain the reason she didn't recognize me was the large bruise across my face. I probably looked terrible. "Is he going to be okay?"

A warm glow radiated from her face. "Yes, the rewarming seems to be going well, but he'll need to stay here for at least a few more hours to make sure his temperature is stable and back up to normal." She held the clipboard in one hand, clicked her ballpoint pen, and hovered it over the paper work. "Do you want to leave a number, and I'll give you a call when he's ready for visitors?"

"Call mine," my dad said and scribbled out his cell number on the back of a business card he'd pulled out of some pocket. His voice softened as he said, "Rory will be staying with me."

Kathy took it. "Will do." Before she headed back to the patients' area beyond the small waiting room, she asked, "Do you know someone named Kilgore?"

I thought back to the short report Jonah had given me on what had happened to Ben's friend, Ian Kilgore. "Why?" I asked.

"He keeps telling me that he killed Kilgore over and over and over." The nurse rubbed her arm. "I heard it was awful out there on the ice tonight. Just didn't know if someone else was involved in his accident or if he was recalling some other stressful time in his life."

That must've been what Ben was seeing when he tried to save Kyle. Kyle's rescue must have brought it all back. I wondered if this might open up the possibility of Ben telling me about what happened, or would talking about it send him into another depression? If Jonah had been right and Ben had suffered PTSD as a result of his friend's death, it had no easy fix.

"When can I see him?" I asked.

Kathy glanced from me to my father, as if he had the right to make decisions for me. "He's not coherent right now. I really think it would better if you go get some rest and come back in a few hours." She touched my arm. "You'll feel better about everything after some sleep."

I knew she was right. Ben had been out of it ever since he rose out of the water with Kyle in tow. Something had shifted inside him when he chose to make that dive. I bit my lip. I didn't want to think about a different Ben in that hospital bed. I wanted *my* Ben back—strong, determined, and fiercely loyal.

"Come on, Rory," my dad soothed. "The nurse is right, you need to rest."

"Make sure you keep your ice pack on that." Nurse Kathy eyed my bruise. "It'll help with the swelling."

The three of us headed out to the parking lot. The storm had quieted some and only a few flakes swirled around us as we made our way to the snow machines. My gaze was drawn to the Zodiac still tethered to my father's machine, where the gun lay hidden beneath Kyle's parka. Its presence was a reminder of the dangers I'd faced, and a shiver of unease coursed through me. I hesitated, trying to decide if I should take it with me or not. It was like finding a stray dog on the side of the road—it came with a mix of curiosity, hesitation, and the weight of responsibility.

I left it there for now, not wanting to deal with everything it represented, but I regretted it the moment we made our way down East N Street and I saw an unmistakably familiar figure—Declan. Illuminated by one of the orange streetlights ringing the parking lot, he stood with his hands in his pockets and watched as we passed by. I turned my head to keep my eye on him until I couldn't see him anymore.

I wished I'd put the gun in my pocket while I had the chance.

Why was he there? Had he heard about what happened to Kyle? Should I be worried about Ben?

The situation with Lola clearly wasn't over yet. The pit that had started in my stomach hours ago grew even deeper. But now was not the time to confront him. I was still too shaken with everything that had happened. If I wanted to close this dark chapter without more people getting hurt, I needed time and rest to think things through before I acted this time.

I leaned into my dad's back and soaked in the comfort it gave me. I felt like my younger self, when things were simpler and my dad taught me how to fight the boys who liked to wind me up. It had been easy to do back then, and just as easy now, apparently. Tell Rory she couldn't do something because she was a girl, I'd pop off. My main goal in life back then had been to become a carbon copy of Buck Darling, and if anyone disagreed, I'd lose my temper.

He throttled up the machine and dug through the deep snow that had accumulated since the storm began hours earlier. It flew up in an arc behind us. The cold flecks fell down the collar of my parka. I flashed back to the dive I'd barely survived—the petrifying blackness all around me and the formidable strength of the ocean pulling me away. If I'd let go of that boulder, I would've drowned.

Did it matter anymore what my father had done in the past? He was there when it mattered. Out on the ice in the middle of a storm when there was no way I could've brought Ben home on my own. Despite the fact I'd felt our relationship was too broken to fix, he'd come.

"Did Jerry tell you we were out there?" I said as soon as he parked in front of his apartment building.

"Ben called me last night after he went to Miner's looking for you. He thought you were supposed to be over at Stella's watching movies and knew something was wrong." He climbed off and held out a hand out so I wouldn't fall into the deep snow. "He sounded freaked out, so I told him to wait for me. But by the time Nate and I got to Miner's, Marla told us he'd already headed back to the yurts. So we drove out there and ran into Jerry who told us he'd seen both of you ride out on the ice and how Ben had borrowed his boat after he'd heard the ice cracking up. That's when we knew something bad was going down."

He uncovered the gun still resting in the Zodiac. Without a word, he picked it up and shoved it in his pocket. I hefted the jar of gold.

"I'm glad he called you, Dad."

I let him hug me to his side. "I am too, kiddo."

Nate took the lead on the steps to the second floor. I hadn't been in the apartment since Kyle attacked me last summer. I tried not to think about it.

As we entered, however, my whole body tightened up, as if coiled like a spring. I found myself needing to take one last glance at the street to make sure neither Declan nor Lola lurked out there. This wasn't over yet.

CHAPTER 26

A strange noise woke me up from a dreamless sleep. For a split second, I thought I was in the yurt and Ben had fallen off his cot. Then I remembered I was on the couch in my father's living room.

"Come on out, you little bitch." A fist pounded on my father's door. "I know you've got our money."

Lola.

My heart froze.

Nate had left for a friend's place after giving up his couch to me, leaving only me and my dad in the apartment. I hadn't seen him, but Declan must've followed us after all.

My dad burst through his bedroom door, carrying a baseball bat. "What in the hell?" His hair stuck out everywhere, and he wore only his long johns. His chest bore an angry red line, proof of his heart surgery only six months ago. "Who is that?"

"Don't, Dad." I blocked him from opening the door. "Call the police. It's the people Kyle owes money to. They must think I have it."

"You thought you fooled us pretty good with your games," Lola said, kicking the door several times. "But now it's time to pay up."

My dad pushed past me and looked through the peep hole, his hand on the doorknob. "You have ten seconds to get out of here before I call the police."

While he said it, I was already dialing.

The kicking stopped. "Your girl owes us, old man. I don't care what the cops think. She knows she fucked up. You can't stay in there forever with daddy."

I wrapped myself up in the quilt I'd been sleeping under and whispered our address into my phone when the dispatcher picked up. The gun stared at me from the coffee table. My dad had left it there once he'd carried it inside, uncertain what to do with it

Buck stood tensely at the door; the baseball bat gripped in one hand.

I reached for the pistol. In Alaska most people—kids and adults alike—have fired a gun before. With so much empty space everywhere, it was easy to find a safe location for some target practice. But it had been a few years, and I didn't trust my aim.

My hands shook. It was as if everything that had happened since Declan kidnapped me off the streets came flooding back in one massive wave of fear.

"Take the gun, Dad."

Buck stared at it.

"Wouldn't want anything to happen to your boyfriend in the hospital," Lola threatened. "Just tell us where the money is, and we're gone."

I rose from the couch and approached the door. "I have a gun. You might want to back off. I already told you, I don't have Kyle's money."

My dad pushed the gun down so it pointed at the floor. "Don't, Rory. The police will come."

"Maybe your daddy would pay his tab. You've got some nice equipment out there, I'm sure it's worth some money."

Nome wasn't that big of a town. The station was only blocks away. Where were the police?

"Stay away from my father's stuff. He doesn't owe you a damn thing. Kyle is dead. It's over. There's nothing left. Everything he had went with him out to sea." I thought about the peanut butter jar of gold, but it was mine, and there's no way I would use it as a peace offering. Lola and her sidekick deserved jail time.

Sirens sounded down the street.

"Fuck you, Rory Darling," Lola said. "I'll be back."

My dad plucked the gun out of my hands and tucked it away in a kitchen drawer. Then he leaned the baseball bat against the counter and hugged me close.

Minutes later the police knocked on the door.

A n hour later I sat in a familiar place at the police station having told my harrowing story of what had happened last night after leaving Miner's. Officer Garber had taken pictures of my face. I knew the bruising and swelling looked bad because Garber had winced when he'd seen me at the door of my father's apartment.

"The Coast Guard are hoping to find Kyle's body today." A younger police officer, whom I didn't recognize, approached Garber's desk to give the news. "Now that the storm died down, they're hoping to track down the ice floe based on your description of the ice shack." The dark-haired Inuit with a nametag that read K. Anawak gave me a nod.

I prayed they'd be able to find it. I thought about Kyle drifting out to sea, never to be seen again. I couldn't imagine his parents not having a body to bury.

"Thank you, Officer Anawak." Garber turned to me. "Even if the Coast Guard locates the ice floe, they won't be able to save any of your belongings. This is only about body recovery."

"I understand." The minute Ben and I had fled the drifting ice, I'd written off the possibility of salvaging anything. Most of the equipment wasn't worth the trouble anyway. "Do you have everything you need from me?" I yawned. My body rapidly lost all energy. I guess fourteen hours of running on pure adrenaline wasn't sustainable.

Garber hit the print button. "Once I print this out, we only need your signature so we can file the complaint. The kidnapping and assault charge should stick on Declan, but the criminal threat charge for Lola—that's going to be a tough one. I don't want to lie. All you heard was a voice through the door. It'll be her word against yours."

He left his desk to pick up the papers from the printer.

While he was gone, my father saw an opportunity and left his position in the little waiting area near the doors. "Have they found Kyle yet?"

I shook my head.

"I gave the authorities his parents' contact information." Buck pulled up an empty office chair to sit next to me. "Had it on file years ago when he first started working for me. Emergency contacts and all that."

I nodded, but my mind was elsewhere. "When I'm done here, can you take me back to the hospital? I'd like to wait until Ben is ready for discharge." Even though I was exhausted, I knew I wouldn't be able to sleep until I saw him. I wanted to make sure he was okay. What if Lola had made good on her threats already?

"Of course." He folded his hands together as if in prayer and bent his head. "Until they arrest these two, I want you to stay at my place."

"What about Ben?"

When he lifted his head, his steely eyes stunned me. "The invitation was for both of you." He placed a hand on my forearm and squeezed. "You and Ben are always welcome in my home."

Officer Garber interrupted by handing me the printed statement. "Sign at the bottom, and then you're free to go. I'd advise you stay in a secure place with sturdy locks until the arrests have been made."

My dad gave me a pointed look.

"It shouldn't take long," explained Garber. "We've brought these two in before for other offenses. Declan McTavitt is facing felony charges and will go in front of a judge for a bail hearing after he's been processed. As for Chang, we can hold her in custody for twenty-four hours before she goes in front of a judge—so I'm hoping in questioning we might get her to trip up and end up with some evidence we can use. But no guarantees."

I signed the statement and stood up to leave. As my dad led me out the door and toward his snow machine, I said to him, "One night. We'll stay one night."

His lips pulled into a smile.

After that, Ben and I would figure something out.

———

When I entered the lobby of the emergency services department, my limbs felt as heavy as firewood. My dad had dropped me off and given me an hour to check on Ben before he'd be back to escort us to his apartment. As the automatic doors closed behind me, the buzz of my father's snow machine told me he'd waited to make sure I got inside safely before leaving to prep for our arrival.

Nurse Kathy stood behind the registration desk talking with one of the ladies who checked in patients for treatment. She looked up. "Are you here to see Ben?"

"Is he awake?" I unzipped my parka and smoothed my hair.

"He won't care what you look like." My favorite nurse smiled. "He's been asking about you."

"He has?" I took a deep breath. If that was true, I knew Ben would be okay. The zoned out, disconnected Ben I'd seen out on the ice had only been temporary.

She nodded. "Also keeps asking when he can leave. I've never known such a stubborn patient. He tried to get dressed while I was grabbing the doc to check on him."

I mustered a weary smile on my lips. "Sounds like him."

"Hey, Rory," a familiar voice said behind me. "I heard what happened last night. Was hoping I might be able to interview you about it. Add it to the piece I'm writing?"

Jonah Tanaka.

Where did he come from?

I whirled around. "I thought you were flying out of here this morning?"

"My flight was cancelled." He held his yellow legal pad in his hand. "I leave tomorrow instead."

Nurse Kathy ping-ponged her gaze between us. "Is he a friend of yours, Rory? He said he knew you and wanted to talk to Ben, but I wasn't sure, so I made him wait here. I knew you'd eventually come back."

"Why would you try to talk to Ben?" I asked him point blank. "I told you he was off limits."

He put up his hands in a surrender pose. "I thought it would make a good story. Pretty heroic stuff out on the ice, I hear. Might go a long way to putting him in a different light with his fiancée's family."

The civil suit. It had slipped my mind with everything else that had gone on last night.

"Fiancée?" Nurse Kathy stared wide-eyed.

Great. More Nome gossip that would fly around this town in minutes. He'd only just come out from under the dark cloud that had hovered over him after the Nome Police had mistakenly detained him for a cancelled arrest warrant. "He's not engaged," I said to Kathy.

My first instinct was to call my sister and demand she call off her boy toy. I'd already given my interview; this was going one step too far.

"True, he's not," said Jonah. "She's dead."

"The fiancée?" Nurse Kathy's face paled.

"Oh my God, can you please stop?" I wanted the whole awful night to be over with. Even though daylight was approaching, the gloom outside matched my mood. "Ben isn't going to talk to you, and I'm not going to talk to you either. Leave me alone." I turned my attention back on Kathy. "Can you show me to his room, please?"

"Rory?" Ben stood at the far side of the waiting room. He'd half-dressed in damp blue jeans and a T-shirt. He held his boots, one in each hand. "Who is that guy? Why is he talking about Laura?"

My stomach bottomed out. Holy hell, this was exactly what I didn't want happening. Jonah and Ben were never supposed to meet. My interview was supposed to be a secret. The story a nothing on the internet that no one would ever see. "He's nobody. Come on, let's get out of here."

"He can't leave until the doctor clears him for release," insisted Kathy.

Ben dropped his boots to the floor and crammed his feet into them. "I'm fine. And, you," he pointed at Jonah with a curdled look on his face, "leave me and Rory the fuck alone."

Nurse Kathy backed slowly away and made a phone call from the reception desk. Probably calling security or whatever they did when things got unruly in the E.R.

"I'm only a reporter here to do a story," Jonah said. "I didn't mean to upset anyone. Sorry, Rory."

Ben swung his head around to look at me. "You know this guy? You're talking to reporters about me? What the hell is going on?"

Ben had risked his life for me. He'd raced across the ice in horrible white out conditions, leapt into the icy waters of the Bering to save my ex-boyfriend, and did it without fear or worry for himself. And this was how I reward him?

"It's not like that, Ben." I reached for him. "It was Zoe's idea. I didn't want to upset you—"

"And why were you out there with Kyle? I thought you hated him. I don't get you, Rory." He backed away.

"I'm sorry," I stammered, my voice laced with regret and a touch of desperation. I thought I'd have more time to explain myself, to make him understand that Kyle had forced me out there. Everything was falling apart.

"We only talked about her family's dredge operation, man," Jonah interjected. "Nothing happened."

"Shut the fuck up!" Ben rushed at him. "I don't want to see your stupid face right now."

At the same moment a male nurse and what looked like a maintenance guy entered the waiting room. Nurse Kathy pointed frantically at Ben, who looked like a raging bull about to gore a matador in the ring.

"Ben, stop!" The words exploded out of me. I wanted to rush in and put myself between him and Jonah, but the two hospital employees were already running up. They managed to grab Ben before he landed more than a single blow—a right hook that glanced off Jonah's cheek, but ended up knocking his glasses to the tile floor.

This all was too much. I just wanted to be alone with him, tell him about Lola and Declan and the police, and my dad's plan to keep us safe. I didn't need a fight right now. But I'd screwed up. I created this chaos. Me, and nobody else.

My sister's reporter friend stood stunned as the two men wrestled Ben to the door. He touched his check to find a bit of blood oozing from a small open cut on his face and bent down to pick up his glasses.

I mouthed the words 'I'm sorry' to Jonah, then followed my boyfriend outside.

CHAPTER 27

When I stepped into the cold, I saw Ben standing on the sidewalk, breathing heavily.

The hospital employees who'd taken him outside were stationed in front of the entrance, blocking any chance of him re-entering.

"Come on, Ben, let's go." I moved to touch his arm, and he flinched. "My dad was going to pick me up. I didn't realize you were going to be ready to leave so quickly. Let's see if Stella can give us a lift to his place."

Ben's gaze remained dark, his body stiff. "Where were you last night? Before—"

My stomach clenched painfully. He meant before Kyle had dragged me out on the ice, before he'd come to my rescue, before Kyle had died. So much had happened between the time I'd told him I was going to hang out with Stella and when he'd found me on a drifting bit of ice in a storm.

But Jonah had outed my lies to Ben, and the story would have to start there. "It was only a meeting."

"A meeting with a stranger—why did you need to lie to me about it?"

I hesitated. I didn't know where to begin. There was no way to keep him from being hurt. If I wanted to save my relationship with him, I had to start telling the truth.

He looked away. "Fuck. I should've known." He scratched the back of his neck, then clenched his fists. "Goddamn, Rory."

My stomach turned queasy. "Hey, it's not like that. I'm so sorry I didn't tell you about it." As I finally mustered the courage to confess, a wave of vulnerability and fear washed over me. Would he believe me or would he bolt? "He's a friend of my sister's—Jonah Tanaka." As the truth poured out, a weight lifted off my chest.

Ben's shoulders slightly tensed, and his gaze held a careful reserve, as if he were gauging the sincerity of my confessions.

At that moment, I was acutely aware the wrong words could jeopardize our relationship. "He wanted to do some dumb inter-view for a story about dredging. I thought it wouldn't be a big deal, that you didn't need to know—"

"That doesn't make any sense. Why wouldn't you tell me if it was all so innocent?" He scrubbed a hand over his face. "I don't understand you."

Ben didn't deserve to be lied to, deceived, and that's all I'd done to him lately thinking I was sparing his feelings. What a crock. "It was wrong. I know. I'm sorry." I wished I could start over, go back to last night, and make different choices. Maybe if I'd done that, Ben wouldn't be hurt, and Kyle wouldn't be dead. "I knew how much you hated reporters. I didn't want to upset you, and I didn't want to disappoint my sister. It all sounds so stupid now. I never meant to hurt you, Ben. Never."

"When you didn't come home, and Stella told me about the call from Kyle, I didn't know what to think. I hitched a ride to Miner's and found the Polaris idling and your phone in the snow. Even your dad didn't know where you were." He turned away from me and stood silent for a few beats. "Not knowing was the worst. I thought maybe you took off because I screwed up with the equip-ment and ruined our plans to build our own dredge boat."

"No, Ben! It had nothing to do with anything you did." I felt hot tears spilling and wanted to will them away. I had no right to cry. I'd hurt him. Me. The person who was supposed to love him the most. I wiped at my eyes with the back of my hand. "When I left Miner's this Declan guy attacked me thinking I was still dating Kyle." I gave him the quick and dirty of Kyle owing Lola Chang thousands of dollars and how I was forced out onto the ice.

I watched his face as I spoke, looking for signs he believed me. His blue eyes were cloudy and a wrinkle marred his brow. The whole story sounded insane.

Uneasy silence followed. Ben's gaze shifted from me to the mounds of snow that had piled up in the hospital parking lot during the storm, and the wrinkle in his forehead deepened as he gauged my explanation.

I swallowed. "I managed to trick Kyle into calling Stella."

He looked down at his boots and nodded. "I couldn't find you." His voice cracked. "Bobby Sykes thought he saw you in Kyle's truck headed back to the yurts. I didn't understand. I only knew he'd hurt you before."

I came up behind him, wrapped my arms around his middle, and leaned my head against his solid back. "And you found me. You saved me, Ben. I would be dead right now if you hadn't shown up." I squeezed him so hard, I thought he'd tell me to stop. "I love you."

He grabbed my hands, pulled them away, and spun me into his arms. "Don't ever do that again. Not ever," he whispered into my hair.

The desperate tone of his voice broke me. I vowed to myself I'd never hurt him and instead, he'd almost died because of me. "I promise I'll never lie to you again, Ben. I can't imagine living life without you. I'm so glad you're okay."

My thoughts drifted over the questions I had about the civil case and the letter he'd hidden from me. But now wasn't the time to discuss it. Ben would find a way to tell me when the time was right.

We stood there in front of the hospital in each other's arms while the watery sun rose in the late winter sky to declare the storm complete. My anxieties fled, and I felt safe again, loved again. Although I knew things were on shaky ground, Ben wouldn't give up on me, and I wouldn't give up on him. We were two injured souls who needed each other, despite the mistakes we made.

"I'd really like my sister to meet you some day," I said.

Ben's lips curved upward briefly, and I knew he'd forgiven me. "I'd like that."

A half an hour later we were in my dad's apartment. After I explained to Ben what had happened with Lola and Declan while he was in the hospital, it hadn't taken much convincing for him to agree to a few nights at Buck's.

Sitting on the couch and looking out the window at the clearing sky ate away at me, though. Not only were we unable to go back to ice diving, my father refused to leave us alone while the two people who'd threatened me and Kyle were still out there.

"Please, Dad, don't waste a good day on our behalf. Ben can take care of me." Ben and I sat side-by-side, our hands woven together. Didn't my dad believe my boyfriend could handle whatever came our way? He outweighed my father by at least fifty pounds and was taller than him by six inches.

Buck leaned against the island that separated the kitchen from the living room and chewed on the inside of his cheek. "I was hoping they would've found Kyle by now."

"I'm sorry, Dad." All my decisions from last night came back to haunt me. "I screwed up. I didn't think about the danger. Nothing would've happened to him if it weren't for me." Sure, my ex had been jailed for attacking me, but that had ultimately forced him into the devilish deal with Lola. If I'd backed off testifying against him last fall, he wouldn't have ended up in so much debt. "He was broke and desperate. I didn't realize—"

"Stop it, Rory," Ben said. "You didn't do anything wrong. Nobody made Kyle pull a gun on you, threaten you, and drag you out in the middle of a storm to go diving for gold." He gave my dad a dark look. "Kyle died because of his own bad choices. You have nothing to feel guilty about."

"It's hard to believe he harbored so much hate toward you, honey." My father's face was unreadable. "And here I gave him a second chance."

"Why did you do that exactly?" I asked. Seeing my attacker on my father's dredge team had been a shock and had felt like a betrayal.

"Nate thought I should."

"Wait, Nate encouraged you to hire Kyle?" Last year Nate had been shocked when he found out Buck had stolen the gold map from Kyle's great uncle. I'd assumed Nate had cut off ties with my ex after that. Then Nate went off to Anchorage for drug treatment and had returned with renewed zest for dredging without all the repressed anger I'd seen over the years. Kyle was in jail, and Nate should've had no contact with him at that point.

"Nate saw himself in Kyle, I think," my dad said. "During treatment, he was working through the steps and made contact with him to make amends for whatever wrongs he thought he'd done against the kid."

I recalled a similar phone call from Nate back in late October. He'd listed some events in the past where he'd felt residual guilt about how he'd treated me because he was jealous of my relationship with Buck. I'd forgiven him, of course. When I'd handed him his half of the money I'd made off the sale of our family's dredge last summer that had been my attempt at forgiveness. "So arranging the job had been an extension of that."

My father always had a soft spot for Nate. Even when they'd had bitter arguments over gold percentages or how to fix a certain piece of equipment. They acted like two brothers—fighting one minute, drinking beers together the next. A twenty-year relationship can sometimes turn into that. They knew each other well. So I shouldn't be surprised my dad would've taken Nate's request under consideration.

"Kyle made a mistake and asked me for another chance. I can't say I don't understand that." My dad's gaze shifted away from me. "Sometimes you do stupid shit, and it's almost impossible to get out from under it."

I knew my dad was referring to himself. A lump formed in my throat. The Buck Darling I knew didn't steal and didn't take advantage of people. Finding out he'd tricked an old man out of his gold map still stung. I had a hard time getting past it.

Ben squeezed my hand. Did he want me to say something? Lately, he'd given the impression I should forgive my dad and move on. That it wasn't worth it to ruin our relationship over one poor choice.

But I wasn't ready for that. Sure, Buck had offered up his place and cared about my safety. That was a step in the right direction.

But I needed something more than an off-handed comment about making mistakes to completely forgive him.

My phone rang.

"It's Officer Garber." I answered it. "Hello?"

"We have Declan in custody. Found him at Lola's place."

Ben and I rode our snow machine to the police station. My eyelids drooped. I wished I had a chance to take a nap. However, knowing Declan couldn't hurt me kicked me into another gear. I could sleep when this was over. I took off the hood of my parka and let the frigid air blow against my cheeks.

Officer Garber had some more questions for me now that they had arrested Declan. He and his partner, Officer Isaacs, the father of one of my high school classmates, had been the ones to handle Kyle's attack on me last summer.

"Aurora," Officer Garber greeted me when we entered the station, "Sorry to see you again so soon and after such a terrible event."

Nobody wanted to say the words aloud: Kyle's death.

"It's all right."

Garber ushered us both to his desk and two empty chairs.

"So this Declan guy is in custody?" Ben asked. "What about his boss, Lola?"

"We're still looking." Garber tapped a pen on his notepad. "We've got a warrant out, but we were hoping you might be able to provide us with more information that could help us figure out her whereabouts. Maybe she mentioned some other names or where she might be going?"

"I don't think I can help." I scanned my mind for any little detail. "Lola and Declan didn't really say anything like that when I was at her place."

"You might be surprised at what we'd find useful. Officer Isaacs is working on tracking down any of her known associates, previous cell mates when she spent some time down in ACC, that kind of thing."

"ACC?" asked Ben.

"The Anchorage Correctional Complex. It's a medium-security facility for low-level criminals," Garber explained. "She was being held there a few years ago for pre-trial reasons. Lola's been causing headaches all over Alaska for more than a decade now. Long before she ever chose Nome as her new stomping grounds."

I chewed on my lower lip. "She wasn't happy when Declan brought me to her place. I think she thought it was a risk for her. She told me that she made money other ways...not just dealing drugs."

"What other ways?" Garber crooked a brow.

"Getting contraband into the prisons for one. Sounded as if she had a contact that made it possible."

"A dirty guard?" Garber asked, his voice tinged with suspicion.

"Yeah. That's why she recruited Kyle when he got his sentence," I explained. "Wherever Kyle was going, she had connections."

Garber nodded, absorbing the gravity of the situation. "This is helpful, Aurora."

"Oh, and something else, she seemed to think it was sort of humorous the local papers thought she was 'just a drug dealer.' As if that was a complete misunderstanding of what she was involved in." The implications of her involvement sent shivers down my spine, and I could see the unease in Garber's eyes as he processed the depths of her criminal connections.

"Okay, thanks." Garber scribbled on his notepad. "She left her truck parked around the block from your dad's place, but she hasn't been seen since. We have someone keeping an eye on her place in Hoodoo Gulch, another at the airport, and someone out by the yurts."

"Why out there?" I asked.

"Just to make sure she doesn't go looking for you."

Ben rested his elbows on his knees and struck a thoughtful pose. "So we can't go back there yet?"

"I wouldn't recommend it. She can't have gotten very far in a few hours. But she seems to be the slippery type. We thought we'd cornered her once before and then she up and disappeared...almost into thin air."

Although I didn't love the idea of staying at my dad's place for more than a night or two, Ben probably wouldn't let me do anything else. If that was the safest place to be, then that would be where we would stay until the police gave us the all clear. I'd have to figure out how to work through the conflicting feelings about my dad while sharing such a small space.

Lola was wily. She'd been underestimated by the police and the newspapers. The idea sent my nerves tingling. Where was she? What was she capable of? And how long would I remain on her radar?

Garber must've seen the worry on my face. "Be assured Declan will be behind bars until trial. He's had enough strikes against him that the district court judge likely won't grant any bail. Especially with his partner missing. The trial should be held in superior court in a few months, and then they'll ship him to Anchorage for whatever sentencing he receives." He leaned back in his chair. "He had outstanding warrants from Sitka and Homer, plus an old one out of Portland, Oregon. He'll be going away for a long time, I think."

"Good," Ben said. He touched the darkening bruise on my cheek. "He'd better know that if he shows his face around here again, I'll be waiting."

Garber shifted his gaze between the two of us, as though he could read on our faces if Ben was capable of revenge.

I wasn't sure what he saw, but I know I felt a lot better with Ben on my side.

CHAPTER 28

As we made our way out of the police station, we ran into Alisha Childress, Matt's younger sister. Per usual, she wore her long, brown hair in a single braid down her back and had on her favorite winter hat—one made from beaver with ears flaps. Her slim build plus the masculine hat made her appear like a young boy from a distance.

"Alisha," I said as we ran into each other, "what are you doing here?"

Ben tilted his head.

"This is Alisha, Matt's sister." I touched him on one beefy bicep. "I don't think you've had the privilege of meeting before. This is my boyfriend, Ben."

Although I'd been over to Stella's a million times since last summer, and Ben had been at their apartment as well, Alisha never seemed to be there. Even though Stella constantly complained about sharing their one-bedroom apartment with her. Her obsession with sled dogs and racing occupied any free time she had when not working at the Northern Lights Inn, a better-than-average motel near the Alaska Army National Guard Recruiting Station on Front Street, where she cleaned rooms and sometimes ran the front desk.

Alisha nodded at Ben in greeting, but her mind seemed turned inward. "Someone stole my sled and my dogs." Her nose turned red, and she rubbed at it with a fist.

"All of them?" I knew she kept her dogs not too far out of town off Hoodoo Gulch, where she'd managed to rent a cheap piece of property to store her gear and house her fledgling race team.

"I'm worried, Rory. Those dogs—they're everything to me."

I gave her a quick hug. "I'm sure they'll be all right. Someone just took them out for a joyride after the storm, maybe."

"Ask for Officer Garber," Ben suggested. "He's a good guy. He'll find them."

"Thanks, I will." Alisha lips twisted. "Wish everyone cared about my dogs as much as you do."

We watched her enter the station, then continued on.

W hen we walked through the door into my dad's place, he had a grim look on his face.

"What's wrong?" I asked.

Ben took my parka and hung it with his in the closet, while I dumped a bag of groceries on the kitchen counter. If we were staying for a while, I wanted some better food choices than the canned peaches and boxed macaroni and cheese in the cupboard.

"The Coast Guard recovered Kyle." His whole body turned inward as if he were shrinking into himself. The tough exterior Buck Darling usually showed to the world had disappeared. "I just spoke with his parents."

I gave him a hug. "I'm sorry, Dad, that must've been awful." Even though we still had our own issues to work through, I couldn't ignore the pain in his eyes.

Ben silently stowed the food we'd bought in the refrigerator.

"They're coming up to arrange for his body to be flown to Texas. They want to meet me—meet us." He swallowed.

My throat tightened, leaving me feeling both apprehensive and burdened by the weight of the impending encounter. "Why would they want to meet me?" Kyle had attacked me, and then later pulled a gun on me. I wouldn't have kind words to say, they had to know that.

"I think they want to apologize to you. They feel awful about what happened and seemed to want to explain things."

I thought about the two teachers who hoped they'd raised a good son who would make them proud. They'd shipped him off to Nome thinking he'd find some family roots, some connection to their history, but he'd only fallen apart without them. Kyle had never spoken negatively of his upbringing and had even flown home for Christmas the year we spent together. I'd assumed they were close.

"If it will help them, I'll be there—you just tell me when." I made a silent promise to myself to set aside my own reservations and support Kyle's parents through the difficult moments ahead. They'd done nothing wrong and deserved my sympathy.

Ben joined us on the living room side of the apartment. His presence next to me soothed. I choked on the thought I'd almost lost him because of my impulsive ways.

"I'll let them know we're open to it." My dad looked at both of us. "By the time the Coast Guard reached the ice floe, the storm had blown the shelter away and the waves had washed it clean. In fact, they had to retrieve Kyle's body from the Bering."

In my mind's eye I could see it—a flat white chunk of ice tossed around in the storm. The heavy generator probably went first, full of expensive diesel we'd purchased only the day before. The sluice box, weighted down with hard won gold sucked up from our secret spot, would've gone next. The last thing I thought of was Ben's carving of the two owls. The one personal thing I'd wanted with me out on the ice. Now lost forever. Whenever I saw it, I thought of the moment I fell in love with Ben, the moment I knew I'd found the right person for me. I'd felt it in my soul.

"We'll find another way," said Ben. He knew I'd be upset at the loss. Our plans for the summer and our future together had been washed away overnight. He stroked a hand across my back. "Won't we, Rory?"

I wrapped my arms around myself and nodded. I couldn't spoil his positive thinking with my own negative mindset. We were striving for independence, but all we had to our name was six grand in gold in a peanut butter jar and a couple of sleeping bags.

The notion of establishing our own business seemed like an insur-mountable mountain at this point.

"I think I have an idea, if you're open to it," my dad said.

I raised my gaze to meet his. "An idea?" My curiosity piqued despite my reservations. We'd only buried the hatchet a few hours ago, and the ground beneath our newfound peace was fragile.

"After spending the last couple of weeks with Nate and Kyle, it's clear to me I need more help to have a chance of making a good profit this winter. I didn't realize how hard it would be to recover from my surgery and manage the dive operations with only two divers." My dad looked down at the cup of coffee in his hands perhaps afraid to see the rejection in my eyes before his whole idea had been voiced.

He paused to scratch his scalp. "You're a good dredger, Rory. I'm sorry if I mouthed off at you the other day. It's not easy seeing your flesh and blood do a better job of dredging than you."

I looked up at my dad, his words catching me off guard. I'd never heard my dad admit when he was wrong or acknowledge my dredging skills so directly. Not like this. Usually it was Buck's way or no way at all. I reached out and gently placed my hand on his. "It's alright, Dad," I said softly.

"I was wondering if you and Ben would consider joining up with Nate and me?" His voice was tinged with a mix of hope and uncertainty.

Ben leaned down and kissed the top of my head. "I'm in, sir."

Although I wanted to give my father an easy 'yes' like Ben, I was having trouble silencing my inner voice of caution.

"I'm not sure if I'll be that easy to work with," my dad admitted, "since I've gotten used to running things my way, but I'm willing to give it a shot." He looked at both of us with genuine sincerity in his eyes. "Let's do this together and make this winter our best season yet."

I knew my father and I trying to mend the rift between us pleased my boyfriend. I wrapped an arm around his waist and looked up at Ben—my beast. "I suppose I could agree to that."

Accepting the offer to work with my dad was ninety-percent a selfish one. Without more gold, our future plans were shot. I'd have to apply for fill-in work to make ends meet without a summer floating dredge—take up Stella on the offer of a job at the Polar Cafe or try my hand at working for someone else.

I gave Ben a sidelong glance. He and my father were already negotiating percentages, work hours, safety rules. Although such talk interested me, I had a hard time taking part when powerful emotions swirled in my head. I wished I could set feelings aside, like Ben or my dad or Nate, and talk business first. But my heart was torn in different directions—clearly Ben already had forgiven my father for the crime I felt he committed against Arthur Stroup, Kyle's great uncle. Arthur had been slowly losing his faculties. A conversation on the wrong day resulted in Arthur being persuaded to give my father the gold map he'd painstakingly put together over the years. It still felt so wrong to me that he'd taken advantage of the man, even after I had given the map back to Kyle as a peace offering.

Maybe it wasn't the same as someone dressed all in black who breaks a window, climbs into someone's living room in the dead of night, and steals a valuable item. But the intent to me was the same —taking something that wasn't yours for your own personal benefit.

"How does that sound?" Ben asked me.

I nodded without even knowing what I was agreeing to. If Ben was willing to work with my dad, then I had to be on board, too. He and I were partners in everything, and I knew he'd back me up if anything went sideways. Plus, my dad would be stupid to cross him.

"Sure. Perfect." My lips quirked in the tiniest of smiles. "Isn't that called a win-win situation?"

My father's eyes crinkled at the corners. I'd pleased him. I was back to being 'his' Rory. The daughter who used to look at him with pride and affection. But a flicker of worry remained. I didn't know if I would ever be that daughter again.

My smile wavered. Didn't I want an opportunity to break out on my own with Ben at my side? Looking at the wreck of my life left behind by Lola, Declan, and Kyle, I knew I had to face my uncertainties head-on and forge the future we wanted. And if that meant extending an olive branch to my father, I could do it. Couldn't I?

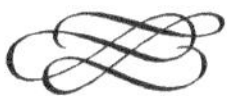

CHAPTER 29

A couple of days later, Ben and I drove the snow machine out to my father's ice shack. The storm had battered everyone's set up and repairs had to be made to continue diving. A quiet settled on the ice that hadn't been there previously. As we drove past other dredgers, the apprehensive gazes that followed us revealed the reason: Kyle's death and my involvement in it.

Did they see me as a bad luck omen? First, Kyle had been sent off to prison because of me, and now he'd died under my watch.

The news had spread quickly after Kyle's body had been discovered. His parents were due to fly in tomorrow for a quick memorial service before they brought him to Texas for burial. Knowing my father and I would be meeting them both in person at Miner's the day after tomorrow gnawed at me. I knew it was the right thing to do—they deserved some information about Ben's attempt to save him, and anything else they wanted to ask. They deserved to know everything—good and bad—about his last hours.

Ben ignored the stares and throttled up the machine to move more quickly. I knew he did that for me. I'd be the one rattled by the attention—not him. He'd soldiered through much worse when he'd been suspected of murdering his fiancée. At least now I had a better grasp of the feelings that tore at your gut when someone close to you died. It was as if an ice cold hand gripped my insides and squeezed.

Nate stood outside my father's shack with an insulated mug in his hand. He waved as we approached.

I remembered the words Kyle said in the middle of the storm when we were alone on the ice: *Nate was right, Rory. You are weak.*

I thought Nate and I had patched things up between us months ago. Then he'd tricked Ben with the bum equipment. When had he turned on me? Or had Kyle only been using Nate's words as a way to get at me?

"Hey, Nate." I slid off the back of the snow machine and reached for our bag of gear. I'd have to use my dad's wetsuit since Kyle had been wearing mine the day he died. Neither the Coast Guard nor the funeral home had contacted me about it, but I didn't want it back anyway.

"Rory." He dipped his head in recognition and continued to sip his hot drink. The steam curled in the air and then disappeared when a small gust of wind blew by. "Did you hear the latest news going around about Lola?"

"No, the police aren't being very forthcoming with information," I said, wrapping my arms around myself against the crisp breeze.

"I heard at Ernie's last night that she's holed up downstate with old pals," Nate said, squinting at the horizon.

Ben asked, "Do you think it's true?"

Nate shrugged, his breath visible in the cold, "That's the buzz, but who knows?"

I gave Ben a knowing look. We'd been feeling the cramp of staying at my dad's place the last few days. Despite the worries about Lola being on the loose, Declan had been the more formidable threat…and if it was true she'd left town? It'd be nice to have a little privacy again. We'd talked about taking any downtime we might have and making a trip out to the cabin. I tried to convince myself the main motivation was to make sure everything was still secure, but I also hoped to reconnect with Ben.

An uneasy silence stretched between us like a taut rubber band, waiting for someone to break it.

Nate rose to the challenge. "Your dad's inside already."

Both Ben and I ducked through the tarp flap. My father sat at the comms. I knew that was his least favorite place to be. He wanted to be in the water, attacking the gold, battling against nature. How long would he be able to stand working as a mere tender on his own outfit?

He looked up from the controls and scanned me from head to toe, as if making sure I was fit to dive. "Good morning. I have coffee in the thermos if you want some." He held up a massive Royal Stewart plaid thermos that was at least thirty years old. The same one he'd always used. The familiarity of the red background with its distinctive black, green, and yellow plaid pattern soothed my prickly nerves. I couldn't help but marvel at the longevity of that old thermos. Its faded pattern and dents told stories of countless adventures and shared cups of warmth. The memories embedded within its worn surface spanned decades, which gave me an odd sense of stability. He raised an eyebrow, a silent invitation for us to join him in a cup.

As Ben stepped forward, a faint smile on his lips, I couldn't help but wonder what shadows he hid behind those earnest eyes. "I'll take some," he said, accepting the offer for coffee. We were still dancing around the edges of this new relationship with my father. The night before, in the quiet intimacy of our shared space, he'd confessed the unease in his heart. "It doesn't feel right," he admitted, "that I hardly know your father at all, but I know that I love you."

I had felt the weight of those words, a sentiment amplified by the scars of his past, especially the civil suit he hadn't yet unveiled to me and the letter he'd chosen to burn rather than share it with me. Perhaps he thought he was sparing me the worry or himself the judgment. The ghost of that unspoken revelation lingered between us, and I sensed his longing for my father's approval.

As Buck unscrewed the cap, a familiar aroma wafted through the air, triggering a flood of nostalgia. The scent of rich, steaming coffee mingled with the scent of diesel.

"I'll have some, too," I said, hoping the caffeine would soothe my growing nerves. I'd agreed to the plan in my father's apartment—Ben and I would dive in exchange for thirty-three percent of the gold after expenses. A fair deal considering. He and Nate would split the other two thirds. But diving in the storm had changed me. My mind revisited the feeling of helplessness under the water as the surge moved me like a mere plaything caught in the grasp of a tempest. Even the memory of the dark ice above me had been causing me nightmares. If Ben knew, he'd insist I stay up top. But that wasn't the deal...

With each sip, I hoped for the tension in my shoulders to ease, for the worries weighing me down to vanish. But as the last drop of coffee disappeared, the black sense of dread only strengthened. My breathing grew shallow, and I stared at the dark hole in the ice. I felt dizzy.

"I can't do this," I gasped. I stood abruptly, the insulated cup slipped from my hands, and I felt myself lose consciousness.

I woke up in the passenger's seat of someone's truck. Several pairs of eyes looked at me through the window.

I startled. "Ben?" A blanket slipped from my shoulders, and I clutched at it as if it could protect me from the people who surrounded me and stared as if I were an animal in the zoo.

A warm hand settled on my thigh. "Hey, it's okay."

Ben. That deep baritone voice was one I instantly recognized.

My mind slowly returned to me. The curious crowd thinned and returned to their repair work and prepping for diving—their entertainment over. "I fainted."

"You hyperventilated." Ben started the truck and drove us back toward shore. "Have you ever had a panic attack before?"

"Who's truck is this?" I took in the dirty interior littered with greasy rags and empty beer cans and noted the faded dashboard was thick with dust.

"That doesn't matter." Ben kept his eyes on the ice, maneuvering around soft spots and leftover blocks from cutting holes for dredging. "You need to get some help."

I sat up, my senses on full alert. "What are you talking about? I'm fine. I feel fine." I threw off the musty-smelling blanket. "Take me back to the dredge. I promised I'd dive."

"You're not diving today."

I bristled at his authoritative tone. "You can't tell me what I can and cannot do, Ben. I'm not a child." I fiddled with the door lock. "Stop the truck. I'll walk back if I have to."

How dare he keep me from diving. How dare he decide for me what I was capable of doing.

He stopped the truck before I launched myself out on the ice at ten miles an hour. "Before you make a decision—"

I glared at him. "I've already made my decision."

"—listen to me for five minutes. Then if you still want to go back to your dad's dredge, I'll drive you back myself."

Blood pounded in my ears. I wanted nothing more than to step out on the ice and run away from Ben and his crazy ideas. I was perfectly fine. I'd fainted. People fainted all the time. Maybe I didn't eat enough for breakfast. Maybe I was dehydrated.

I clung to the door handle.

"Please, Rory."

Those beautiful blue eyes that could be clear as the sky one minute and dark and cloudy the next drew me in. I couldn't deny him anything when his eyes looked like that. "All right," I said quietly. "Five minutes."

Ben gripped the steering wheel. "You know that I was in the Iraq War when I was in the Navy."

I nodded. In the seven months since I'd known Ben, he'd told me very few details about his service. I held my breath, worried I'd spook him. The documents Jonah had shown me the night of my interview leapt to mind. Some kind of accident, and his diving partner had died. That's all I knew. The report had been sparse.

"I was stationed on a carrier in the Persian Gulf with my best friend and partner."

"Kilgore," I filled in. He'd told me that much around the time we first met.

He nodded. "We went through the diving course together and then EOD school."

"EOD?"

"Explosive Ordnance Disposal...we cleared explosives like mines underwater."

I knew Ben had a dangerous job when he was in the Navy, but I had no idea it included explosives. "Damn."

"When I first joined," he began, his eyes distant as he recollected earlier times, "the idea of it was exciting to me. I had this bad ass thing going on. I was eighteen and stupid. I thought I was untouchable. Every challenge they threw at us, Kilgore and me, we came out stronger than before." Ben gave me a half-smile and then focused his gaze on the ice as he drove. "Eventually, you start to forget the danger and work the job—just like anyone else."

I thought about when I first went diving for gold. My father had lectured me for years about the dangers of cold water diving and the risks of underwater dredge mining. For most of my dredging career I'd been untouched by tragedy. Until my dad's near fatal heart attack under water...and now my brush with death when Kyle had forced me to dive during the storm.

"When we were completing an operation in the Persian Gulf, there was a really bad accident." His chin dipped. "And Kilgore didn't make it." Ben wiped his eyes with the back of his hand.

"You don't have to tell me anymore." I reached for him. I wanted to wipe away the tears and kiss him until he came back to me. Even though I wanted to know everything, he didn't need to revisit his pain just to help me.

He brushed me away and navigated the truck around a patch of particularly uneven ice. "Rory, listen to me. This is important. Kilgore and I were clearing mines. We'd done it a dozen times before without a problem. Attach explosives, detonate from a safe distance. But these were booby trapped."

A lump formed in my throat as Ben's voice trembled. "The explosion...it was devastating. The force threw us back, and the shockwave reverberated through the water. I tried to reach Kilgore, but the chaos and debris made it nearly impossible. I... I couldn't save him."

I could see the pain etched on Ben's face, the guilt weighing heavily on his shoulders. I knew he blamed himself for not being able to save his friend. The plain words in the report Jonah had handed me in no way captured the true horror of the event. I wanted to offer comfort, but I knew that nothing I could say would heal the wounds he carried.

"I was hit with some of the shrapnel," he said.

"Your scar." I remembered the first time I saw the scar on his back and asked him about it. He'd shut me down with a look of pure grief.

He continued without acknowledging my words, "But I didn't

even realize it until I was back on the ship." His voice grew thick with emotion. "They recovered Kilgore's body, and we held a memorial service on board. He was a kid just like me, but I'd lived and he died. It didn't seem right. It wasn't fair."

Ben took a deep breath, his eyes were wet. "I wanted you to know, Rory, because it's a part of who I am now. Kilgore's sacrifice, it changed me. It made me realize the fragility of life, the importance of cherishing every moment we have."

I reached out and took Ben's hand, offering my silent support.

"But for a long time I was in a really dark place. I came back from that tour and had nightmares about it—over and over and over I'd see the mine exploding, Kilgore's body ripped to pieces. I couldn't handle it. For awhile I found some peace at the bottom of a bottle, but even that didn't help for long." His gaze held mine for a few moments before he parked on shore beside the yurts. "Then a doc at the VA asked me some questions, and I found out I was suffering from Post-Traumatic Stress Disorder—PTSD. Sometimes it can manifest with panic attacks, like yours back there in the shelter."

"That wasn't a panic attack—" But I thought about what had happened before I felt lightheaded, before I lost consciousness. The dark scary hole in the ice...thinking about diving, remembering the helplessness I'd felt in the storm clinging to a rock, waiting for the ocean to carry me away never to be seen again.

"Rory." He lifted my chin and searched my face. "You need help. What Kyle did to you—and that thug Declan—I don't want it to take you away from me."

"I'm not going anywhere, Ben, I'm right here."

"I saw a look in your eye, Rory," he said softly. His fingers lightly grazed my bruised cheek, a tender gesture that betrayed the depth of his concern. "I recognize it. You need to talk to someone before it takes over your mind."

The weight of his words settled on me like an anchor, and I struggled to hold back tears.

"I don't know if I could stand to lose you," he confessed, his voice trembling with emotion. "I love you too much."

As the raw vulnerability of his words hung in the air, I reached out and clutched his hand, squeezing it tightly. "I love you, too." I leaned toward him and we kissed. The wintery scene outside disappeared, and I lost myself in the sensation of my mouth against his. Every kiss we shared was like coming home and made me forget that night in the storm.

When he broke away, he brushed a thumb to wipe away a tear that had rolled down my face. "I think you need to stay away from diving for a while until you deal with this."

The little girl inside me who wanted nothing more than to be exactly like her father, Buck Darling, came out scratching and screaming. She didn't want anyone telling her what she could and couldn't do. And if it were anyone but Ben who asked me to seek mental health help and stay out of the water, I would've fought that person like a wild animal caught in a trap.

But Ben was different. He knew me inside and out. No one knew me as well as he did.

"You're right," I found myself saying. Relief swept over me the second I gave up the need to be brave, to be tough. "I need help." I let all the fear and horror I felt that night come to the surface and threw my arms around Ben's neck and bawled.

CHAPTER 30

Ben, my dad, and I entered Miner's to meet with Mr. and Mrs. Stroup—Kyle's parents. They'd flown in yesterday, and we'd agreed to a conversation before the funeral the next day. A rock formed in my stomach. Would they blame me for Kyle's death?

I took a deep breath and attempted to use some of the techniques I'd learned in my first therapy session yesterday to find some calm and center myself.

One hour in therapy in a judgment-free environment had helped more than I thought it would. But so much more than my experience on that stormy night came to the surface.

Ben had been right; I needed someone to talk to. I'd relied heavily on him as my emotional touch point since we'd met last summer, yet I'd kept deeper feelings to myself. The news about him hiding the civil suit from me added a layer of uncertainty and weighed on my mind. I was oddly looking forward to my next session with Therapist Sarah, curious about her perspective.

As we approached the table against the far wall, I shook off thoughts of therapy. Kyle's parents had heartache in their eyes, but attempted to smile. I could see a bit of Kyle in each of them, and it made me sad to think they'd lost their son in such an awful way.

Mr. Stroup stood. "Thank you for being willing to meet with us."

My father shook his hand, and we all sat at the table.

Marla kept her distance, but a pitcher of beer and glasses of water already waited. Maybe Mr. Stroup had ordered that before we'd arrived.

Ben reached for the pitcher.

"Yes, please, help yourselves," Mrs. Stroup said. "We also ordered some appetizers."

"Hopefully not the muktuk," Ben said as he poured himself a generous glass of beer.

"Muktuk?" Mr. Stroup had a quizzical look on his face.

"Whale chunks breaded and fried," my dad explained, scooting his empty pint glass in Ben's direction.

Mrs. Stroup turned a little green.

"Ben's pulling your leg," I said. "They don't serve that here."

As if on cue, Marla placed two platters of steaming food in front of us—mini crab cakes and reindeer sliders.

After a few minutes of pleasantries and sampling the appetizers, Mr. Stroup cut to the chase, "We knew that Kyle had problems. We were hoping his move to Nome might be the thing to shake him out of it. But I think he had deeper issues he didn't share with us."

Mrs. Stroup set down her half eaten slider and pushed her plate away. Her eyes grew red and watery.

I didn't want to go there. I didn't want to hear about Kyle's issues. We all had issues, but it didn't mean you threatened someone with a gun and forced them to dive at night in frigid waters during a storm. I dropped my fork on my plate with a clatter.

Several patrons in Miner's turned to find the source of the loud noise.

"Kyle was a hard-working kid." My father kept me from making a scene. He read the outrage on my face, I guess. "He was a great diver, and I'll really miss him. I'm very sorry for your loss."

Mr. Stroup nodded. Mrs. Stroup put a napkin up to her mouth and nose and covered a sob.

Ben settled his hand on my thigh, and I relaxed.

"Thanks—" Kyle's dad drew his brows together. "I feel weird calling you 'Mr. Darling,' as if you were my high school science teacher." A ghost of a smile drifted across his face.

"You can call me Buck."

"Right, Buck." Mr. Stroup grabbed another crab cake off the platter. "Kyle really seemed to look up to you."

Mrs. Stroup had gotten control of her emotions enough to speak. "I really appreciate how you took him under your wing when nobody else cared."

We spent another hour telling stories about Kyle—the good times before his arrest last summer. By the end of it, my anger toward my ex had dissipated. He was dead. He'd suffered the worst punishment possible for his mistakes. Did his parents need to suffer, too? I had to figure out a way to forgive their son and move forward.

It made me think of my stepfather, Henry, and what he'd suffered after my mother had left him. He'd spent years paying the price for her selfishness—a single dad raising two girls on his own. And I wasn't even his blood. I was the product of an affair during another one of my mother's 'blue periods,' as Henry liked to call them. The ways she had humiliated him shocked me. Had he loved my mother that much? When she came to her senses, he'd always welcomed her home.

But why didn't she come home that last time? Where was she? Did she even care what had happened to Zoe and me?

I had to find out. I had to fix me. Because I couldn't wake up in the middle of the night anymore drenched in sweat and dark thoughts filling my mind. My insecurities about myself, my relationship with Ben—was I destined to be the same kind of woman my mother was? Incapable of working through the hard stuff?

The facade I'd built since I was twelve years old was beginning to melt away, and the real me was about to be exposed. What would I find once the exterior me crumbled? Would Ben stick around? Would he run away? What if I was a weak, frightened little rabbit underneath it all?

The trauma I'd experienced with Kyle, Declan, and Lola had unlocked something inside, and I couldn't put it back in the box. The only way to get over it was to go through it. I needed to rebuild a sense of safety and control in my life, and it all began with middle school me feeling bereft, unloved, and ugly when my mother left us. A child grieving for a person who'd never been that great a mother; she'd been self-absorbed and neglectful. But that void she left behind had echoed throughout my life, shaping my relationships.

"What do you think, Rory?" Ben asked, pulling me back into the conversation.

I quickly realized I'd missed a question, and with a slight panic, I attempted to gather myself and salvage the moment. "Sure. Great," I replied, mustering a smile. I didn't want the Stroups to think I hadn't been paying attention as they poured their hearts out.

"Wonderful," Mr. Stroup said. It was evident he appreciated my agreement, even though I had missed a crucial detail. Mrs. Stroup, ever perceptive, shot me a compassionate smile, understanding that my mind may have wandered temporarily.

As we wrapped up the evening with Kyle's parents and headed out the door, I whispered to Ben, "What did I just agree to?" My body tensed. The cool air outside soothed me after the suffocating warmth inside Miner's.

"You agreed to speak at Kyle's funeral service tomorrow." He let out a lungful of air.

"I did?"

"You did." A pained expression marred his features.

Did I detect a bit of hurt in his voice that I'd do some kind of eulogy at my attacker's funeral?

"Shit." I scratched the side of my neck and then slid my hand up under my chin. My jaw muscles ached. Had I been clenching my teeth again at night?

"Right." Ben led me to our Polaris we'd parked outside. "You said yes before I had a chance to stop you."

"What am I going to say?"

He shrugged. "You mean it's going to be weird for Kyle's victim to say nice things about him?" The sarcasm that laced his voice was unmistakable. "Shocker."

How could I explain to Ben how my mind had wandered? That my thoughts had been elsewhere and not on the conversation at the table. At best I'd appear aloof, at worst I'd appear coldhearted. Kyle's mother had worked the whole evening to keep from crying.

Kyle's dad kept refilling everyone's mugs with beer maybe hoping we'd think better of him for raising such a mess of a son.

"I'm sorry, Ben, maybe I can get out of it?" As I said the words, a familiar figure entered the bar and grill a mere twenty feet away. "Jonah?"

"Who?" Ben was about to start the Polaris. "Is that the reporter dude?"

I slipped off the back seat. "Sorry, I have to go talk to him."

"What?" My boyfriend gave me a quizzical look as I trotted back inside. "What the hell, Rory?"

When I stepped back inside the bar, I saw Jonah Tanaka making a beeline for the Stroups' table. Mr. Stroup was paying the bill, and Mrs. Stroup was checking her make-up in a small compact from her purse—probably worried her mascara had run.

"Hey, Jonah," I called out. Why was he still in town and what interest did he have in the Stroups?

The reporter turned and had a look of shock on his face when he saw me. "You're all right?"

"Why wouldn't I be all right?" I crossed my arms. The mix of drunk gold miners and rock music made it hard to hear. Dinner hour was over, and Miner's began its shift from family dining spot to local beer hall. "And why are you still here? I thought you were supposed to fly out days ago."

"I decided to stay a few extra days. I heard you collapsed on the ice. Zoe's been worried." He shifted his backpack to his other shoulder. "If it weren't for the lack of seats on the flights to Nome, she'd be here already with your dad. Wanted me to check on you."

"I'm fine." My gaze slid to the Stroups who were headed our way. "Why were you going to talk to Kyle's parents?"

Jonah flushed. "I thought I could interview them."

"You seriously have a problem." Mrs. Stroup saw me standing in the middle of the bar and gave me a sad smile. "They've been through enough without you poking around. What is it? A new story you're chasing? *Local Miner Drowns in Horrific Winter Storm?*"

Jonah gave me an odd look. "No."

Before he could expand on his answer, the Stroups reached us. Kyle's dad touched me on the shoulder. "We'll see you tomorrow at three. Thank you so much for agreeing to speak. I know it's an odd request, but you were one of the people who knew him best. Before all of the..." He cleared his throat. "...troubles this past year."

"Bless you, Rory." Kyle's mother gave her a hug. "It warms my heart to know you've forgiven him."

I hadn't said those words to her, but if it made her feel better about the loss of her son to think that, I wasn't about to correct her. My therapist would be proud. I'd have to add it to the journal she wanted me to keep.

After tomorrow, I'd never see these people again. Giving them a bit of kindness seemed to be the right thing to do.

As Kyle's parents headed out the door, Ben came roaring in with eyes of blue fire.

CHAPTER 31

"Leave her alone, Tanaka." My big burly boyfriend towered over the leaner, smaller reporter. "When are you going back where you came from? We've had enough of this crap."

Jonah stepped back with both hands up in a surrender pose. "*She* came after *me*. I only showed up here to try to talk to the Stroups about the accident. I'd heard they were in town."

"She's done talking to you." Ben's finger poked into Jonah's chest.

"Ben." I still wanted to know what Kyle's death had to do with some stupid story about a female dredger in Nome, Alaska. Was he going to dig into everything about my life? "Please don't. He's right. I'm the one that chased him down."

My quiet words drained Ben of his bravado. He lowered his hand, and his chest deflated. "Are you sure?" His gaze softened as he looked at me. "He isn't bothering you?" His eyes flicked back to Jonah, simmering with lingering suspicion.

Jonah, sensing the shift in the atmosphere, cautiously interjected, "Look, I understand your concern, Ben. But I promise you, I mean no harm to Rory. I only wanted to gather information about the accident, to understand what happened to Kyle, and to get a feel for the real danger out there on the ice."

Ben's protective instincts were still on high alert, but my plea had touched a chord in him. He took a step closer to me, his hand reaching out to gently touch my arm. "Rory, I think you need to take a break from all of this," he murmured, his voice filled with genuine worry.

I nodded, appreciating his concern. He was right. I needed to work on my mental health. "The police should have my report available soon. You can ask them for a copy. That will give you all the details you need to know."

Ben's grip on my arm loosened. "Let's go back to the cabin like we talked about."

"Tonight?" It would take us a couple of hours, and it must be almost eight o'clock. But it was my safe place, my refuge. Lola was long gone, according to Nate's friends, so why not? A flicker of relief warmed me as I reached out and squeezed Ben's hand. "Okay. That sounds good." I turned to Jonah, who had been observing the exchange. "Tell Zoe I'm fine and that I'll call her tomorrow after the funeral. I need some time away from all of this." I gestured at the room full of miners, half of them staring at me and knowing exactly what had happened out on the ice. The weight of their judgment was almost too much.

"I'm glad you're okay," Jonah said, his voice filled with genuine relief. "When I'm back in Seattle and the story's all done, I'll send you a link so you can read it."

I didn't have the heart to tell him I really had no interest in reading whatever little story he was going to write. If he emailed me a link, I'd probably send a thank you and delete it. But he didn't need to know that. "Sure. Thanks."

Ben and I walked out the door. This time when we found ourselves outside, I looked up at the sky—the clouds had cleared away and a black sky above glittered with stars. For some reason, the cold winter nights in Nome made the stars appear almost within reach.

As Ben drove us out to his cabin, I kept my gaze on the sky and thought about how Kyle would never see a night sky again. It pricked my heart, and my tears dried in the cold air as we sped into the tundra. I leaned into Ben's back and wrapped my arms more tightly around his middle to try to forget all the sadness that surrounded me.

"We need to take the trail slow if we hit deep snow on the way,"

I said into Ben's ear as we headed out of town. "Not sure how much has changed since the storm."

He nodded and tightened his grip on the handlebars.

Winter on the tundra was different than summer. Under the star-filled sky, a span of white spread out in front of us as we peeled away from Nome-Teller Road and headed down a familiar trail that took us farther away from civilization. A few rolling hills, bare of vegetation, echoed the bluish white all around us. We had miles to travel before we arrived at our cozy hollow protected by a few stunted trees. But the winds had blown the snow from the storm into drifts making the drive difficult.

Each gust of icy breath from the Arctic wilderness seemed to whisper warnings of the challenge ahead. As Ben steered us expertly through the drifts, our snow machine worked hard. The engine whined, and the crisp air was filled with the high-pitched churning of treads battling the resistance of the snow. The world became a blur of white and wind, and I forgot about everything but the two of us as we drew closer to our cozy haven, a place of warmth and safety that I longed to see again.

From somewhere distant, I thought I heard a chorus of howls over the engine noise. Wolves? Strange to hear out this way, they usually lived farther out on the tundra beyond Pilgrim Hot Springs. Maybe I was imagining things.

Ben drove over the hill on the less-traveled road that led to his grandfather's cabin, and I let my mind wander as the eerie howling continued.

Instead of dying away, the howling grew stronger as we closed the distance to Ben's cabin. The hairs on the back of my neck stood up. We'd stayed here all winter and never had we heard any wolves.

Ben made the turn to reach the cabin and almost ran head on into a group of sled dogs who were hitched up to an overturned sled that blocked the road.

"What the hell?" He slid to the right to avoid colliding with the lead dog who had a distinctive all-white coat with a single black spot on his back.

"That's Smudge." I recognized Alisha's favorite sled dog. She'd raised him from a pup in high school, convinced that because he was from a winning line of sled dogs that he would be a future Iditarod champion. "What are they doing all the way out here?"

I held on as the snow machine swerved and then came to an abrupt halt.

We both climbed off, and I immediately began to check each dog to make sure there were no injuries. The team merely appeared to be tired and hungry. "Wait, didn't Alisha say that her dogs had been stolen?"

Ben flipped the sled right side up and touched a broken runner. "Matt's sister?"

"Yeah." I scratched Smudge under the chin. He wagged his tail and panted. "She'll be so glad we found them. Maybe they just ran off."

"Ran off tied to the sled?" He plucked at the gangline that connected the team to it. "That doesn't make a lot of sense."

The recognizable sound of the racking of a shotgun stilled us both. "Leave my dogs alone."

Lola Chang.

My insides froze. She was standing on the small front stoop of Ben's cabin, the shotgun pointed straight at us.

The dogs, who had grown quiet after our arrival, began to whine and cry again.

"Shut up!" Lola lunged at the dogs, swinging the butt end of the shotgun at them. The stock caught one younger pup on his back legs, and he yelped in pain. "They're driving me crazy."

"They're hungry," Ben said quietly. "Have you fed them?"

Lola snorted. "Fed them? I hadn't eaten in three days before I found this place. They're fine."

I stood farther back in the shadows. Lola had yet to recognize me, I was so bundled up in my cold weather gear.

Ben moved to his left to stand in front of me and protect me from direct line of fire. "Eat all you want. I can water the dogs while you fill up. At least that would fill their stomachs, and then you are more than welcome to move on. We don't want any problems."

"This your place?" Lola lifted the shotgun to her shoulder, finger on the trigger.

He held up his hands. "I don't care who you are or what you want. I think we all want things to go well, don't we?"

Lola gestured with the shotgun. "Who's that behind you? I want to see both of you."

Nausea filled my stomach. I thought this nightmare was over. I thought Lola had run away, and I'd never see her again. My refuge had turned into my nightmare. I slowly stepped around Ben. The little bit of moonlight shone on my face.

"Rory Darling. Well, fuck me." Lola smile was a wicked one. "Isn't this a fine turn of events?"

Ben had no idea what we just ridden into. He probably thought this woman was only a thief looking for food or weapons at an empty cabin who then would be on her way once she got what she wanted. He couldn't be more wrong.

"Who is this?" Ben asked, keeping his eyes focused on Lola and her shotgun. "Why does she know you?"

"Rory wrote herself a death sentence when she talked to the cops. You think the money Kyle owed us belonged to *me*?" She laughed derisively. "Hope you had a nice ride out here, because I think I'll be taking your snow machine and this shotgun."

Keeping the barrel pointed at us both, Lola made her move toward our snow machine.

"Where you are going to go? There's nothing out there but tundra for miles," I said. The police would be scouring the area for her, and she couldn't travel too far on half a tank of gas. "You might as well turn yourself in. They already arrested Declan. It's over."

"You don't get it, do you?" Lola swung one skinny leg over the machine, somehow keeping the shotgun aimed at us both. "Without that money I'm fucked. You're fucked. We're all fucked." She started it up, shoved the gun through the straps of our gear bag attached to the back, and took off into the dark.

As the sound of the engine grew more muted in the distance, the dog team howled and howled. Ben swept me up in his arms and held me tight until I stopped shaking.

CHAPTER 32

TWO DAYS LATER…

Alisha drove up to my dad's place in her brother's truck. The ten dogs, tied to a sign post in front of my dad's apartment, yelped and leaped excitedly when they saw her climb out. She'd arrived alone, which seemed a little odd. Where was her brother?

"How did you find them?" Alisha asked kneeling down and giving Smudge a hug as he licked her face. "The police told me you had them but didn't explain anything to me."

Ben and I had had to figure out how to slowly sled our way back to town after giving the dogs a well-deserved rest and a bunch of food—whatever seemed dog-friendly from our larder: rice, ground moose, a few cans of chili. They'd done quite well sheltered in the shack where the snow machine usually sat. But our attempts at being mushers had been an epic fail. We'd spent half the time figuring out how to keep the dogs on the trail and how to slow them down without crashing—they had been so eager to go home.

"Lola Chang stole them to slip past the cops," I said. "Guess the rumors she'd headed downstate was just that—rumors. She'd holed up at Ben's place, and we ran into her there. To be honest, she seemed more worried about someone higher up the criminal food chain than getting arrested."

"Wow, and you guys are okay?" She looked up at us with awe in her eyes.

I nodded. "Lola wanted to get out of there. The minute she saw the Polaris, she took it and headed toward the Blodgett Highway."

"How far do you think she'll get?" Alisha began to unclip her dogs one at a time from the line and load them into the back of the pick-up.

"She only had a half-a-tank of gas," Ben said.

"The highway's closed in the winter, but she maybe could've made it to Teller," I surmised. I didn't want to tell her that I didn't care. I was glad Lola was gone and out of my life. She ran off with the police on her tail and maybe some gangbanger looking for his money, and I hoped we'd never see her again. To disappear into Canada or the Lower 48 and lose herself where nobody knew who she was would be her best bet. She'd be stupid to stick around Nome. Teller had a small airport, so she'd probably find a way to barter for a ride. Lola was resourceful like that.

"We're just glad everyone's all right," said my dad. "Including your dogs." He scooped up a tan-and-white sled dog and carried him to the truck. "You have a nice team here, Alisha. Hope that woman didn't do any damage to them."

She checked the paws of her lead dog. "I don't see any cracked pads or blisters. But I'll have to have the vet check them out. Could be soft tissue damage I can't see."

Stella was right. Alisha had an obsession with her dogs. Every extra penny went toward their care and training. She'd likely never move out into her own place at this rate.

"I'm glad to hear it," I said.

After the back of the pick-up had been loaded up with yipping, howling dogs, no room was left for the sled.

"Is it okay if I come back for this in an hour or so?" Alisha asked.

"I don't mind hauling it for you." My dad surveyed the sled and the gangline, and I knew he was figuring out the best way to fit it in the back of his truck. "You're down Hoodoo Gulch, right?

"Yep. That's right. Thank you, Mr. Darling." Alisha smiled. "That would be so helpful."

Had the tension between Stella and Alisha created bad blood between her and her brother? It could be possible Matt was at work, but seemed a little cold nobody from the Childress clan was helping Alisha with her recovered dogs and sled. The whole incident from my kidnapping, Kyle's death, and Lola's daring escape using Alisha's sled team had run through town within hours of our return. But it seemed no sympathy came from Alisha's own family. Odd.

As my dad and Alisha drove away, Ben steered me toward my father's apartment on the second floor. "I'm sorry you missed Kyle's funeral yesterday."

"I'm only sad because I promised his parents I would be there." I waited for Ben to catch up to me at the top of the stairs. "But I think they'd understand the circumstances we were in. No way was I going to run Alisha's dogs after what they'd been through to make it to a funeral. Those poor animals. Besides my dad got my text and let them know I couldn't make it."

He nodded. I knew his silence meant I hadn't given a satisfactory answer. He wanted to know my mental state. After the unexpected encounter with one of my assailants, maybe he was worried I'd have another panic attack.

I sighed. "Right now, I feel fine." I wasn't ready to admit to him that I'd felt a surge of relief knowing I'd miss the funeral. All eyes would've been on me: the survivor. The one who'd been there when Kyle died. No matter the circumstances and my innocence, there would always be people in town who would wonder at how everything really went down. "But I don't know what I'll feel like tomorrow. Does that help?"

"Yes."

We stepped inside my father's apartment. We'd be staying here until we could arrange for the purchase of another snow machine after our insurance paid out. Then we'd head back to the cabin. Ben and I had come to an agreement that winter diving was off the table for both of us until I had more time to wade through my emotions and work on my mental health.

"I'm probably having a harder time thinking about giving up dredging, to be honest." My second session with Sarah, my therapist, had been postponed until tomorrow. But while Ben and I were holed up at the cabin for a couple of nights, we'd discussed our future, the money we'd made, and what was our best path forward.

Ben pulled me into his arms, and I breathed in his scent. "You don't have to give it up, Rory. I only want you to take some time to deal with what happened to you. You need a break. I can dive for the both of us this summer. Your dad already offered me a job on his dredge if I want it."

I pulled away. "He's made enough money this season to buy a new dredge boat?" It was hard to believe. To build a floating dredge took tens of thousands of dollars and with ice season dwindling away, I couldn't figure out how that was possible.

"I offered up my half of our gold as an investment," he said quietly.

"What?" My stomach twisted into knots. He'd made this decision without me?

"I'm good at this dredging thing, Rory. This winter is the first time in a long time I've felt good about diving, and I think I need to keep at it."

"And last summer?" I'd hired him off the plane last year, and he'd seemed eager enough to dive—arrogant even. Had he been dealing with his demons even then?

"Last summer proved to me there was nothing to fear under the water." He sat in my father's recliner chair and pulled me onto his lap. "What happened to Kilgore was a horrible accident, and I was lucky to survive."

"You were lucky to survive that dive into the Bering." Had he forgotten so soon his recklessness when attempting to save Kyle? He could've died from hypothermia that night and left me with a lifetime of guilt.

"I was lucky to survive or I wouldn't be here with you," he whispered in my ear.

I leaned back, and his arm snaked around my torso. My pulse quickened. I wanted him. I needed the reassurance he wasn't going anywhere. "Ben," I sighed.

He slipped his hand beneath my shirt and massaged my breast. "Kilgore would want me to live my life to the fullest. That's what I learned, and you helped me figure it out." He kissed the sensitive place behind my ear.

The stroke of his hand stilled me, and I closed my eyes so my mind could fly away from the awful thoughts that consumed me since Kyle died. I centered around the physical, and my body softened. The fear and sadness buried itself, and I let everything go.

I shrugged out of my shirt and rolled to one side. We scrambled to undress. Our lips met in a hard, heated kiss, and I sighed with relief when he entered me. When Ben and I made love everything else disappeared. He was my solid place. He was my anchor in the stormy ocean. And when I was in his arms, nothing else mattered.

Afterward, I smiled and snuggled into his chest. It was hard to think about giving up diving for the summer while I worked through things. Was that really the right choice? Or would I be admitting I couldn't hack it out on the water with the guys?

"I know what you're thinking." Ben's deep voice rumbled under my ear.

"You do?"

"Hm-mm." He stroked my hair, and a warm satisfaction flooded through me. "That I'll never be as good a gold dredger as you."

I smiled. "You better believe it, Ben Abel."

We lay there together for a long while. After a few minutes, my smile began to fade, and I felt a cold fear settle inside me. A fear that I wasn't sure I could ever escape. One that would maybe haunt me for the rest of my days. The moment during the storm when Kyle talked to me over the comms and said, "You are weak, Rory."

And I feared he was right. I'd never amount to anything. I was a dredger who couldn't dredge. And without dredging, what good was I? And who would want to stay with me if I had nothing to offer? But Ben didn't need to know these fears. I could push them down and deal with them later. But in the back of my mind Kyle's white face and wide open eyes haunted me.

I shook my head, hoping it would shake the memory of him out of my head. I would find a way past this. That's what Buck Darling's daughter would do, and for all our troubles, I was still his daughter.

Five months later, Ben and I sat in a booth at the Polar Café while Stella served us breakfast. She came up to our table with a gleam in her eye that I recognized. "Did you see the latest on Lola Chang?" She pulled out her cell phone and scrolled through the *Nome Nugget* Facebook page.

"No." That was a name I hadn't heard since ice season. She'd fled with our snow machine, which had been found abandoned on the road to Teller, and the police hadn't seen her since. "Is she finally in custody?" My stomach rolled. I'd worked through most of my anxieties about that night with Lola and Declan and thought my last session with Sarah the therapist had gotten me past the worst of it. Ben and I had actually been talking about our own dredge again after a blow-out summer on my father's new operation, and the idea of diving again didn't sound nearly as scary as it had the day of my panic attack. Yet, there was another weight I hadn't confronted with Ben—the looming civil suit he'd kept from me, a conversation I'd been avoiding despite Sarah's gentle nudges toward openness and honesty.

"They found a body." Stella tapped on the story she wanted and handed me her phone.

My worries about the civil suit fled my mind.

Ben leaned in to read with me.

"It's a pretty decomposed one," Stella said. "But it's definitely a woman with black hair with the same build as Lola. And only about ten miles from where the snow machine was found."

As I read the sparse details of the story, I had a fleeting feeling of sadness for the woman who'd caused me so much pain and who'd ended up indirectly causing Kyle's death. No one deserved to die alone on the tundra like that. Not even a criminal. "She should've turned herself in when we found her at Ben's cabin. Is a prison sentence really worse than freezing to death?" The thought lingered in my head—perhaps, for Lola, someone higher up the criminal food chain was scarier than the prospect of prison.

Ben took the phone from me and re-read the story. Maybe he wanted to reassure himself that the last person left who could hurt me was no longer alive.

The bell rang at the pass-through from the kitchen. "Order up!" yelled the short-order cook.

"That's your food." Stella returned the chair to the table across from us and trotted off to grab our plates—I had pancakes and bacon; Ben had the reindeer sausage and eggs. Somehow he'd gotten a taste for reindeer since he arrived last summer. I grimaced.

Ben set down Stella's phone. "Looks like Lola got what was coming to her."

"I don't know." My mind returned to the day we found her at the cabin and what she told us. Was it really over? "What do you think she meant when she said that the money Kyle owed didn't belong to her?"

"A bluff." Ben drank more of his coffee. "She wanted us to be scared so we wouldn't come after her." He leaned in and kissed me on the head.

I did my best to let go of my worries. What did Sarah say?

Letting go of worries is a process that takes time and practice. You have the power to control your thoughts and reactions. Worrying about the future or dwelling on the past won't change anything in the present. Instead, focus on what you can do right now to take care of yourself.

I took a deep breath and attempted to focus on the present: sitting in the cafe with my boyfriend and enjoying a delicious breakfast while we dreamed of our future together and what that might look like. Lola was dead. Declan was in prison for a long time. And Henry and Zoe would be here soon to visit for the first time in a long time.

The past was the past. It couldn't hurt me anymore.

"You're right." I grabbed the maple syrup container off the table and poured a healthy amount over my pancakes. Then I cut off a hunk of buttermilk pancake, drenched it in sticky sweetness, and ate it. The Polar Cafe had some of the best pancakes in town. "Want a bite?" I said noticing Ben watching me eat.

He cupped my chin in his hand and kissed me, tasting the syrup on my lips. When we broke apart, he said, "I love you, Rory."

I smiled, and my heart warmed. "We should leave soon for the airport."

We ate our breakfast together and watched Nome come to life beyond the plate glass window before heading out.

We waited inside the Nome airport for the flight to arrive from Anchorage. Ben squeezed my hand. It must've been clammy because he asked me, "When's the last time you saw them?"

"My stepfather? Or Zoe?" I tugged at my blouse. I felt over-dressed, but working with Alisha at the Northern Lights Inn had forced me to add some more professional clothing to my closet. My regular jeans and T-shirt had seemed too informal for the event.

"Either one."

"In middle school and high school, I used to fly to Seattle every Christmas, Buck insisted on it." A smile tugged at my lips. Henry, my stepfather, would circle the airport while Zoe had the fun job of waiting with me at baggage claim for my massive suitcase. My dad always made me pack too much and bring weird gifts—yak jerky or sealskin gloves or some tacky T-shirt that said 'Don't Moose With Me.' "And Zoe's been up here maybe a couple of times since then."

"That's kind of sad."

The tinge of wistfulness in his voice surprised me. "Is it?" I'd been content being Buck Darling's daughter until last summer. I'd idolized him in every way. It had taken me a long time to under-stand Henry, and with my therapist's help, I was still learning more.

"Yes, so we'll have to fix that," Ben said. "I've never been to Seattle. Maybe we need to take a trip."

A familiar duo exited into Baggage Claim—a thin woman with a dark bob and an equally thin older man wearing khakis and a polo shirt. "Zoe!" I waved. Her face lit up. Our relationship had been strained for many years after I'd chosen to leave them and live with Buck, but we'd repaired things over the last year. The look on her face was one I didn't remember seeing when I entered a room.

"Aurora!" Zoe ran toward me, her lanky limbs reminding me of a newborn colt learning how to use its legs. She hugged me tight. We'd never been the huggy kind of family, so the warm gesture surprised me. "I'm so glad to see you're okay." She leaned back still holding my arms and examined me from head to toe.

Henry Pomeroy hung back with arms limply at his sides.

Ben stepped forward to shake his hand. "Nice to meet you, sir, I'm Benjamin Abel."

My stepfather accepted the handshake and said, "You can call me Henry." Relief washed over his features when the baggage carousel began to turn. "Excuse me. Our bags."

Not surprised he'd rather hunt for luggage than engage in conversation.

"Dad." Zoe threw up her hands. "Give Aurora a hug. When's the last time you saw each other?"

"It's okay, Zoe." I redirected her attention to me and Ben. "Let him do his thing. It'll calm him down after all that flying." I grabbed Ben's hand. "This is Ben. Ben, my sister, Zoe."

My half sister looked up at my beastly boyfriend. I almost thought I heard her gulp. "I'll bet you're no match for the grizzlies up here."

"They don't have grizzly bears in this part of Alaska." Ben's brow wrinkled.

"That's my sister's way of saying you're an intimidating guy," I said.

Before Ben could respond, my stepfather joined us towing two roller bags. "Did you tell Aurora about the story?"

"Story?" I asked and looked up at Ben. This didn't sound good.

Zoe blushed. "Jonah's article. Didn't he email you?" She dug in her leather tote bag. "I thought for sure he said he'd email you. But maybe he was too excited."

"No, he didn't email me." The hair stood up on my arms.

My sister pulled out a magazine and handed it to me with a wide smile. "He got the cover story."

I stared at a copy of *Pacific Northwest Life* with my picture splashed across the front that read:

Bold, Brilliant, and Breaking Barriers: Meet Nome's Fearless Feminist Icon of the Bering Sea!

"Isn't that exciting?" Zoe took her suitcase from my stepfather and flashed all her teeth in the widest smile I'd ever seen from my sister. "I have extra copies to give you when we check in at our hotel."

"Motel," I corrected. I'd gotten them a deal at my workplace—twenty percent off for family—but the magazine cover drained me of any triumph I felt at getting them a bargain. "Not so fearless anymore," I mumbled to myself. I'd be the joke of Nome when this magazine made the rounds. They'd probably stock up on *Pacific Northwestern Life*, if the gas station didn't already carry it.

"Rory," Ben said softly. He grabbed my hand and squeezed. "You look amazing in that photo. All the Nome girls will be jealous you clean up that good. The secret's out." His face shone with pride.

But how could I be proud of my face next to a lie of a claim—I hadn't done any dredging since the winter and who knows if I'd ever be able to do it again. My confidence had been blasted to smithereens that stormy night on the ice. All summer I'd worked with my therapist to find satisfaction in other areas of my life, to push past my reckless need to prove myself out on the water. Now, seeing my face next to the outlandish title, I was ashamed. This 'fearless feminist icon' had folded under the smallest amount of pressure. I'd failed. Even Ben, who had more than enough reason to avoid diving, had made peace with his past and found a way to move forward.

I was stuck, and the magazine article was one more reminder of it.

Zoe hadn't noticed my changed demeanor. Her words came out

a mile a minute, "Jonah's been nominated for a Livingston Award. It's very prestigious...it celebrates journalists under the age of thirty-five, recognizing excellence in local, national, and international reporting. He only found out yesterday."

"Wow," I said, my mind numb. Why did I ever agree to the stupid interview? That's what I needed—even more publicity on the story. Great for Jonah, not so great for me.

"That is a wonderful picture of you," my stepdad said and squeezed my shoulder. That was the closest thing to a hug in his world.

The touch of his hand brought back a memory: after my mother had left I was in shock. Nothing made sense. Mothers didn't just abandon their daughters. I automatically assumed it must be something I'd done. A mother would only leave a child if that child were really really bad. Henry must've noticed the change in me, and how a quietness settled around me weeks after she'd gone. One night he sat on my bed, touched me on the shoulder, and said, "Honey, you didn't do anything wrong. I want you to know that." And I'd cried and cried.

He'd done his best with his quiet ways and simple words.

When I'd decided to live with my real dad, it must've hurt. His wife had left him, then his daughter. Therapist Sarah had led me through the feelings...things I hadn't considered. It made me view Henry in a completely different light. He'd let me go free, even though he probably wanted to hold onto me as tightly as he could.

I smiled at my stepfather—a real, genuine smile. He deserved it. I needed to repair our relationship to find healing, and this visit was a good first step for us both. I had to let go of my worries about some stupid magazine article. Why care so much about what other people thought? The people that mattered most to me, besides Buck, were all here with me. The rest of the world could go screw themselves for all I cared.

After a beat, my stepdad clapped his hands together. "All right. Who's going to give me a tour of the town? We're only here for a few days, and I want to make sure I see it all. Can you take us to the sign where this picture was taken?" He pointed at the magazine in my hand. "The view looks spectacular."

"Sounds like a plan," Ben said. "I've got the rental outside. Good thing you visited in the summer, we have hours of daylight left." He took Zoe's suitcase and rolled it toward the exit doors.

We'd rented a van for the week. Ben and I were used to getting around on the ATV. Not exactly enough room for four. Instead of making the daily trek back and forth from the cabin, we'd continued to rent the yurt down on the beach. Ben could walk to the docks for his diving job on the *Alaska Darling II*—he, Nate, and my father had pooled their money together to make it happen. While my job at the Inn was our steady paycheck—something I hadn't experienced much in my life. Sarah had told me stability was important in my recovery, so I'd set aside my guilt at not being part of the operation and settled into my new daily routine. Stella had been over the moon that we could hang out more often, now that I had regular hours.

As we exited out into the fine Alaskan summer air, I took a deep cleansing breath. I'd figure out the stupid magazine thing. I wasn't about to let it hamper my progress. The only way through something was to move forward. Ben opened the back of the van and began to load the luggage. My stepdad joined in. Zoe and I stood on the curb.

"I'm so glad you're here," I told her. It was an honest statement, and I never thought a year ago I'd say something like that to my older sister. We'd bumped heads over every little decision I made since I'd chosen to live with Buck. What a waste of emotions. She was the only sibling I'd ever have. Life was too short to waste on petty disagreements.

A grin split her face. "I am too, sis."

A content feeling came over me as I walked out with the man I loved and the family I'd spent too long staying away from. For the first time in many months, I felt happy. I knew that feeling might not have been possible without Therapist Sarah, and Ben for making me see I needed her.

I hugged him close to me as we went to the van. With Ben by my side, I knew I could do anything.

The End

❀ Created with Vellum

ABOUT THE AUTHOR

K. J. Gillenwater has a B.A. in English and Spanish from Valparaiso University and an M.A. in Latin American Studies from University of California, Santa Barbara. She worked as a Russian linguist in the U.S. Navy, spending time at the National Security Agency doing secret things. After six years of service, she ended up as a technical writer in the software industry. She has lived all over the U.S. and currently resides in Wyoming with her family where she runs her own business writing government proposals and squeezes in fiction writing when she can. In the winter she likes to ski and snowshoe; in the summer she likes to garden with her husband and take walks with her dog.

Visit K.J.'s website for more information about her writing, her books, and what's coming next. www.kjgillenwater.com.

If you enjoyed this book, K. J. Gillenwater is the author of multiple books, which are available in print and in eBook format at multiple vendors.

- Aurora's Gold (Book 1 in the Aurora Series)
- The Genesis Machine Trilogy: Inception, Decryption, and Revelation
- Automated
- Revenge Honeymoon
- Illegal
- The Ninth Curse
- The Little Black Box
- Acapulco Nights
- Blood Moon

Short Stories & Short Story Collections:

- Skyfall
- Nemesis
- The Man in 14C
- Charlie and the Zombie Factory

www.ingramcontent.com/pod-product-compliance
Lightning Source LLC
Chambersburg PA
CBHW072123300726
48975CB00003B/904